THE
FASCINATORS

THE
FASCINATORS

ANDREW ELIOPULOS

HARPER TEEN

An Imprint of HarperCollinsPublishers

HarperTeen is an imprint of HarperCollins Publishers.

The Fascinators
Copyright © 2020 by Andrew Eliopulos
All rights reserved. Printed in the United States of America.
No part of this book may be used or reproduced in any manner whatsoever without
written permission except in the case of brief quotations embodied in critical articles
and reviews. For information address HarperCollins Children's Books, a division of
HarperCollins Publishers, 195 Broadway, New York, NY 10007.
www.epicreads.com

ISBN 978-0-06-288804-4

Typography by David Curtis
20 21 22 23 24   PC/LSCH   10 9 8 7 6 5 4 3 2 1

First Edition

If you've ever cast a spell alone in your room in the dark,
wishing you were somewhere—or someone—else,
this book is for you.

PROLOGUE

TWENTY MINUTES NORTHWEST OF AUGUSTA, GEORGIA, in a suburb where you're more likely to see someone praying in public than using their magic, Liv Honeycutt was trying to sell her diamond cross necklace at the King of Pawns pawnshop on Highway 104. She needed a hundred and fifty dollars—thirty to cover the car to Augusta, and the rest to cover the bus ticket to New York. The ten-dollar bill already in her purse would have to be enough for three meals during the twelve-hour trip. Maybe a Chick-fil-A sandwich for lunch and the side of waffle fries for dinner.

But the guy working today did not want to give her a hundred and fifty dollars. The guy working today was sure Liv's cross necklace was fake.

"They're plastic," he said, pointing at the gemstone inlays with his ballpoint pen. "Or glass, maybe. Cubic zirconia at best.

They're definitely not diamonds."

"How can you tell?"

"It's like a special ability I have."

"You mean . . . like magic?"

"Yes, like magic. *Not* magic, I reckon. But like it."

Liv let out a sigh. She'd gotten excited for a moment there, at the prospect of a rare power. Any real power at all was rare, in this part of Georgia. People with real power never stuck around here.

"My mom gave me this necklace for my sixteenth birthday," Liv said. "Isn't there some test or machine you can use to be sure?"

The cow bell over the door clunked behind her, heralding the arrival of a new customer. The guy working the counter took a look over Liv's shoulder, his impatience to be rid of her already clear on his face.

"Listen, sweetheart, you can take this little necklace to Bob's Pawn or Mike's place, and I guarantee neither of them is going to give you more than twenty dollars for it. We can't resell sentimental value at a pawnshop, do you understand what I'm saying? That watch, now—*that* looks like it might be worth something. If you're that desperate for money, I mean."

Liv felt her heart drop into her stomach. She'd almost forgotten she was wearing the watch at all, because she wore it every day, always putting it on while she brushed her teeth. And if it was all too easy to believe that the cross necklace—like everything else her mom had ever given her—was worthless, well . . . It wasn't surprising that her grandmother's watch would be worth quite a lot.

She put her hand over the watch, as if to shield it from this man's gaze. The new customer walked up to the counter beside her, and out of the corner of her eye, Liv could see that he was a young man, probably here to buy a gun or something. The guy at the counter turned to give the man his full attention.

"How much?" Liv said.

The guy at the counter paused. He stared at Liv's hand, like he could still see the watch underneath it, no doubt tapping into his *ability*—like magic, but not.

"A hundred even."

"But I need a hundred and fifty."

She was about to cry. She knew she was about to cry; she could hear it in her voice, and she hated that. This man didn't seem like the type to take pity on someone in need. She'd have better results if she bargained from a place of strength. But these past few days—the fights with her parents, the reaching out to friends who'd all taken her parents' side, everyone turning their backs on her after seventeen years—well, she didn't really have any strength to draw on at the moment. Some days Liv thought she was on track to have real power, if she worked at it. Today did not feel like one of those days.

"A hundred twenty. Take it or leave it."

One hundred and twenty dollars. That was the value of the only thing she had left to remember her grandmother—her grandmother, Emilie, who used to read her palm and her tarot and who used to tell her that her magic was as clear on her face as sunshine. One hundred and ten dollars, plus the twenty in her pocket—if she walked to Augusta, she could get the bus ticket and still have money left for food.

"Fine," she said, undoing the metal clasp. She set the watch on the counter, while the man reached into his pocket and pulled out a large wad of bills. He flipped through them until he found a hundred-dollar bill and a twenty-dollar bill, and he handed them over to Liv like he was giving her a real gift.

She took the money and ran, the clunk of the cowbell the last indignity of the encounter. Though that wasn't quite true, was it? As she walked along the side of Highway 104, the sun beating down on her face, hot and miserable, she realized she was suffering the indignity more with every step. She pulled out her phone, hoping at least that Uncle Theo had responded to her Friendivist message by now. If anyone would understand the soul-crushing ordeal that had been her week, it'd be him. She was counting on that.

But no, no response. She tried to steady her breathing. She was still okay. As long as he responded before she got to New York, or before her parents realized they had the power to stop paying for her phone—since they'd said she was quote unquote "dead to them"—then everything would work out. Even if he didn't respond, surely she'd be able to find *some* way to track down his address once she got to New York. Or maybe she'd start sending Friendivist messages to his New York friends if she hadn't heard back by the bus ride.

She was walking a few feet off the shoulder of the road, hardly paying attention to the cars that sped by. Even when she heard the crunch of gravel just ahead of her, she barely looked up; she didn't care why this silver Honda was pulling over. She just wanted to get to the bus stop and get the hell out of this state.

"Hello there."

It was the customer from King of Pawns, leaning out of the passenger side window. Now that she got a good look at him, Liv realized that he was more of a boy than a man—he couldn't be that much older than she was, in fact. He had a military buzz cut and a thick neck, but there was something about his smile that seemed genuinely friendly. Liv had been catcalled plenty of times before; this guy was at least smart enough not to lead with a come-on.

She still didn't trust him.

"Hello," she said, but she didn't stop walking.

"I know it's none of my business," the guy called to her retreating back, "but I think I have something that will cheer you up."

There it was.

"Let me guess—it's in your pants."

"What? Oh—ha. But no. Actually, it's in my hand, it tells the time, and it has a little engraving on the back of it that makes me think it's something special."

That got her attention.

Liv turned around, her eyes narrowed, and when she saw her grandmother's watch in his hand, dangling out the window, her first reaction, even before suspicion, was rage.

"What are you doing with that?" she snapped.

"Whoa, hey—I was just trying to bring it to you. I didn't like the way that guy was taking advantage of you. Especially since he tried to cheat me the same way after you left."

"Well, aren't you a knight in shining armor," she said, but her voice lost a little bit of its edge. If this wasn't a trick, it was the first nice thing anyone had done for her in a very long time. She walked back to the car.

He held out the watch to her, and she accepted it gratefully, not taking its familiar weight for granted as she tightened the band across her wrist.

"How did you get this?"

In answer, the boy weaved his hands together, then pulled them apart. A tiny light seemed to be flickering to life between his palms, but just as Liv squinted to get a better look at it, a bright flash in her peripheral vision caught her attention and made her spin. When she realized there was nothing there, and when her heartbeat slowed, Liv turned back to the boy.

"Like that," he said.

"Well, damn. I mean—thank you."

"Where are you headed anyway? Can we give you a ride?"

For the first time, Liv peered past him into the car. An older woman, maybe his mom, was sitting behind the wheel. She was watching their interaction with a kind of bland curiosity, but she hadn't spoken, and she didn't speak now. She did smile, though, like it was fine by her if Liv took them up on the ride.

And Liv really wanted to. Her shirt was sticking to the sweat on her back, and her legs were sore from all the walking she'd already done this morning.

"Are you sure? I'm going to the Greyhound station in downtown Augusta. I wouldn't want to trouble you."

"No trouble at all," the boy said. "We were going to head that way on an errand anyhow."

"Okay, then," Liv said. Her hand hesitated on the handle of the back door, but only for a second.

"I'm Isaac, by the way," the boy said as Liv took a seat and the car got moving. "And that's Grace."

Okay, so probably not his mom, then.

"Nice to meet you," Liv said. Grace only nodded. "It's not often I meet other magickers in real life who would or could do what you just did. Everybody I know thinks magic is the devil's work."

"Is that right?" Isaac said. "Well, now you've met two. Grace and I live in a kind of co-op situation with a few more, as a matter of fact." He paused, considering her. "I take it when you say 'other magickers,' you mean you can do some spell work of your own?"

"That's right," Liv said, a hint of pride creeping into her voice, in spite of everything. "But my parents, well. They're basically the mascots of the people who think it's the devil's domain. My mom barged into my room a couple nights ago when I was trying to do this spell to make my eyes green instead of brown. One look at the mess of candles and whatever was happening with my eyes and she started screaming her head off. Yesterday, my parents told me to leave and never come back. So now I'm headed to New York, to live with my uncle. They disowned him too, when they found out he was gay."

It felt really good to say all of this out loud. She'd been feeling a little unhinged, keeping it to herself, like it was some awful nightmare she'd had and not her new reality.

"Wow, that really sucks," Isaac said. "I'm sorry. We got a couple people at our place who don't talk to their parents anymore, either. Actually, one of them just ran off. We're hoping it's to live with an uncle type, maybe, but we're not really sure. He didn't leave a note or anything. That's why we had to sell a few things at King's. We've got to come up with his rent for the month, living in a co-op. I just hope he's okay."

Grace shot Isaac an inscrutable look. Maybe she wasn't feeling quite so sympathetic to this boy who was costing them on the rent.

Liv felt her phone vibrate in her pocket. It was a Friendivist notification—Uncle Theo had responded. With shaking hands, she opened the message and read it as fast as she could.

. . . and I sympathize, Liv, I truly do. But I live in a studio apartment with my boyfriend, and really it's more his place, because I'm between jobs, and his couch is so small, you'd

have to sleep in a sleeping bag, and we could put you up for
a few days, maybe a week, but no way could it be permanent,
and New York is so expensive, I don't see how you would . . .

"How much is the rent?" Liv said. "On the room that guy
left, I mean."

"Why, you want to live there?" Isaac said, laughing. But then,
when Liv didn't laugh, he added, "It's three hundred a month."

"And it's here in Evans?" Liv said. Ready as she was to start
over far away from her parents, she hadn't been thrilled with the
idea of dropping out before graduating, and now, if she could find
a job, maybe at Starbucks or something, she could complete senior
year and leave Georgia on her own terms, the way she'd always
planned. And better than she'd planned—she'd be spending the
year until then living with other practicing magickers. Maybe
they'd teach Liv what they knew.

"It's pretty close. Only a couple minutes outside of town."

"I don't have a job yet, but I can get one," Liv said.

"We were planning to pay this month's rent anyway. You think
you could have three hundred by next month?"

"Easy," Liv said.

Grace shot Isaac another pointed look.

"I *am* eighteen," Liv said, interpreting Grace's hesitance as
misgiving.

But Isaac just grinned.

"Well then, Liv. Forget the Greyhound station. Why don't

we take you to see the place? See how you like the others? Fair warning—they're not all as cool and personable as me and Grace, but they're all right."

"Understood," Liv said, laughing. Laughing! She hadn't laughed in days, but this sudden reversal of fortune was so unbelievably perfect, so exactly what she needed, that it felt like some kind of divine intervention—and the irony of that revelation was just too much. Laughter was the only reasonable response.

It would be a few months before she would look back on this moment and recognize it in a different light—not divine at all, but a result of very human magic, self-serving, deceitful. By then, she would know that "not personable" was a gross understatement for describing the others; by then, she would wonder if maybe her parents had had a point, thinking magic was of the devil. By then, of course, it would be too late.

CHAPTER 1

THE SPELL WASN'T WORKING, NO MATTER HOW MANY times Sam tried.

Surely, that meant he was doing it wrong.

The incantation was tricky enough—two whole pages of words that looked like gibberish but turned out to be Welsh, which was basically gibberish except harder to pronounce.

But Sam had spent all summer practicing those words—transcribing them phonetically, then reciting them in his room, over and over until he'd almost memorized them. Since he still hadn't gotten the spell to work, he could only assume it was the short first step—the association—he was managing to screw up:

"Make of your mind an empty vessel. Let it sing with silence, leaving space for your dreams."

Which—sure thing, spell book! Let me get right on that!

That was often the case with high-level spells, though—that

they required feats of figurative language, metaphorical thinking. Associations, if you wanted to get technical, but James often called them the "touchy-feely parts." (Sam wished he wouldn't. As a redhead with pale white skin, Sam was prone to blushing.)

Anyway, it was somehow the last night of summer, and Sam still hadn't mastered this high-level spell, despite all his efforts. It had been his one and only goal for the past three months. The single item on his to-do list, besides sleeping in and hanging out. This didn't bode well for the goals he'd set for senior year.

"Trying again?" Sam's mom said from his doorway.

Sam sat cross-legged in the middle of his bedroom floor. In front of him were the Celtic spell book—overdue from the library and open to the page where his transcription lay next to the original entry—and a stick of sandalwood incense, burning down slowly.

"Apparently, I'm a glutton for punishment. I'm starting to think I should've spent my summer on something simpler, like time travel or mind control."

"You do love a challenge. Which reminds me, have you talked to James since we got back?"

Three days ago, Sam and his parents had returned from a weeklong vacation in Gulf Shores. He had begged to stay home and miss the trip entirely so that he could go to Mike's party with James, but his mom had pointed out that this was likely their last family vacation while Sam was a high-schooler, whereas he and James had many more parties ahead of them, if not this year, then when they got to college.

Roommates at UGA—that was the plan. Or at least, for two years, that had *been* the plan, and Sam was pretty sure that it was *still* the plan; he just felt a little unsure about where things stood with James after that awkward whatever-it-was at the bowling alley three weeks ago. And James had been so busy, between helping his dad with his roofing business and volunteering at his church's Vacation Bible School, they hadn't really had a good moment—or *any* moment—to hang out in person and clear the air. Mike's party could have been the exact moment they needed.

(Sam may or may not have sulked for the first few days of the vacation, before the gulf breeze got the better of him.)

"You're hilarious, Mom."

"Who said I was kidding?"

"Well, the answer is no. I haven't heard from James since we left, and he hasn't posted any v-clips in the last week, either. For all I know, he's been abducted by aliens, and I'll never see him again."

Sam's mom frowned. She was a real estate agent with surprisingly sharp empath abilities, which she called her secret weapon. She could always spot the difference between a joke and a desperation vehicle.

"I'm sorry, sweetheart. You know this is why I think you should just talk to him directly one of these days. Get all your feelings out in the open."

"I do know that's what you think," Sam said.

His mom always made it sound so easy, like it was one more negotiation with a compromise at the end that would work for all involved parties. As Sam had tried to explain to her numerous times over the years, there was nothing to negotiate; he was perfectly happy with his friendship with James as it was. Or as it had been. As it would be again. The funny thing was, Sam hadn't even told her about what had happened at the bowling alley. She just had a sense for these things. Again: an empath.

And sure, James had the exact sleepy eyes, messy hair, and slantwise smile that his mom had (correctly) identified as Sam's "type," based on his favorite movies. And yes, there had been times when Sam had found himself daydreaming vaguely about cooking a nice meal with a guy who could make him laugh and believed in him unequivocally, the way James could and did. But no, that did not mean that Sam was so desperately in love with James as to sabotage one of his few close friendships.

Besides, if there ever *was* going to be some great romance between them, it was still in the ember phase now, and if Sam blew too hard, he would only blow it out before it had a chance to get going. (His mom always countered that his relationship with James was less like a fire and more like Schrödinger's cat, and Sam was just afraid to open the box to find out whether it was alive or dead.)

"Well, suit yourself," his mom said now. "The real reason I stopped by is that your dad and I both have to be at work on the early side tomorrow. Are you going to be okay to wake yourself up on the first day of school?"

"As long as I can actually fall asleep, yeah."

"Right. Cherish those butterflies—it's your last year to get them."

"Why? You don't think I'll get into UGA?"

"It's different in college. In college, all the days run together, and your first class of the week starts at noon, if you even remember to go."

"Wow. Suddenly I see why you put so much effort into keeping me away from parties. You were the biggest partier of all."

"Goodnight, sweetheart."

"Night, Mom."

She shut the door behind her, and Sam started back at the beginning of the incantation, determined to give it one last try before school kicked into gear and everything got in the way.

Not three words in, his phone buzzed on his desk.

Sam scrambled over to it, but even before he got there, he had this feeling that it wasn't going to be a message from James. It was the next best thing, though—a message from Delia.

You still awake?

You know it, he replied. What's up?

Is it weird that I'm nervous for the first day of school?

Sam smiled. He could just picture her, her chin-length brown hair falling to either side of her face as she held up her wrist to her mouth, gnawing on the magically reinforced friendship bracelet he'd made her freshman year. She hadn't taken it off since.

Not weird, he said. *I'm* nervous, and I'm not trying to get into Pinnacle. ☺

Thanks. Now I'm even more nervous.

It hardly mattered that Sam had known her his whole life—it was still hard to read Delia's tone in text form. In stark contrast to Sam, she never used emojis, even to denote sarcasm, because she wanted her words to speak for themselves. In this case, Sam suspected she was a little bit sarcastic but mostly serious. She really had been working herself ragged these past few years, her heart set on getting as far away from Georgia for college as she could, even though her parents had made it clear that she would have to pay her own way if she was going to pass up the HOPE scholarship covering in-state tuition. If anybody could make it happen, Delia could. It was their guidance counselor, Ms. Berry, who had suggested in passing that Delia might even have what it takes to be a Keeper one day, and that the Pinnacle School of Magic could help her get there. Their program was generally considered to be the best in the world, because it was free to all accepted students while being rigorous enough to open the door to pretty much any career for its graduates. Delia had once quoted to him and James this unbelievable statistic about how something like seventy percent of Keepers—like, all Keepers, around the entire *world*—had gone through the Pinnacle program. No surprise, then, that it was mind-numbingly competitive to get in.

I'm excited for the Fascinators tryout ;) Sam said, changing the subject.

I hope I make the cut! Delia wrote.

Good—she was back to joking.

Delia, James, and Sam were the president, vice president, and treasurer-slash-secretary of their high school's magic club, respectively. They were also the only three members, and had been since their freshman year.

That inaugural year, in the weeks before their first Georgia State Magic Convention (when it was starting to sink in that they had no chance in hell of placing, let alone winning), James had encountered the word *fascinator* in a book. The word, it turned out, was not only a type of British hat but also an archaic synonym for magicker—to fascinate was to charm, enchant, beguile. Instantly, James had seen the potential for a much-needed in-joke and point of pride for their club. With only three members, they might never put up a good overall finish at convention—that podium would be dominated by the bougie Atlanta schools that had dozens of members and dedicated magic classes, not just extra-curriculars. But sure enough, when the announcers that year were forced to read out James's and Delia's names for top-five freshman finishes in their individual events, and in both cases said, "of the Friedman High School . . . Fascinators?" the three of them and their sponsor—again, Ms. Berry—had screamed loud enough that everyone in the giant auditorium had looked at them like they were insane.

Their club had officially been called the Fascinators ever since.

Did you print the flyers? Delia wrote.

Ah, the fliers. Sam's favorite to-do every year—not even kidding.

One for every building!

Cool. Thanks, Sam.

The conversation might have ended there. The reminder about the fliers was clearly the real reason Delia had messaged him. (Sam's memory for details was two slices shy of a pizza.) But since he had her . . .

Have you talked to James lately?

Not since the bowling alley.

For a second, Sam thought this was a pointed comment. That she'd somehow heard about what had happened outside—maybe talked to Bethany, or even James himself. This was another case when an emoji would have been extremely helpful—a winky face to mean that she'd heard all about it, no thanks to Sam, or a scratching-chin face to mean that she truly hadn't talked to James in three weeks, why do you ask? Sam was sorely tempted to come right out and ask her what she knew, though that would make it a little harder to pretend that it hadn't been a big deal, which he was determined to do, so everything could go back to normal. Mercifully, before he could give himself an aneurysm from this knot of indecision, Delia moved on.

Did you get your dream spell to work? she said.

No ☹

Well, it would have been remarkable if you had. That spell seemed hard as shit.

18

It really is! Like, Welsh!

Welsh! Ok, I'm going to sleep. See you tomorrow, Sam.

Night.

She didn't know.

Sam exhaled.

He went back to where his book lay open on the floor. He tried to make of his mind a vessel, and then he recited the Welsh. Then he attempted to go to sleep, crossing his fingers that the spell had worked this time—that when he dreamed tonight, as he assumed he would, he would be present and aware, able to think and see and remember.

That last part, to Sam, was the most important.

Sam hadn't been able to remember any of his dreams. Not one. Not ever.

As if an out gay magicker in Friedman, Georgia, needed any other reason to feel weird.

It hardly mattered the next day that the spell still hadn't worked. As he pulled into the senior parking lot at Friedman High, Sam felt a tiny but very real spark of hope that this year was going to be different—that it would be the year when everything went his way. It was such a small thing—the senior parking lot was maybe twenty yards closer to the school than the general parking lot was—but Sam didn't need for his life to be drastically different. Twenty yards' difference felt like enough.

Sam had gotten to school early to put up the fliers. He pinned one to the bulletin board in each of the main halls, which at Friedman were divided by subject—English, science, math, etc. Sam's first-period class this year was economics, so he saved the last flier for the social sciences hall.

The morning went by in a blur of new teachers and new textbooks, plus all the same classmates Sam had known his whole life. He didn't have a single class with Delia or James this semester because he was a B-minus human being while they were in Advanced or AP Everything, but the three of them had the same lunch period, and Sam could actually feel his heartbeat speeding up as he entered the noisy, linoleum expanse of the cafeteria.

James and Delia were already at their usual table, talking away, having clearly made full use of their three-hour head start on senior year to get back in the rhythm of things.

"Hello, hello," Sam said brightly, taking a seat across from his friends.

James turned to greet him, and his face lit up. Sam had to admit it: he had missed that smile.

"There he is," James said. "My man Sam."

"Happy first lunch of senior year," Sam said.

"It truly is the first day of the rest of our lives," Delia deadpanned.

"Okay, Captain Cynical," Sam said, holding up his hands in surrender. "Sorry I am feeling an actual emotion because I have an actual heart."

"Thanks for soldiering on and putting up the fliers," she said without missing a beat.

"How was Mike's party?" Sam said to James.

"Oh, yeah. It was fine. A little weird. But fine. How was Gulf Shores?"

"It was great," Sam said.

"You're such a liar," Delia said. "I saw your v-clips. It looked like it rained half the time you were there."

"But it was sunny the other half," Sam said. "Plus, when it rained, I stayed inside and caught up on TV. Did y'all see the finale of *Last Keeper Standing*? No? Well, the woman who won had to do this spell to lift a car over a pit full of spiders, while her brother and sister were *inside* the car. It was wild."

"Sounds wild," Delia agreed.

James laughed, maybe a half-second too late to be real. Now that Sam was looking for it, it seemed like James was a little tired, distant. Or maybe Sam was looking too hard for any sign of residual weirdness; maybe things had just gone back to normal, no further discussion required.

Sam said, "I was planning to stop by Ms. Berry's office before the tryout, to check if she's going to be there today or not."

"She never comes," Delia said.

"She came freshman year," Sam replied.

"Yeah, but that was the first one. We didn't know what we were doing then."

"Wait, we know what we're doing now?" Sam said.

Delia laughed, and then a moment later, James did, too. Like he'd been waiting for the translation.

"Everything cool?" Sam asked him.

"What? Oh, yeah. Everything's fine. Sorry, just have a lot on my mind."

"On the first day of school?" Sam said with a smile, aiming for low-key.

"Yeah, I guess." James smiled back. It didn't reach his eyes.

"Do you want to talk—" Sam started, but he didn't get a chance to finish his sentence.

A girl had walked up behind James, and she was tapping him on the shoulder. Sam knew the girl to be Amber Williams—a junior this year, and a varsity athlete. Amber had dark brown skin and black hair that she'd worn in a ponytail for as long as Sam had known her, which meant since second grade for him, first grade for her, when she'd told some boys who were making fun of Sam's purple backpack that they should mind their own business. These days, she played soccer and hung out mostly with other soccer players, including the ones in the Fellowship of Christian Athletes. How she knew James was anyone's guess.

Amber held a crumpled-up brown paper bag in her hand, like she'd already finished eating and had been en route to throw away the trash.

"Hey, James," she said.

"Oh! Amber! Hey! Amber, this is Sam and Delia. Y'all, this is Amber."

"I know," Sam said.

"Hey, Amber," Delia said.

"Amber goes to my church," James explained.

"That's funny," Amber said. "I didn't realize it was *your* church. I thought it belonged to everybody."

This was apparently very funny to James—not delayed-reaction funny but whole-body-clouds-have-broken-laugh funny. James was all sunshine now.

"You know what I mean," he said. To Sam and Delia: "We both helped out at Vacation Bible School a few weeks ago. We had to feed, like, fifty kids a day. We were in charge of snack time."

"Yeah. Snack time," Amber echoed.

What fresh hell was this? Sam had gotten the impression from James's texts that he was miserable having to do Vacation Bible School; certainly, he hadn't mentioned living it up with Amber Williams. Not that Sam expected James to tell him *everything* he did when they weren't together, but something about this effusive, stumbling introduction made it sound like "snack time" had been a significant omission.

"Is this seat taken?" Amber said.

"It's all yours," James replied smoothly.

Amber sat down. She said, "Don't let me interrupt. Feel free to talk about whatever y'all were talking about."

"What *were* we talking about?" Sam said to James.

"You were just saying—about the tryout? And Ms. Berry?" James prompted.

"Well, that was it," Sam said. "That was the whole story."

"Is this the tryout for the magic club you told me about?" Amber said.

"Yup. The one and only."

"You thinking of joining?" Delia said, her tone unreadable.

"One hundred percent no," Amber said. "James did make it sound pretty great, but we actually start training for soccer way before the season begins. Three days a week practicing magic is a lot. No offense."

"Yeah, we take it pretty seriously," Sam said.

"Do we?" James said.

"I do," Delia said.

"That's true—you do," James conceded.

And, okay, was Sam understanding this correctly? Had James actually tried to convince someone new to join the Fascinators? Someone from church? Sam thought James hated going to church. That he only went because his parents made him.

With one quick glance, James seemed to register that Sam was upset. His eyes widened by the tiniest fraction of an inch; they reflected a trace of something like guilt. Sam had collected a lot of these looks over the years. They were often his best indication that he and James were, if not on the same page, at least reading the same book.

"I hear you want to go to Pinnacle?" Amber asked Delia.

"That's step one," Delia said. "Though since the academics suck so hard at this school, my magic convention results are basically the only thing I can put on my application to give me a shot at getting in. I don't think Pinnacle takes many applicants who work at Chili's four days a week. Not to worry, I've got my backup plans ready."

"Pinnacle doesn't care if you have a perfect résumé," James said, an oft-repeated reassurance to an oft-repeated insecurity. "They just want people who made the most out of what was available to them. They know not everyone is on the same playing field."

"From your lips to the dean of admissions' ears."

The bell rang then, as if to ratify Delia's hope. Sam's lapse into moody silence went unacknowledged. His friends weren't ones to indulge him in his sullen moods, and Sam supposed that was for the best. If they asked him what was wrong, he wasn't even sure what he'd say.

As they picked up their trays to take to the trash can, Amber turned to James.

"By the way," she said, "what ended up happening with those guys from Mike's party?"

Sam's ears perked up.

"Uh, which guys?" James said, not stopping in his steps.

"You know, those guys by the cooler? The jerks with the pipe? Farah said she saw you get in the car with them, so I figured you went to that other party."

"Oh, uh. Nah, those guys weren't so bad. We talked it out after you left."

Delia caught Sam's eye and raised her eyebrow, which at least reassured him that he wasn't the only one picking up on the weird vibes here. But now they'd reached the fork outside the cafeteria, where Sam would have to go left to Trig while his friends went right to Calculus. He wasn't sure which direction Amber would go.

"Well, okay then," she said, shrugging it off. "Glad you sorted it out."

"So, see y'all in the gym at three forty-five?" Sam said, as if he were oblivious to whatever was happening here. "First practice of senior year?"

Delia gave him a two-finger salute, and James flashed him his best smile—*nothing to see here*. Which—fair enough.

But their group dynamic did feel twenty yards different today. It was just twenty yards in the wrong direction.

CHAPTER 2

THE THING ABOUT PRACTICING MAGIC IN FRIEDMAN,
Georgia, was that you never knew who was going to hate you for it.

The closer you got to Atlanta—and for sure, the closer you
got to the North—the more you encountered people who saw
magic for its progressive and artistic possibilities. Down here,
in the Deep South, you were still more likely to get an I-saw-
Goody-Proctor-with-the-devil.

It was no secret to Sam's classmates that he was a practicing
magicker. Most of them also figured he was gay, tipped off by
his careful pronunciation and penchant for fitted jeans, or else
by the bumper sticker on his car (an unsubtle rainbow, just in
case they didn't know that "Q-Atl" stood for Queer Atlanta, a
monthly support group on the south side for kids, teens, and
parents). But there was an unspoken understanding between
Sam and his classmates that the key to his peaceful existence at

school was to keep himself to himself. Save for his parents and a small handful of teachers and friends, which included James and Delia, Sam was never sure when he was talking to a Friedmanite if that person was actually okay with him or if they were just being polite, waiting until he was out of sight to cross themselves and pray for his immortal soul. Sometimes they didn't wait. Who could forget the time sophomore year when some seniors in the Fellowship of Christian Athletes had taken offense to his existence and launched a brief but intense campaign to try to defund and disband the Fascinators?

(They might have been successful, too, if Sam's mom hadn't threatened to rain down the full force of the ACLU upon the school. That had been a trip.)

All of that was to say, Sam never took the experience for granted when he walked into the gym at three forty-five—it was something special he had going here, with James and Delia. They were practicing magic. It was sanctioned with a practice space by state and school.

Sam was the first to arrive today, but he wasn't waiting long on the bleachers before Delia and James came in together, talking amiably—no sign that they were dwelling on the weirdness from lunch. They hardly paused their conversation as they walked up to Sam, and Delia managed to keep talking even as she brought her backpack around to her stomach and unzipped the main pocket, removing a stack of loose papers.

" . . . which is when I said that if he wanted me to go on a real date with him, he was going to have to try a little harder," Delia concluded, earning an admiring laugh from James and a serious eyebrow raise from Sam. "I was just filling in James on what happened at the bowling alley that night, after you two left," she explained.

There was that disorienting blip again, in the split second before Sam realized that she couldn't be referring to what had happened with him and James, because James would hardly need her to fill him in on that, and besides, James seemed totally at ease right now.

"Ah, right, with Jamal. You told me about that." Sam took a steadying breath. The only way things would start feeling normal again was if he started acting like they were normal again. He nodded at the papers in her hands. "What are those?"

"These," she said, handing one collated stack to James and one to Sam, "are copies of Professor C. January's freshman-year Applied Magics syllabus. Who is Professor C. January, you ask? Well, she, he, or they are a professor at none other than *the* Pinnacle School of Magic. You may have heard of it?"

"How did you get a copy of their syllabus?" Sam asked, leafing through the pages and finding references to all kinds of spells that, according to C. January, could be found in about fifteen different books and on dozens of different websites and apps. Some spells were written directly into the syllabus; most of those were in English, and they were all attributed to C. January themself. Original designs—a fact that seemed to confirm all of Sam's notions about Pinnacle.

"Well, Pinnacle has a Friendivist group for prospective students, and I dug around until I found some of the members who joined a while ago and were just starting first semester now. I private-messaged a couple of them, nothing too pushy, saying that I wanted to see whether the syllabus was too challenging for a Georgia nobody like me. You know, appealing to their own sense of how smart and accomplished they are."

"Good thinking," James said.

"And a little scary of you," Sam added.

"You don't even know," Delia said. "Turns out they're *too* proud of themselves up there; none of them wanted to share with me. But this guy, Vikram, and this other guy, Mark, both mentioned having the same teacher, so I made up an email address as Mark and told Vikram I was locked out of the student portal, so could he please forward the syllabus? It was a longshot, but surprise, it worked. And now that we have these, I can make *sure* that the coursework isn't beyond me. If it's all right with you two, I was thinking this semester we could alternate between practicing our convention categories and then practicing from this syllabus. Come Thanksgiving, convention will be behind us and I'll know if I got accepted, and then we can figure out what we want to do with our last six months, since we won't have a convention next year to practice for."

"Sounds like a plan to me," James said.

"Am I the only one who's not ready to think about our last

six months on the first day of school?"

"Sorry, Sam. You know living in the moment is a luxury I literally can't afford." Delia hugged her copy of the syllabus to her chest.

"Right, well, before we get too far down the road of planning our Christmas-slash-graduation party: James, what was all that about at lunch?"

"All what?"

"At Mike's party or whatever?" Sam said. "Sounded like I missed a lot. Of course, I've had all afternoon to wonder about it, so I'm sure the truth will be totally underwhelming."

"Oh, well . . . ," James paused and looked around, as if someone might be hiding in the wide-open—and very empty—gym. "It's nothing, really. Nothing worth getting you two mixed up in, anyway."

"Mixed up in?" Sam said.

"You obviously have to tell us whatever it is now," Delia said.

James bit his bottom lip, then let out a sigh.

"All right. But it's really nothing to worry about. I've got it all under control, okay? So. Last week, I went to Mike's party—"

"Is this the tryout for the magic club?"

In unison, they turned to find a boy in a blue plaid shirt, at least six feet tall plus another few inches of sandy blond curls. The boy was frantic and winded, as if he'd just sprinted here. Sam didn't recognize him, but the boy didn't look like a freshman, either. He stood a few steps inside the doorway, and he took a few more steps toward them, interpreting their silence to mean that they hadn't heard him, and not that they'd stopped expecting new potential members so long ago that they were having trouble processing the appearance of a stranger.

"Is this—"

"Yup, you're in the right place," Sam said. "I mean, assuming you are looking for the magic club yourself, and not just . . . asking . . . for someone else . . ." Sam felt his face go red. Delia gave him a look like she was embarrassed by proxy.

"Awesome," the guy said. "Yes, I am looking for the magic club. For myself."

Sam blushed even redder, which was apparently very amusing to James, judging by his roguish grin. If he thought he was off the hook for finishing his story later, he was sorely mistaken.

"I'm Denver, by the way." The boy reached out to shake hands with all of them, starting with Delia.

"I'm assuming you just moved here?" Delia said.

The boy stretched to his full height and smiled. Which, goodness. He had literal dimples.

"What gave it away?"

"It's a small school. We're the only three members of the club, and have been since we started it."

"Mostly because of how religious everybody is here," Sam explained, not wanting Denver to think that they were the weird ones or something. "People in Friedman think magic should only be used in worship. Anything more than that and you're trying to rival His power."

"I did get that sense around town this summer," Denver said. "One simple levitation spell to reach the top shelf at Publix, and suddenly everyone's looking at me like I summoned a lesser demon."

"You know how to summon a demon?" Delia said, with what Sam considered an alarming degree of excitement.

Denver laughed. He had a good laugh, warm and inclusive.

"No, no. Are those even a real thing? Either way, no. But I'll tell you what, it's a good thing Ms. Berry mentioned this group when I came in to register for classes last week. Even if Friedman is a Shirley Jackson story waiting to happen, I'll bet the main reason y'all don't get more members is that you hold your tryouts on the first day of school, with no announcements or anything."

Delia and James turned to Sam.

"Hey—I don't know why y'all are looking at me. I put up the posters, as you know."

Denver smirked. "Would those be the posters that said, 'Down with the patriarchy, up with magic, join the Fascinators'?"

The holding of a tryout was a necessary formality, following school and state magic club bylaws, and the bylaws said that tryouts had to be open and advertised to the whole school. But since they truly didn't believe anyone else at this school cared, Sam, as treasurer-slash-secretary, got to interpret "advertised" however he wished, which over the years had meant fliers containing PG innuendo, obscure anti-humor, and subtle liberalism.

"Clearly, they worked well enough," Sam countered.

"Ms. Berry stopped me on my way out to my car and gave me the heads-up," Denver said. Sam avoided eye contact with all of them, letting the beat that might have been filled with his apology be filled with the humming of the gym lights instead.

"Why *are* y'all called the Fascinators, by the way?" Denver finally continued. "Ms. Berry tried to explain it, but it didn't make any sense. At my old school, we were just 'the Magic Club,' and I thought that was a standardized thing, like Beta Club or Key Club. Lets people know what they're joining."

"It's just a word James found," Sam said, earning a mild look of betrayal from James. "We all liked it, though," he quickly clarified. "It's taken on new meaning in the years since."

"And who wants to be standardized?" James said, throwing down a smile like it was a challenge.

Which was Delia's cue to swerve. "So where was your old school?"

"Nashville. You been there?"

"Once," Delia said. Sam shook his head.

"It's a mixed bag. My mom and I did use magic in worship, but we're not zealots—we're Episcopalian. And my school's magic club was pretty diverse."

"Was your club any good?" James said.

"We were all right. I only joined it last year, as a sophomore, but we came in eighth overall at our state convention. Why? Are you three really good?"

Sam started to reply that if Denver had placed in the top ten in his state, he'd need to leave his hopes, dreams, and expectations at the door of the Friedman gym, but James spoke first.

"Honestly? Yeah, kind of," he said. "We don't have enough

members to field a full team, but Delia's never met an incantation she couldn't do exactly right, and Sam always gets the touchy-feely parts when Delia and I don't."

"He means the associations," Sam mumbled.

"Plus," James went on, "Ms. Berry never comes to practices. We've basically taught ourselves everything we know."

That was true, strictly speaking, although Sam was tempted to point out that their lack of a teacher could also be the reason for his own deficiencies. Whatever James thought of his figurative strengths, Sam wasn't a quick study like James and Delia.

"I respect that," Denver said. "Does that mean you judge your own tryout, too?"

"Yes," James said, before Sam could interject that there *was* no tryout—the only requirement was to show up. That was the whole joke.

"It's actually pretty simple," James continued, deliberately avoiding eye contact with Sam and Delia. "We've all done it before. You just have to tell us how much cash Sam has in his wallet, without touching him in any way. You can use whatever magic you want, as long as you don't hurt Sam and as long as you give back any money you take."

Delia and Sam exchanged an uneasy look. Neither of them knew what James was playing at here, and what he was asking was hard. Unless Denver had X-Ray vision—and Sam hoped he didn't, under the circumstances—he would either have to levitate an object he couldn't see and had never seen, or else he would have to read Sam's mind.

"Oh," Denver said, daunted but determined. "Okay, then, sure. Straightforward but tricky. I like it. I think."

He squared his feet with his shoulders and stared into Sam's eyes, like maybe he really was going the mind-reading route. He seemed so sincere, with his hands down by his sides. Sam's aggressive anti-awkwardness reflex manifested in the form of a powerful urge to look away.

More than that, though, he felt an urge to help. Denver might not need to pass this tryout to make the club, but he didn't know that, and Sam found that he didn't like being on this side of a joke at someone else's expense, however lighthearted it was intended to be.

I don't carry cash. I don't carry cash. I don't carry cash.

"James—" Delia started.

"Wait—don't mess up his concentration," James said, enjoying this far too much for Sam's liking.

Denver had broken a sweat.

I don't carry cash. I don't carry cash. I don't carry—

"None," Denver said, as if it had come to him suddenly. "He doesn't have any cash in his wallet."

Sam sighed, too relieved to be impressed, although there would be plenty of time to realize how impressed he was later.

"How did you do that?" James said in disbelief, and Sam could swear he was looking at him, too, like he knew that Sam had contributed somehow.

"A good magicker never reveals all his secrets," Denver said.

Then he winked at Sam—actually winked, like a black-and-white movie star, instead of a person.

"Well, Denver," Delia said, "however you did it, as club president, it is my executive privilege to speak for all of us and say welcome to the Fascinators." She shot James a matching executive look. "I imagine we all have a lot we can learn from you."

If the addition of a fourth member into their tight-knit group made their first practice feel a little stiff and stilted, forcing the three of them to articulate things that had long since become routine, it was all lost on Denver, who seemed at ease right away. He even already had lots of ideas for the rest of the year, which he was more than happy to share, one after the other, as they all walked out to the parking lot at the end.

"Maybe we can keep a shared drive going with all the spells we're working on, so we can help each other between practices? Oh, and do y'all do a fundraiser before convention? We did at my old school, and we were able to completely cover our hotel rooms and meals."

"We don't," James said.

"Though that *is* a great idea, actually," Delia said. "Don't you think so, Sam? Sam's our treasurer. Last year we stayed at James's distant cousin's place during convention. We had to sleep on a couch and an air mattress while Ms. Berry stayed in an Airbnb on her own dime."

"It was a very comfortable air mattress," James said.

"What do you think, Sam?" Denver said. "How much money would we need to raise?"

"Well, let's see . . . every year, I take the hundred dollars the school gives us, then use it to pay for our entry fee to convention. With the five dollars that's left over, I reimburse myself for the tryout posters and, if I'm lucky, the markers. But now that you mention it, I was thinking this year I could push Ms. Berry for an extra ten bucks to help buy us some T-shirts. Seeing as how it's our last year and all."

Denver didn't know Sam well enough to tell if he was kidding, so he offered a smile that could pass either way. To be fair, Sam wasn't kidding, he just couldn't stop his voice from defaulting in that direction.

Finally, they got to the row where their cars were waiting. All except Denver's—he'd have to keep walking the twenty yards to reach his.

"Well, I'll see y'all next time, I guess?" Denver said.

"See you then," Delia said, while James and Sam waved.

Sam turned to say goodbye to his friends, but for some reason, without discussing it, Delia and James were both climbing into the back seat of *his* car, not even waiting for Denver to get ten steps away before gossiping so loudly, Denver probably could have heard them from the football field. Sam jumped into the driver's seat and rushed to roll up his windows all the way, the least he could do.

"—and then making him try out?" Delia was saying.

"Oh, come on, that was totally harmless. Not to mention it didn't work, thanks to an assist from that one." Sam caught James nodding his way in the rearview mirror. He didn't think he liked being referred to as "that one."

"We could really use some new blood," Delia said. "I think he's going to be an asset to the group."

"I'm *sure* you do," James said suggestively. "*Quite* the asset."

"Oh, please, James. My type is a little less bright-eyed. Besides, I got the distinct impression that he plays for Sam's team. Didn't you think so, Sam?"

"Um, I don't know what to think, having just met the guy. But what I do know is that y'all better wait until he's at least out of earshot before you draft him onto any team, or we're going to scare him away before our next practice, and possibly find ourselves in Ms. Berry's office."

"So, you're also happy he's joining," James said. It sounded like a trick question, if it was a question at all.

"I mean, sure," Sam said. "Why not?"

"Nothing, it's just . . . I mean . . . I just . . ."

James's voice became faint until he fully trailed off, and at first Sam thought he was looking for the right words to express his disappointment. But when the silence stretched on and Sam turned in his seat, he found James staring blankly ahead, his eyes glazed over. His mouth hung slightly open; he didn't blink. Sam snapped his fingers, but no response.

"James?" Delia said, shaking him gently by the shoulder,

which only had the effect of making him slump forward against the passenger seat, his whole body limp.

"What the hell?" Sam said, unsettled but still clinging to the hope that this was another prank, like the tryout—that James was just in a joking mood.

Delia clearly didn't think so. She began muttering the words to an incantation Sam didn't recognize—something rough and guttural. Urgent. Circular. Sam wasn't sure what it was doing exactly, but finally, in the exact moment that he felt his own stomach fly toward his spine, a visceral revulsion, James rocked suddenly back against his seat, and when he regained his balance, he was himself again.

"Oh no," he said. "No, no, no."

"What was that?" Sam said.

"*Who* was that?" Delia added.

In the twelve years that Sam had known him, James had never been one of those guys who hid his emotions. He couldn't if he wanted to—his emotions were too big. (The words to go with them were a different story; James always said he didn't like to share his problems, because it only made the problems bigger.) On three different occasions, Sam had seen James cry, and he'd lost count of how many times he'd seen James clenched-fist angry, usually about something his complete monster of a father had done.

But never—not once in twelve years—had Sam seen his friend look scared. Not when they'd broken Mr. McDougal's window playing catch with James's little brother, Benji—not even when

James had had to go to the ER with an arm so broken it jutted out at a weird angle.

Right now, in the back seat of Sam's car, James looked absolutely terrified.

"James, does this have something to do with what happened at Mike's party?" Sam said.

"Maybe," James admitted.

Sam raised his eyebrows.

"Okay, yes."

"You have to tell us what's going on," Sam said.

"Agreed," Delia said. "I'm no dark magic expert, but that felt like one powerful curse."

James wrung his hands and stared into his lap. Sam knew what was happening; James was afraid to make the problem bigger. Finally, he looked up at them. "Do you have time right now? It might be better if I show you."

CHAPTER 3

IN FRIEDMAN, GEORGIA, THERE IS ONE MAIN ROAD, right off the interstate exit, that gives the appearance of a town that's developed but generic. A pit-stop exit and not much more. In short succession, there's a movie theater, a Chick-fil-A, a Waffle House, etc.—oh, and the Chili's, the one where Delia works—and if you were just driving through on your road trip from Tennessee to Florida, you might think that Friedman was a cookie-cutter, forgettable town. No deep wells of magic here.

If you took the time to head farther in, though, you'd start to notice the tiny box homes sitting right off the road, often dilapidated, yes, but many of them unchanged for a hundred years. You might catch glimpses of the sprawling farmhouses and colonnaded mansions at the end of long driveways, mostly hidden through the trees. (The houses Sam's mom sold were somewhere between these two extremes, and she always said that this was by design; she hated that the super-rich people who made their money outside of Friedman didn't want you to know they lived here, while the lower-income families couldn't afford any privacy.)

You'd see that, beyond that main road, hardly any of the town's restaurants belonged to chain franchises—instead they had singular possessive names like Mo's or Mary Ellen's.

You'd see at least ten churches, if you made the full tour, some of them one rectangular room plus a steeple, but some of them sprawling, the size of a big-city block.

To Sam, who'd grown up here, everything in Friedman had a hard-to-pin-down quality that did have a kind of magic in it. A uniquely Friedman-like, beautiful magic. Even that main drag. It was something in the town's bones—a jigsaw puzzle that needed every single piece to make sense.

And even if Sam often felt like an extra piece in that puzzle— like the town didn't want him; like he didn't fit—still, it was hard not to feel as if the town's magic coursed through his own veins, a part of his DNA.

Perhaps that was why, when the end of James's circuitous directions at last found them driving by a long stretch of land that Sam had never seen before, containing what appeared to be a repurposed warehouse a ways off the street, Sam knew they were outside the Friedman city limits without even having to check his phone. This place was silent and strange.

"I don't understand. Does Mike live around here somewhere?" Sam asked, leaning over Delia to try to get a look at the building.

So far, on the drive here, James had been trying to set the scene with a story that kept circling around three facts: (1) He had been to Mike's party last week, where (2) He had drunk way more than he should have, and okay, he'd even gotten high, when he *really* should not have, because (3)—and this was in answer to Sam's question—yes, Amber was at this party as she'd hinted at lunch, but no, she hadn't gotten drunk or high with him, because, in fact, she didn't approve of anyone getting high, so James's being stoned had caused a bit of an issue between them. Number three didn't seem to be a main point of the story James was trying to tell, however—he didn't get why Sam kept asking about Amber at all—so there was that, at least. Whatever dangerous things James had gotten mixed up in last week, Amber wasn't mixed up in them, too. That was some consolation.

"Don't slow down," James now urged from the back seat, startling Sam and causing him to jam his foot on the accelerator, earning a complaint from his transmission. "No, Mike lives back by Stillwater Creek."

"Then what are we doing all the way out here?" Delia said, craning her neck to keep an eye on the warehouse.

There were tall windows on the first floor, but they appeared to be covered from the inside. There was a parking lot around back that Sam could see in his rearview mirror, now that they had driven past. It had three, maybe four cars in it, none of them very new or very nice.

"Keep going and I'll tell you," James said, also watching the building. "There's a little turnoff up here on the right, coming in . . . right there, see it? Pull in there."

Sam turned right onto a narrow dirt road, one he would have certainly missed if James hadn't been here to guide him, since two arching trees by the street covered it almost completely, a hidden doorway in the wood.

The trees only grew denser as the road continued. Though Sam had turned off the main street in broad daylight, it was as if he'd driven into a world where it was always night.

Sam was more than a little relieved when James said, "You can stop here." He figured the chances of another car coming in either direction and needing to get by them were low; the chances of going so far into the wood that they never came back out again seemed significantly higher.

"Okay," Delia said. "Now can you tell us what in the hell we're doing here?"

"Right. So, like I said, this all started at Mike's party, where I got completely blasted—like, seeing double, walking backward, high. Backing up a little bit, though—there were these three guys there, guys I'd seen at a couple other parties this summer, always standing off to the side, keeping to themselves. One of them had offered me a light once, I think. They seemed fine. Maybe a little old to be at a sophomore party, but I was, too, so."

"Yeah, I won't pretend I'm not judging you for that part," Delia said. Sam was more hung up on the "couple other parties" that James had apparently attended without them this summer.

At least he'd known about Mike's. At least he'd been invited.

"Judge if you want," James said. "I needed to get out of my house. Anyway, so these guys were standing right by the cooler when I went to get another drink, which of course was also when Amber got there, saw the empty and the new beer, and gave me this look because she knows from church that I'm trying to cut back. Right away, the guys are like, 'Oh, somebody's in trouble,' 'somebody's in the doghouse,' that sort of shit. So Amber heads inside, and I end up starting a conversation with these dudes, partly to save face but also to tell them they were being complete assholes to my friend. But then we started talking, and they actually seemed pretty cool. They're the ones who had the pipe."

"James, please tell me you did not take a hit of something a stranger gave you," Sam said, exasperated.

"Not until after I'd seen them take a few hits of it first," James said. "I'm not a complete idiot. Anyway, somehow we got on the topic of magic; I think I mentioned something about the Fascinators, I don't know. And it turns out these guys are magickers, too. And they say, hey, you should come with us to this other party, at this place where all these magickers hang out and learn new spells."

"And let me guess, that creepy abandoned warehouse we just passed was that place?" Delia said.

"Not abandoned, but yes."

"You went to a magicker party without us?" Sam said. For some reason, this was even worse than going to a regular party—

magic was *their* thing: Sam, James, and Delia. It was what set them apart.

"How many times do I have to say it? I was high out of my mind. Even if you had been at Mike's, y'all hate being around me when I'm high." Which, fair enough. Delia and Sam didn't do drugs of any kind. Delia had stopped being around them altogether because of the potential impact on her college applications if she got caught. Sam didn't have strong feelings about alcohol or drugs in the abstract so much as he had strong feelings about what everyone in Friedman became when they consumed them. Drunk people were way more likely to let their homophobic flags fly. James never got that way, of course, but he wasn't pleasant to be around either—he became more avatar than person, ecstatic one moment and then hating the world and his life the next. Sam preferred the small, sober, and separate world the Fascinators inhabited when they practiced magic. That was why the news of this party, populated by other magickers, felt like such a betrayal.

"Anyway, backing up again, that's when Amber and I kind of had our thing. She didn't want me leaving with these guys, because I was so stoned and because she didn't trust the one guy who said he hadn't been drinking to be the designated driver."

"At least someone was thinking straight," Delia said.

"Look, do you want to hear the rest of the story or not? I'd been watching him. He hadn't had a drink since I'd gotten there."

"Go on," Sam said, even if inwardly he was having the same horrified reaction as Delia.

"So we get to that warehouse, and there are all these cars in the parking lot, which is weird, because I'm thinking there can't be *that* many practicing magickers around here. Surely we'd know if there were. And then we walk in the back door, into this huge, open room, where I can see two floors above me, almost like the ground floor of a prison or a mall or something. Right away, I notice that of the thirty or so people there, only nine or ten look like they're our age. Everybody else is a grown-ass adult. Then this guy comes up to us with a clipboard, asks for our names, and I think we're about to get kicked out, but the three guys have their names on the list and say I'm with them. Say I'm really good at magic, which struck me as funny, because what are they basing that on? At this point, I was starting to come down, and my internal alarm bells were going off, just a little bit."

"'Just a little bit?' What the hell, James." Delia looked like she was ready to smack some sense into him. Sam had to agree. Showing up and then *staying* at a sketchy adult party in the middle of nowhere sounded insane, even for James, and the fact that he could recount this story in such a calm voice—the fact that he'd been planning to not even tell them about it—made Sam worry that maybe it wasn't that insane for him. Unlike Delia, though, Sam was trying to contain his surprise; if James saw how cool Sam was being with this news, maybe next time he'd let him in a few steps before things got so out of hand. (It hadn't escaped him that James had confided in Amber about wanting to cut back on drinking—something he'd never told Sam.)

Outside Sam's car, it was growing ever darker. The sun must have been going down beyond the trees, though none of the pinks and oranges of sunset were able to penetrate the forest; in here, it only went from gray to grayer. The three of them all seemed to notice this at the same time, and James's face creased in concern.

"Look, I know, it's not great. I wish I could say I left the second things got out of hand, but I didn't. And I can keep talking about it all night, but before we lose the little light we have left, the real reason we're here is to look for something. A giant leather book. It has this symbol on the cover."

With hardly any effort, because little prestidigitations like this came as naturally to James as breathing did, James guided his fingers through the air and left a trail of light in their wake—a trail of light in the shape of a jagged V, like two lightning bolts striking the same point from different angles. The shape stained the air for a moment and then was gone.

"Oh, hell, no," Delia said. "I am not going out into *these* woods and looking for anything until I know exactly what it is. What is in this giant leather book? Dessert recipes? Your grandmother's journal?"

"I can explain more as we're looking," James said. "But that thing that happened to me back in the parking lot? The curse or whatever? It's going to keep happening—and it's going to get worse—until I find this book."

Sam was already opening his door and stepping out into the woods.

"Brown leather or . . . ?" he said.

"Green, actually. Might not be real leather. Looks like something you'd buy at the renfest."

"Gotcha."

"James," Delia said. "Is this a *spell* book we're looking for?"

"See, I knew you wouldn't need more explanation."

"James!" she protested.

They were all out of the car now, but Delia was standing her ground beside the passenger side door. Sam was scanning the foliage and trees right beside the road; it was hard to take even a step farther into the forest, because the underbrush got so thick so fast. Sam saw more than a few bramble bushes whose thorns looked sharp enough to pierce his jeans.

"Okay, okay," James said. "So, once everybody on the list got there, they started this group spell, right? And shit got weird really fast from there. Like, five people were supposed to stand in the points of a pentagram—"

"What would Amber say about that, I wonder?" Sam asked before he could stop himself.

"Sam, focus," Delia said.

James barreled ahead like he hadn't heard Sam's comment. "—and one stood in the center, while the guy who was in charge stood off to the side with this giant spell book. When his six people were in place, he started reading from it. I didn't recognize the language. Meanwhile, his helpers told the rest of us to start making associations like ripping, cutting, tearing—scissors, knives, paper, whatever. Maybe if I'd still been high, I could have done all that touchy-feely stuff. But in that moment, hell no. And I could tell I wasn't the only one there who hadn't known what to expect and was getting a little freaked out. A few of us were looking at each other like, Um, sorry, no?

"The good news is, the spell didn't work, whatever it was supposed to be. The guy with the book was getting super frustrated, shooting these death-stares at those of us who weren't into it. Finally, he called it off, and everybody started milling around, trying to get the party started, while the leader guy took his book and stormed off into another room, like he was having a temper tantrum."

As he spoke, James tromped around the woods, slicing through the air with his hands, clearing a path with his magic as if he really did have scissors, a knife, a machete. The weeds fell at his feet, though he didn't venture too far off the road.

There was no sign of the book, or of anything not belonging to the forest. Everything here looked like it had always been this way—untouched, unchanged, until now.

Delia didn't budge. "And how did we get from that point in the warehouse to the book ending up out here?"

"Well, almost as soon as the spell failed, I went back to the guys I came with and asked to get the hell out of there."

"The first good decision you made that night," Delia said.

"It would have been, except the guys didn't want to leave. I ended up wandering around the first floor, doing my own thing, until finally I went into that room where the guy had taken the book."

"So it was also the *last* good decision you made that night," Delia said.

James shrugged. "The door was unlocked, the guy was nowhere in sight, and the book was just lying there, so I figured they wouldn't care too much if I read through it. But as soon as I put a hand on it, the leader guy and two of his buddies, like, *appeared*. The door didn't even open, they were just there. And I swear on Mary Ellen's biscuits and gravy, they were ready to kill me. Really and truly. I've never seen faces look like that, so full of hate, and y'all know my dad, so that's saying something."

It was getting darker and harder to see by the moment. Sam closed his eyes and imagined that he was the moon, reflective, willing. When he opened his eyes, a soft, blue glow emanated from his palms, casting everything in a somber light.

Bathed in blue, James stood stock-still, his face beyond haunted—the distance Sam had detected at lunch now clearly a reflection of sleepless nights since last week. Sam believed James about what those guys would have done to him. James didn't exaggerate about stuff like that. Sam was suddenly overwhelmed with gratitude to have James here, alive.

"I panicked like a bear in a trap. I wasn't even thinking. I did this spell that I hadn't done since I was a kid—hadn't even *thought* of since I was a kid—when my dad almost walked in on me playing with my mom's makeup, and I wanted to make it disappear. All these years later, the spell still worked. At least, I'm assuming it did, because the book disappeared. Either way, I told the guys that I was the only person who knew where it had gone, and if they ever wanted to see it again, they better let me leave the warehouse, unharmed. They were pissed. You could tell they didn't trust me to give it back, but they didn't really have a choice, and they didn't want to make a scene in front of the other guests who weren't part of the main group. I guess the book is a big fucking deal for them."

Sam and Delia swayed on their feet, stunned. Sam couldn't stop picturing his friend, trapped and alone and afraid—last week in that warehouse, but as a kid with his mother's makeup, too.

"So you don't actually know where you teleported the book to," Delia said, two steps ahead of Sam, as usual.

"I hadn't done that spell in so long. The first time, all the stuff went back to my bedroom, so I thought the spell would work the same way now. But when I got home last week and the book wasn't there, I did the spell again—experimented with it some more—and *nothing* went to my bedroom. It's hard to explain, but I think all the associations for this spell are about safety—a safe place. And I guess there was a time when that meant my bedroom, but that hasn't been the case for a while now."

Delia sighed. "And you really think this dirt road in the forest is the last place you felt safe?"

"As soon as I left the warehouse that night, I used that camou-flage spell you taught us in seventh grade, then booked it down the street until I found this road. I called a Lyft to take me back to Mike's and then waited for like thirty minutes in complete darkness for it to get here, the whole time thinking that those assholes were going to come after me. Not exactly a safe place, no, but I've checked everywhere else I could think of in the last week. My nana's house, church—I even came into school during freshman orientation to look around."

"Forget the book," Sam said. "Can't you report these people to the police?"

"Report them for what?" James said.

"I don't know. Were they drinking? Maybe providing alcohol to minors?"

"Nobody was drinking as far as I saw. Besides, if this goes to the police, I'd probably be the one to get charged with robbery."

"Now that you mention it, why haven't these guys reported you to the police?" Delia said.

"That's the thing. I think they really were up to something shady. I don't think they want the police involved any more than I do. And I'm willing to bet they don't want the police to see what's in their book, wherever it is. I'm betting there is some serious illegal magic in there. Like, the-Keepers-would-come-after-them level shit."

"So now you're in a checkmate. Or stalemate. Or something," Sam said.

Darkness had fully descended now. They stood in a triangle, lit only by the fairy light of Sam's hands.

"It might be a stalemate, but they are on the offensive," James said. "Ever since that night, I've been having these . . . dreams. More vivid than normal dreams, and I have less control over them, too. I think somehow these people are behind them. It's like my brain has been hacked. Like they're threatening me in my own mind. I had another one in the car this afternoon. It's the first time I've had one while I was awake."

James didn't need to tell them the specific contents of these dreams. Their aftereffects were clear on his face.

If these people were capable of the long-range dream magic James was describing—when Sam couldn't even cast a lesser dream spell on himself after a whole summer of trying—what hope did the three of them have of defending themselves if it came to that?

They had to find the book. That was all there was to it.

"Well, the book's definitely not here," James said, defeated. "Can you drive us back to the parking lot?"

Sam nodded, happy to have something concrete he could do for James—something unmagical. After everything that had happened on this very long first day of school, Sam almost wished his sense of self weren't so wrapped up in the magic thing. It didn't leave him on the surest footing in moments like this, when the magic didn't feel so fun anymore.

CHAPTER 4

SAM DIDN'T SLEEP VERY WELL THAT NIGHT, AND HE spent the second day of school in that semi-delirious state where everything was a little funnier than it should have been and a lot more exhausting. He might have put his head on the table and fallen asleep at lunch, except that Amber joined them again—this time at the beginning of the period—and Sam felt an immense pressure to sit up and be at least as charming as she was. Which, that would have been hard to do even on a full night's rest. Amber was basically charm city.

Maybe because Amber was at their table, James was doing an admirable job of acting like everything was fine, though the deep bags under his eyes gave him away. Sam wished there were more he could do to help; it was torture watching James fake smile and fake laugh when he must have been scared out of his mind, and even Amber seemed to be picking up on the fact that

James wasn't totally on his game.

It was all Sam could do to make it to his locker in one piece at the end of the day.

When he got there, it was to find the new boy, Denver, his thumbs hooked under the straps of his backpack. He was apparently waiting for Sam to arrive. All six feet of him, plus the dimples.

"Hi," Sam said, painfully aware of how his voice sounded, even on such a short syllable.

"Hey, Sam. What's up?"

"Me, but only barely. I mean—I'm tired. Hi. Sorry, I said 'hi' already."

Denver laughed. A small mercy.

"How did you know which one was mine?" Sam said, nodding to his locker.

"Louise Baxter. She didn't know which one exactly, but she said it was around here."

"Ah," Sam said, though really his heartbeat was skipping like a rock on a lake. Denver had gone out of his way to ask a random senior where his locker was. That was an astonishing and flattering amount of effort.

"In all the excitement yesterday, I didn't realize until I got home that we never actually said when the next Fascinators practice was going to be."

"Oh, right. Of course you wouldn't know. We usually just coordinate over group text once Delia gets her schedule from Chili's for the week. We do whatever three days she isn't working.

We'll have to add you to the text."

"Does that mean we can exchange numbers?" Denver said. "Or will James make up a reason for me to guess that, too?"

Sam blushed. Maybe Denver wasn't as bright-eyed as they'd thought yesterday. (But maybe Delia was right about him not being straight, because p.s., was Denver flirting with him? People didn't say "exchange numbers" in the real world unless they were flirting with you, surely?)

"You heard about that, huh?" Sam said.

"Ms. Berry stopped me in the hall to ask how it went. When I said I passed the tryout by the skin of my teeth, I could tell by the confused look on her face that I'd been initiated, chump style."

"Sorry about that. If it makes you feel better, we were all super impressed."

"Yeah?"

"Yeah."

Denver smiled. "That does make me feel better. Anyway, I know I'm the new kid on the block, and you three have been friends for a million years."

"For better and for worse."

Denver quirked an eyebrow.

"You know how it is, I'm sure," Sam said. "From your friends in Nashville. I couldn't survive Friedman without James and Delia, but sometimes—like this year, when I don't have them in any of my classes—I remember that not everyone speaks our weirdo language, and I think maybe I should have spent more time practicing being a normal human."

"Well, sign me up, I guess. All I need is your number."

Sam held up his phone for Denver to see his contact info before he could ruin it by saying anything else. Almost immediately, he received a text from Denver that read, **Hello** ☺.

"Hey," Sam said. "About yesterday? I totally understand if you want to keep most of your secrets, but you have to tell me one thing. You can't, like, full-on read my mind, right?"

"The day I can read minds is the day I drop out of school and take this show on the road. Until then, let's just say the thing my old magic club found most useful was my affinity for luck magic. That, combined with the fact that James most likely wouldn't have thought to call out the money in your wallet unless it was some exceptional number, like a thousand dollars or zero dollars, et voilà."

"Well, hot damn," Sam said.

Denver waved the phone in his hand and turned to go.

"Talk to you soon, Sam."

"If you're lucky," Sam said, earning surprised smiles from both of them.

Just as she refused to sell the mansions of Friedman, Sam's mom refused to live in one of them, too, even though she and Sam's steel engineer father could easily have afforded one if they'd so chosen. Instead, Sam lived in one of the newer subdivisions, which Delia had once described as Variations on a Theme of

Vinyl Siding. Still, out of the three friends, Sam's house was the nicest, and Sam's parents were easily the coolest, too, keeping a fridge stocked with Cokes and staying out of their way during practices in Sam's basement.

When Sam pulled up to his house that day—with Delia and James following right behind him—he saw that Denver was already there, standing awkwardly in the driveway.

"Someone's excited to see you," Delia whispered through a smile as she came up beside Sam. She'd given him no end of hell at lunch when he told them about the incident by the locker, by way of explaining how Denver came to be in their group text. (Thankfully, Amber had gone back to eating with her own friends.)

"I will cast an eternal binding curse on you if you don't stop that right now," Sam whispered in return.

"Sorry," Denver said as they approached. "It took less time to get here than I expected. I almost drove around the block another time, but then I thought, why waste the gas?"

"No worries. Sorry you had to wait out here. My parents are still at work."

The four of them made their way straight for the basement. They'd barely reached the bottom of the stairs before Delia started pulling papers from her backpack. At first Sam thought it was the Pinnacle syllabus again, but then he realized the stack was way too thick for that.

"This is every finding spell I could pull together in time,"

Delia said. "I even used some of the finding spells to find additional finding spells."

Denver laughed.

"I'm not kidding," Delia said.

"Why do we need finding spells exactly?" Denver said right away, trying to pretend his laugh had never happened.

"Because James—" Delia started.

"Because James lost the spell book we put together last year with everything we were preparing for convention," Sam cut in. He'd seen James's face go pale from the first moment Delia mentioned finding spells. He suspected it was because James didn't want to loop in Denver on this secret yet, if ever. To Delia's credit, she seemed to pick up on that now.

"Oh, damn," Denver said. "How'd you do that?"

"Not all of us have your gift for good luck," James said, and even though his voice was friendly enough, Denver shot Sam a look, surprised that he had shared that tidbit with the group.

"Sorry," Denver said. "Just thought a little backstory might help us find it. This is why I suggested the shared drive, by the way. This exact thing happened at my old school the year before I joined the club."

"And after today, I think we should absolutely take your advice," Delia said. "For now, I've arranged these finding spells in order from most advanced to least advanced. I figure the most advanced spell would probably work perfectly if one of us could pull it off, but if we can't, we'll need to move on to an easier one. Hopefully the first spell we're able to do will still be strong enough to find the book."

"How methodical of you," Denver said.

Sam smiled. "There's a reason she's president."

"Are you sure we should be doing this right now?" James said, with a pointed look Denver's way. "Maybe it would be better if we all took some of these home separately and only attempt them together when we know what works?"

"Merlin's Law," Delia said. "The more the merrier the magic."

Denver wasn't stupid. He could see there was something else they weren't telling him. But Sam had a feeling his mind wasn't going as far afield as the truth.

"Whatever," James replied. He really did look the worse for wear today, like a stranger in a James suit—like he'd forgotten how to James.

Delia said, "Why don't you describe the book more. For most of these spells, the associations are more about the thing you're trying to find than they are about the act of finding itself, so it helps to have as clear a mental image as possible. Obviously, this is for Denver's sake, since Sam and I already know what the book looks like."

James clenched his jaw, no doubt wishing he had shared his predicament with better sneaks—or not shared it at all. But he said, "It's green leather, about yea big, with this symbol on the front." He replicated the spell to produce the lightning-bolt *V*. "Does that give you an idea?"

"I guess," Denver said. "I'll do my best."

"Same," Sam said. "For what little that's worth."

James frowned reflexively. He hated when Sam was down on himself, no matter how many times Sam said he was kidding. James was the consummate protector, which he always said came from being a big brother.

Either way, it turned out that this time, Sam wasn't kidding. His best, and Denver's best, and even Delia's and James's best, altogether weren't enough to make the first finding spell work, or the second, or the third-through-sixth. Sam suspected this had a lot to do with all four of them having slightly different mental images for the book they were trying to find, and also something to do with the fact that three of them were concealing the full story of what they were doing from the fourth. Real magic, in Sam's experience, never worked as well on a foundation of dishonesty.

There was nothing about the seventh spell in Delia's stack that suggested it was going to work better. Like a few of the others, it would require them all to close their eyes and picture the book. Also like the others, it would require them all to recite a simple chant. Unlike the more powerful spells, this one didn't even promise to illuminate the exact location of the object in question. It promised a strong mental image of the object's immediate surroundings; if you didn't recognize what you saw, well, tough luck.

Delia read the associations out loud. "Picture the object in your mind, then poke at the periphery of what you see. If you can conjure the details, the feelings, the *associations*, you will start to recall the object itself, and once it has been recalled, it can be reclaimed."

Which—all right, then!

This wasn't the first time Sam had done a spell whose associations suggested a link between imagination and memory. And in a way, the connection always made sense—once a thing was in the past, it might as well have been imaginary, since it existed in the mind in the exact same way.

But sitting in a circle on the thinly carpeted floor of his basement, Sam was finding it incredibly difficult to conjure the feelings and associations he had for this book he'd never seen in real life. His mind kept wandering to something more immediate: James's and Denver's fingertips on his. (After the third failed spell, Delia had insisted that they all hold hands going forward, even though Sam didn't remember this being one of the tenets of Merlin's Law.) Holding James's featherlight hand while simultaneously having his hand held in Denver's firm grip was not helping Sam concentrate on a giant green spell book—not one bit.

But, as often happened, Delia's suggestion proved ingenious. The longer Sam held James's hand, and chanted the chant, and pictured the book, the more he could start to see James in the darker moments of that night last week, following his impulse to slip into the side room and see this book. Because why? Because James couldn't help himself. Because for as long as Sam had known him, his anger at his dad, the pressure he felt at having to be a responsible big brother and role model for Benji, meant he resented his own life too much to make safer decisions, starting with the drinks that night but only snow-balling from there. Because it never occurred to James that there were people who cared about him so much that it hurt. Or maybe because James knew about these people, and that only made the pressure worse.

Suddenly, Sam could see it all so clearly—James with the book that night, his reckless curiosity driving him into danger. He could see James having gone there in search of a good time, and then, having failed to find it, wanting to take something with him, a kind of anarchist's revenge. He could see James walking into the side room, an orderly office space with filing cabinets full of books, all surrounding a central, circular table that looked like it was set up for a card game.

The lights began to flicker—in Sam's vision, but maybe also in the basement of Sam's house. Sam had the sense that the flickering was just beyond his vision, and that if he could only open his eyes, he would see what was causing it.

But he couldn't open his eyes.

And he couldn't direct his vision.

Suddenly, it wasn't James in the side room—it was him. The door to the room opened, and at least five people poured in, though it was hard to say the exact number, as the flickering intensified, painfully bright with each pulse. The people were faceless—there was no other way to say it. Where their eyes and mouths and noses should be, there were only blurs. The people swarming and surrounding him turned their blank no-faces as if to get a better sense of him, there in the room that was only what Sam was imagining and not a real room—*the* real room—surely? Surely? It was a powerful association and nothing more?

But then why did it feel like Sam was confined to the room? Couldn't leave? That he wasn't controlling what he was seeing, and that the faceless ones were walking toward him, reaching, a hair's breadth away—that Sam couldn't move, that his feet were welded to the spot.

Sam heard his name being called from just beyond the doorway, and the faceless ones heard it, too. It made them hurry. It made them lunge for Sam with their not-quite-hands, and Sam had to spin and dodge to avoid them. He made a dash for the door, the faceless ones hard on his heels, while the voices outside grew louder, calling his name.

In the exact, heart-stopping moment when one of the faceless ones reached Sam and wrapped itself around him, Sam threw open the door, and there were James, Denver, and Delia.

"He's awake," Denver said.

"What the hell, Sam." Delia's voice was gruff with panic.

James couldn't speak. His face was ashen and slow to register relief.

"I saw them," Sam said. "I didn't see the book, but I saw them, and they saw me."

"Who's 'them?'" Denver said.

"You're sure the book wasn't there?" Delia said.

"I'm sure. It was like my brain had been hijacked—like I wasn't controlling where my mind went. They were. Is that what a dream is like? Lord, how terrible. It felt like they knew I was trying to find the book, and they wanted to know what I knew. It was like, if I'd ended up finding it, they wanted to be the first to know."

"They who?" Denver repeated, as if they hadn't heard him.

"This is exactly what I've been dealing with," James said, his voice quiet with fear and guilt. "This is exactly what I was afraid of, telling you two."

"Maybe this is because of a spell they've put on the book," Delia said, her mind practically whirring behind her eyes. "You said they came back into the room as soon as you touched it, right, James? Maybe they have some kind of tracer or tracker or something, and a finding spell triggers it just like touching the book in the physical plane would."

"Hello," Denver said. "Metaphysical plane to you three. Could someone please tell me what the hell is going on here, now that I've basically risked my life for a spell without any prior warning as to what I was actually getting into?"

"What's going on down here?"

Sam's mom. In all the excitement, they hadn't noticed her coming down the stairs, and now she stood across the basement. Who knew how much she'd heard.

She walked right up to them and gave Sam a puzzled look. To be fair, he was lying faceup on the ground. The other three stood over him.

Whatever her assessment of the situation, she must have realized that any immediate danger had passed; she turned in her comforting, measured way to Denver and said, "I don't think we've met." She stuck out her hand and smiled.

"I'm Denver," he said. "From Nashville."

"Nice to meet you, Denver from Nashville. James, Delia, good to see you both."

"Mrs. Fisher," Delia said with a nod, while James mumbled a hello.

She turned back to look at Sam, who'd managed now to perch on his elbows and look a little less dazed.

"This wouldn't be the result of some high-level, dangerous spell, I hope?"

Denver, shocked, barked out a laugh. James and Delia gave away nothing with their silence.

"Just based on the way you put that, I'm gathering that the correct answer to that question is 'no,'" Sam said.

"You are gathering correctly," his mom said, with a look that added, *Smartass.* "Now if I go make pizza bagels, will you all still be alive when they're finished?"

They nodded—Denver picking up fast from the others that Mrs. Fisher could read into every word, tone, or gesture, so it was best to leave most of the communication to Sam.

Sam half wanted to tell her the truth—to blurt out that James had gotten mixed up with some sort of cult, and to get her advice for how to handle the situation.

But the memory of the faceless ones stopped him cold. The last thing he wanted to do was plant that vision in her mind, too. She was a powerful empath. If he told her what he'd seen, she'd probably end up on the floor right beside him.

They took their time finishing off the pizza bagels, none of them too eager to try any more new magic after Sam's close call. During a lull in the conversation—and attempting to pass it off as if it hardly mattered—Denver asked again who it was that Sam had seen in his vision.

Slowly and carefully—and also truthfully—Sam replied, "These people who were there the night James lost the book. He told us about them."

"You mean, these people *stole* the book?" he asked.

"No, we wouldn't go that far," Sam said, while James watched him with wide eyes. "But they were there, so I just think it's funny they helped with my associations."

And by funny, of course, he meant the opposite of funny. There was an unspoken but deeply felt thrum of fear in the room, and when the eighth finding spell yielded no immediate results in their first attempt, they were quick to give it up and move on to showing one another spells they could do without trying.

As James, Delia, and Denver gathered up their things to go, Sam noticed that Denver was making an effort to be the last one out. He literally bent over to tie his shoelace, even though Sam could have sworn that the shoelace had already been tied.

Unfortunately for Denver, James appeared to be waiting around as well.

"What's up, Denver?" Sam finally said. "Something you wanted to say?"

Denver glanced James's way, considered him for a second, and then spoke quickly. "Oh, well, I was only going to ask if we know when the next practice will be, or if it will be decided on the group text again."

Delia paused on the staircase, nearly at the top. "The group text, for sure," she said.

"Yeah, I can't meet again until Monday myself," James said. "Let's just see how we're feeling this weekend."

"Okay, okay," Denver said, re-entering the game of chicken with James, before finally seeming to come to some resolution in his mind.

He turned to Sam.

"Do you want to come to a concert with me this Friday? This girl Ellie from some of my classes—she lives in my apartment building, actually. I saw her a couple times this summer. Anyway, she plays drums in this band, and they're playing at the fall festival downtown. On Friday night."

"Oh, man, the fall festival," Sam said. "We haven't been to that since freshman year. But yeah, that could be fun."

"Awesome," Denver said.

Sam felt suddenly and painfully aware of the fact that James was watching them with a funny look on his face, and Delia hadn't moved from her place on the stairs. Denver seemed to recognize this at the same moment, too.

"Delia? James? Do you want to come, too?" he said.

"I can get behind it," Delia said. "A last hurrah for senior year and all that."

"Excellent," Denver said.

"Yeah, excellent," Sam echoed, though if he was being honest, there'd been an undeniable moment there when he'd been excited at the prospect of a night with Denver, one-on-one. Not as a date, mind you. Not when he and James still needed to figure out what that night at the bowling alley meant for their friendship—something they would do as soon as all this business with the spell book was behind them.

"James?" Denver said. "What about you?"

"I, uh—I actually was planning to be there already."

"You were?" Sam said.

"Yeah, I . . . Amber is the lead singer of Ellie's band."

"Oh, you know Amber?" Denver said. "She also lives in my building."

"Oh, yeah?" James said. "You live in Maplewood?"

Denver nodded.

"Well, sounds like we'll all be there, then," Delia said. "Sam, can you pick me up? From what I remember, parking there is a nightmare."

"Yeah, sure," Sam said, his head swimming. He felt like they were playing a four-way game of chess, and each of them kept outmaneuvering the others, whether on purpose or by accident. Maybe it was more like Connect 4. Whatever it was, he was losing.

"All right, then," Denver conceded. "I'll meet y'all there on Friday." He headed to the stairs behind Delia, pausing just for a moment to observe that James still wasn't moving, and then he was gone.

Sam turned to James, taking in his bashful posture and crooked grin. If this was a play for forgiveness, (a) it was working, and (b) Sam didn't want it to. "Did *you* want to talk about something?" he said.

"What? Oh, yeah." James ran a hand through his hair and looked everywhere but directly at Sam. "It's funny. I actually was going to ask if you could give me a ride on Friday, too. My mom has to use the car to go visit her sister, so I thought, I mean, if you didn't mind joining me to hear Amber's band . . ."

"Not at all," Sam said, a little ashamed of how relieved he felt. There had been infinite question marks between them over the years that they'd been friends, because the line between boys being boys and boys being attracted to boys was never easy to walk, but until this week, Sam had never doubted his place of prominence in James's life; never doubted that he was James's go-to for all the things that really mattered. This week, hearing about "snack time" and Mike's party and all the other parties before that, he had started to feel like a thing on the side.

But James had wanted him there on Friday all along.

"Just tell me when you need me to be at your house. We can

stop by Delia's on the way in."

"Thanks, Sam. You're the best. You know that?"

James smiled. There was a moment in which Sam thought he was going in for a hug, but in fact he was simply scooting past Sam in very tight quarters.

"James?" Sam said, right as his friend reached the bottom of the stairs. He turned back to Sam, and his eyes were so sunken and tired, they practically looked bruised.

"Mm?"

"We're going to find that book, I promise. Then everything will get better."

James nodded, accepting this. "Thanks, buddy," he said.

If Sam thought he'd had trouble sleeping before, it was nothing compared to what he experienced that night, tossing and turning, the faceless ones always waiting behind his eyelids and in his peripheral vision. Was it memory or imagination? Imagination or a spell? It hardly mattered. Sam had shown them his face; they knew who he was. He was in this now. For better or worse.

CHAPTER 5

IT HAD BEEN ELEVEN DAYS SINCE MR. GRENDER'S BOOK GOT taken—and four since she would have gone back to school, if school were still in the cards—and Liv was starting to second-guess her decision to live at the compound. To be a part of True Light.

"I don't understand," she said to Isaac. She was standing in his doorway as he circled his room, packing a messenger bag full of spell components, plus a flashlight, a crowbar, and a piece of rope. "Why do we have to drag his friends into this, too? Isn't it enough that we're going after him?"

"I told you," Isaac said, noticeably less patient than he'd been in their first weeks together, "we're not the ones dragging his friends into this. He dragged them into this just fine on his own. All we're trying to do is make sure they give us back Mr. Grender's book."

He paused in his packing, glancing around his room like there was something he was forgetting, or else couldn't find.

"What's in that book that's so important, anyway?" Liv asked.

"Spells," Isaac said tersely.

"Yeah, I figured that part," Liv said, trying to keep it light. Trying to get back to the place where they'd been before that disastrous party, when the book had been stolen and the vibe in the compound had taken a serious nosedive. "But *what* spells? The way everyone around here has been acting, you'd think they were spells you couldn't find anywhere else."

"That's just it," Isaac said. "You *can't*. Mr. Grender has been collecting the spells in that book for decades, and half of them came from Grace herself—stuff she could never replicate."

This had been a recurring thread during her weeks at the compound, always deployed lightly, danced around: Mr. Grender was smart and imposing, their group's de facto leader, but it was Grace who channeled the more powerful magic. Never mind the fact that she had yet to say a word out loud within Liv's hearing, for all the times Isaac had come by her room to say that Grace was wondering if she was practicing her craft (and more, if she was "getting better")—Grace had a power you could feel just by being around her, like a sad song you'd put on repeat so many times you forgot it was playing in your ears.

"Why can't she replicate them?" Liv pressed.

"*Because*," Isaac said, finally spotting what he'd been looking for—a spiral notebook, hidden under a small pile of clothes.

What Liv was really trying to get him to admit was that Grace thought her magic came from an angel. She'd heard this from Carl, one of the five other full-time residents of the compound, besides Liv and Isaac. There was Carl, Grace, and Mr. Grender, plus the married couple, Alex and Alex, and there used to be a lot more extended guests in and out of the compound as well—guests who came to one of Mr. Grender's big parties and stayed for a few days—but that was this summer, before three such guests had brought the thief to a party.

It was at a similar party two weeks before that Carl had gotten drunk and told her about the angel.

"Why do you think we call ourselves True Light?" he'd asked her through a hiccup, and it had caught her off guard, because the truth was, she didn't know that they did. She'd never heard that name.

"It's ironic," Isaac had explained to her later that night, when it was just the two of them again, and he could tell she was freaked out. "It's the true light that's opposed to the false light of organized religion. Don't worry, babe. We're nothing like your parents." He hadn't denied the part about the angel, though. That hadn't escaped her attention.

"Well," Liv said now, reminding herself that Isaac's frustration was about the missing book far more than it was about her, "I guess I see why we need to get that book back, but is scaring these guys really the best way to do that? Couldn't we try another finding spell?"

"Maybe we could, if we were at the top of our game."

This *was* a dig at her; there was no mistaking it. Every time they'd attempted a finding spell so far, focusing on the book, it had ended in disappointment, with everyone else in the circle ultimately staring at her like she was the obvious weak link.

"Why don't you try again without me?" Liv had suggested after one such attempt.

"We're only as good as our seventh member," Mr. Grender had replied, and while that might have sounded like positive reinforcement coming from another person, a nod to the importance of teamwork, Mr. Grender was brusque and impatient, like the smart kid in class who didn't play well with others and didn't want to show his work. Without his book he was miserable, and he wanted the rest of them to know it.

The compound had even been on something of a lockdown since the book had been taken. No more parties for the out-of-city and even out-of-state guests who stayed for a while; now, the seven of them weren't even going to work. Isaac fronted her the money she needed for rent, and he promised to get her another job like the one he'd gotten her bagging groceries, since three days missed in a row had led to a voicemail on his phone from her manager: "Tell Liv she's fired." (Her parents had finally cut off her cell phone, with no attempt to contact her first. She was planning on buying her own phone plan as soon as she had enough money saved, which was reason enough to either find Mr. Grender's book soon, or else admit that this co-op situation was more *cooperative* than she'd signed on for, angel or no angel.)

"Well, suit yourself," Liv said now, as if suiting himself weren't already exactly what Isaac was doing. "You and Carl go scare whoever you want. Get your vigilante justice. Get the book back by any means. But if I'm gone when you get back, know that it's because I'm out looking for an apartment that doesn't come with any cult strings attached."

Isaac moved faster than a fire on pine straw, getting up in her face until she had to take a step back into the wall.

"Don't you ever call True Light a cult," he said. "Mr. Grender is a great man. He took me in when no one else would, and Grace has brought more magic into this world than everyone else in the state of Georgia combined."

That doesn't prevent them from leading a cult, Liv might have said, if she weren't so scared, her shoulder throbbing from where she'd banged it against the doorframe. She'd never seen anything close to this side of Isaac before, and why was it coming out tonight? Because he was on edge? Or because she was the weak link in their group?

"I'm sorry," she said, and it was like those were the magic words. Isaac's face became Isaac's face again. He looked like himself.

"No, I'm sorry," he said, taking a step back. "I don't know what came over me. I just get so defensive of them, I guess." He ran his hand over his head. "Do you forgive me?"

"Yes," Liv said, and she almost meant it.

They needed to get Mr. Grender's book back. The sooner they did, the sooner Mr. Grender would be in a good mood again, and the sooner Mr. Grender was in a good mood, the better it would be for all of them.

She didn't know what it would mean if she stuck around here and the book never came back. She couldn't let her mind go there.

Not until it had to.

CHAPTER 6

IT WAS STILL LIGHT OUTSIDE WHEN SAM PULLED INTO JAMES'S driveway on Friday, and Sam couldn't help feeling a little infantilized by that fact. Couldn't help picturing the hypothetical cool kids who wouldn't be caught dead going out this early on a weekend. This pretty much summed up his memories of the fall festival—and explained why they hadn't gone the past two years. It was a glorified back-to-school fundraiser for Friedman Elementary, with wholesome bake sales and plywood-based games run by the teachers, and with a few of the mainstay Friedman restaurants offering half their normal portions at double the price. Not long after dark, the kids would start to thin out, and the adults who remained would get progressively rowdier as they kept going back to the restaurant stands for more beer, at which point the whole thing became a real shitshow.

But who knew, maybe it had changed since the last time Sam had been.

Sam texted James to let him know he'd arrived. It was hard to shake the deeply ingrained feeling that this was rude, that he should get out of his car and go knock on the door. But after years of brusque and often vaguely homophobic interactions with James's parents, Sam forgave himself for a little rudeness (more than once, James's mom had said—from a place of what seemed like genuine forgetfulness but was never any less hurtful for that—"Do you have a girlfriend, Sam? Oh, I'm sorry, pretend I didn't say that!"). Even James always said, "Don't feel like you have to be nice to them."

James wasn't responding to Sam's text tonight, though. And he kept not coming to the door, no matter how intently Sam watched it. So finally, assuring himself that he was not being nice or polite but *concerned*, Sam got out of his car and walked up to the door.

Right away, Sam could hear the yelling coming from inside.

"—from church, Dad. She goes to our church!"

"Don't you fucking bring church into this, there's nothing—"

"—can't even believe you. Do you hear what you sound like?"

It sounded to Sam like James and his father were moving through the house, their voices oscillating between right-behind-the-door loud and so distant Sam couldn't hear them. Sam might have known they'd be getting into one of their blowups, with James's mom out of the house. James had told him about countless fights over the years, and Sam had been unlucky enough to be present for a few of them. James always became surly and unreachable afterward.

Sam knocked on the door. Not even knocked—pounded, really. It was like some primal, protective instinct had awakened in his brain. James was a big brother, but Sam, as an only child, was stubborn as hell. He didn't care if he got yelled at, too—he only cared about saving James.

The yelling didn't stop. He heard "Go to your room!" followed by an "Are you fucking kidding me?" from James, in the exact moment Sam was thinking the same thing.

But even as he stood there waiting to hear the sound of footsteps, the door creaked open, and there stood Benji, looking hollowed out and scared in jeans and a T-shirt with pro wrestlers on it.

Benji was in first grade. He was old enough to have a personality and interests of his own, although as far as Sam could tell, his interests were basically whatever James was interested in, and his personality was basically the closest approximation to James that he could get. (Yes, James enjoyed professional wrestling; it was something about him that Sam would never understand.) Much like his brother, Benji had more emotions than he had words to deal with them. This made more sense in Benji's case, given his age. But given his age, his parents' pig-headed distrust of magic and their firm insistence on the sanctity of gender norms—attitudes that had only hardened with *their* age—took a much greater toll on Benji than they did on James. It was hard to witness. James couldn't stand it.

"Hey, Sam," Benji whispered. "James can't come to the door right now."

"That's what it sounds like to me, too," Sam whispered back. "Maybe I could come in and talk to him?"

"I don't think that's a good idea," said a voice just beyond the door, which swung all the way open to reveal Mr. Dawson, in his Final Boss state, his eyes bloodshot and hard. He nodded a hello but barely made an effort to mask the rage that had so transfigured him. Sam didn't see any sign of James, which meant he must have stomped down to his basement bedroom by now.

"Mr. Dawson. Hi. I'm, uh. I'm here to pick up James for the fall festival."

"Hate to waste your time, Sam, but James won't be leaving the house tonight, and that's that."

"Uh," Sam said, his heart still racing in anger. "Okay, then, I guess."

"Something you want to say to me, son?"

Sam looked back and forth between Benji and Mr. Dawson. The absurdity of those spandex-wearing wrestlers on Benji's T-shirt was really getting under his skin. He wanted desperately to respond to Benji's tyrant of a father in a way that would model a real way out, if it existed.

"Nah," Sam finally said, but at least he didn't break eye contact.

"All right, then," Mr. Dawson said. He pulled Benji back by the shoulders, and then he slammed the door.

Which.

What. An. Asshole.

Sam stomped back to his car, already furious with himself for staying silent, for not taking the opening to clap back after so many years of wanting that moment. It probably wouldn't have done any good—it might've even made the night harder for James—but those felt like paltry excuses for not trying a little harder. Benji's future was at stake, too, and there was nothing more important to James than that.

Sam was just backing out of the driveway, the volume on his music cranked up to an obscene level, when a voice in his ear, distinct over the noise, whispered urgently, *Sam, wait.*

Sam slammed on the brakes so hard they squeaked. Which was a good thing, too, because they drowned out his unbecoming scream. Sam looked in the back seat and confirmed he was alone in the car. He'd been looking over his shoulder a lot this week, jumping at things that weren't there, but a bodiless voice seemed like a new low, even if it was a voice he recognized. Even if it was James's voice.

He turned off his music.

Finally, when he was ready to accept that he'd imagined it—that two sleepless nights in a row had gotten to him more than he'd realized, and maybe he shouldn't be going out tonight, let alone driving—he detected a hint of movement coming from the side of the house.

It was James, crouched down and hustling like he was in some video game that would have "Ops" in the title. He climbed through the passenger side door as quickly as he could and said, "Go, go, go," bringing the military fantasy full circle.

"How did you do that?" Sam said, even as he peeled out of the driveway and sped down the road.

"I'll explain on the way," James said. "Can I see your phone?"

"What? Oh . . . sure, I guess." Sam rooted in his pocket and handed over his phone. Without looking away too much from the road, he tried to keep an eye on what James was up to. It wasn't like Sam had a text or a note-to-self anywhere that spelled out, *I'm secretly in love with James,* but who knew what all he'd said to Delia over the years? He knew there was at least one message in there from her this summer, asking Sam where he and James had run off to after leaving the bowling alley . . .

"My dad took my phone before I could ask Amber where we're supposed to meet her. But first things first, I'm going to text my phone from yours—**Sorry you're not coming tonight. Hope your dad isn't too mad** . . . because you know that asshole will be reading every message that comes in on my phone—and now I'll text Amber real quick."

"You have her number memorized?" Sam said.

"It's public on Friendivist."

"Ah."

They drove in silence as James finished typing his message. Sam almost suggested that maybe James should just call Amber, since it seemed like—based on the amount of time that had passed—he might have received her response, texted again, and started a whole conversation about God-only-knew-what.

Finally, Sam gave up on waiting.

"So, what was that spell back in the driveway? It was a spell, right?"

"Yeah, sorry—it's hard to send more than a few words with that, which makes it way creepier. You remember freshman year, when I did the Sights, Sounds, and Smells event at convention? Well, that was one of the spells in my brief that year. You had to send a code word to the judges in the other room."

"Gotcha," Sam said. "And the fight with your dad. Same old, same old?"

"Yeah, pretty much," James said. "I swear, I am at the point where if I could think of another place to live, a place where I could bring Benji, I would leave."

"I wouldn't blame you. Was he mad that you were going out, or . . . ?"

"Basically."

"Okay."

James apparently received another message on Sam's phone. He tapped out a quick response, smiling into the screen.

"Don't you think he's going to notice you're gone?" Sam said.

"I doubt it," James said, still absorbed in whatever was happening between him and Amber. "He hardly ever goes into the basement, and if he does, my door is locked, and I cast this spell to make it sound like I'm shuffling papers around on my desk."

"Cool, cool. But—"

"Look, Sam," James said, finally turning away from the phone, "I'm sorry. I feel like my dad has already ruined the night enough. I don't want to give him any more time than I have to, you know? I just want to forget about him and have a good time."

"No, yeah, I get it. No problem. I can switch to good-times mode. Done and done. It's just . . . before good-times mode activates, like *officially* officially, I have to ask—any luck with the book? Or with the counter spell?"

This had been Delia's breakthrough idea at lunch today, based on something she'd read on the Pinnacle syllabus. If they couldn't locate the book with a finding spell, maybe they could reverse engineer the spell James had used in order to make a counter spell. Arnauld's Axiom, she called this process—if you could replicate a spell, you could make a counter spell. It seemed worth a shot. The only problem was, the spell had been so instinctual for James—a reflex out of panic. He hadn't been sure he'd be able to talk through the steps to replicate it if he tried.

"No dice," James said now.

"I figured you'd tell us if it worked, but you never know. Are the visions getting worse?"

"And good-times mode activating in three, two, one."

"All right, all right," Sam said. "We've definitely earned a Friday night. And to that point, about good times, etcetera—Amber's band. What do you know about them? Are they any good?"

"*I* think so," James said. "I mean, they're not like a band you'd hear on the radio, but Amber's got a great voice, and then they have a guitarist and a drummer. Both of them are pretty tight."

"Right. Denver's friend, Ellie."

"Yeah, that's right."

"Seems like you and Amber are really close all of a sudden," Sam ventured.

"I don't know about 'really close,' but yeah, she's cool. She's one of those people who genuinely cares, you know? Like, she doesn't just do things because everyone else is doing them. Her parents don't make her go to church—she goes because she wants to. She doesn't play soccer because it will be good for college apps—she plays soccer because she likes playing soccer. She really helped me with stuff this summer."

Sam couldn't help that his knee-jerk reaction was a defensive one. That all he could hear in James's words was the fact that Sam didn't go to church at all, or the fact that Delia spent a lot of time talking about her college applications. Or the fact that, if Sam was being totally honest, he'd always thought that James only drank and smoked as much as he did because that's what everyone else in Friedman thought was cool. Somehow, Amber was succeeding where all three of them failed.

"Right, she helped you. With snack time. And the drinking."

"You'll like her," James said. "Once you get to know her."

"Can you text Delia and let her know we're almost there?" Sam said.

"Yeah, okay."

James went back to Sam's phone, and Sam turned up the volume on his music, just a little bit.

Delia's memory was correct—parking was a nightmare. The funny thing was, Sam didn't remember that at all from freshman year, but then again, Sam's mom had dropped them off that time, so it was hard to say if things had truly gotten worse or if it was all a difference in perception now that Sam was the one driving.

Finally, they found a parking space, then headed off toward Mary Ellen's stand, where James had arranged for them to meet Amber. On the way, they ran into Denver. Sam spotted him a good ten yards before Denver spotted them; he was leaning against the wall of the Hick Country Café (its real name), alternating between checking his phone and scanning the crowd, and he looked so out of place in his black skinny jeans and black T-shirt, so utterly alone, that it finally sank in for Sam that this boy had moved to Friedman with no friends and no history here, and Ms. Berry had directed him to the Fascinators, counting on them to be welcoming. In return, they had promptly initiated him, "chump style," before luring him into a battle of wits with dark magickers. Sam wanted to die.

Then Denver saw them and grinned his confident grin, and Sam determined that there was still time to fix this.

"There's my Fascinators," Denver said, all suave.

"'Your' Fascinators?" James said.

"Honestly," Delia added, "it just doesn't work with a possessive, 'yours' or anyone's. It's *the* Fascinators or no Fascinators at all."

"Okay, okay, give the guy a break. He's new."

"Thank you, Sam."

"No problem. So, have you already played Plinko and cornhole, or were you waiting for us?"

"Oh, yeah, me and Bubba over there in the hunter's flannel made a great cornhole team. We won lots of tickets, and we were going to combine them to buy a huge stuffed unicorn, but I told him, sorry, Bubba, I need to wait until Sam gets here in case he'd rather I get him a Friedman water bottle or something."

Sam blushed outrageously. James snorted and then looked away, as if he had never seen downtown Main Street before.

"Hey," Delia said, "that's my cousin in the hunter's flannel." She looked stone-faced and insulted, but when Denver's face blanched in mortification, she said, "Denver, I'm kidding. You think I have a cousin named Bubba?"

"I don't know!" Denver protested, laughing with relief. "I barely know you, but based on the fact that you live in Friedman, Georgia, home of this here Hick Country Café, I wouldn't put it past any of you to be cousins with a Bubba, if not that particular man, with whom I did *not* play cornhole, just so we're clear."

"I think I see Amber," James said, picking up the pace as he led them the rest of the way to Mary Ellen's stand.

She was talking to two girls whom Sam had seen at school but never talked to, presumably Ellie and the guitarist. You could tell they were a band from the way they were standing, synchronized in their effortless coolness, two of them smiling and leaning at complementary angles whenever the third was talking.

There was an awkward moment as they all came together

and introductions were made—it turned out the guitarist's name was Carrie—because a group of seven was honestly too big for a single conversation. James ended up in a clump with Amber, Carrie, and Delia, while Sam somehow found himself on the far side of the circle with Denver and Ellie.

"It's so cool that you're in a club all about magic," Ellie said to Sam. "I'm so bad at it, I don't even try, but I think people who're good at it are amazing."

"Thanks," Sam said. "I wasn't all that good at it either until I started hanging out with James and Delia. Now I'm good by association."

"Bullshit," Denver said. "You're good on your own, too."

"How would you know?"

"Just a hunch. If you believe it, you can achieve it," Denver said, ridiculously. "That's like the number-one rule of magic."

"I thought it was 'Don't dream it, be it,'" Sam said.

"No, that's *Rocky Horror Picture Show*," Denver replied.

"I think he knows that," Ellie said, sharing a grin with Sam.

"Yeah, we have movies and culture down here in Friedman too, you know. Even though we wear plaid and attend elementary school fundraisers on our Friday nights."

Denver smiled, as if to say, *Touché*. Sam didn't even know why he was defending Friedman, exactly, since it would never defend him; he only knew it was fun to disagree with Denver.

"Speaking of fundraising," Ellie said, "can we go get some food and play some games before I have to be on? I always like that game where you have to go fishing for rubber ducks with a magnetic pole. It's fun because you can't lose."

"Magnetic rubber ducks it is," Denver said. "The epitome of culture if ever there was one."

It turned out Amber's band was one of a few musical acts lined up for the evening. The Friedman Elementary chorus kicked things off with rousing renditions of "This Land Is Your Land" and "Over the Rainbow," and damn it, Sam actually got sort of emotional during the second song, watching all those innocent little souls who hopefully had no idea yet what it felt like to want to be somewhere else that badly; although of course, if Benji's face tonight and Sam's own memories from elementary school were any indication, they probably did. Then a trio of brothers with two fiddles and a guitar made a valiant effort at "The Devil Went Down to Georgia," a song that Denver had apparently never heard before, because he looked at Sam with bug eyes and mouthed, *What the hell is this?*

Sam shrugged. It was a good song, even if—to be fair—it was taking on a more menacing air than it normally did, given the things Sam had seen at the corners of his vision this week. Things he was trying not to think about tonight. Good-times mode and all that.

By the time Amber, Ellie, and Carrie got up onto the little raised platform in front of Kelsey's Florist, a pretty sizable crowd had gathered, and the floodlights had come on, making everything and everyone look just a little more intense than they had before. You could start to feel the energy shift as a few adults here and there went unchecked in their tipsiness. James bent over like he was trying to read his phone while keeping it in his pocket, and in the same moment Sam remembered that James didn't *have* his phone, he realized that James was sneaking a sip from a silver hipflask. Which—damn. So much for cutting back on the stuff.

"Hey, y'all. I'm Amber. These are my girls Ellie and Carrie. We're In His Name, and we're going to play a couple songs we wrote."

Hold up.

In His Name?

Did that mean . . .

Amber started singing, and it wasn't clear from the first few lines, but . . . yup, there it was.

" . . . always have a home in the heart of the Lord . . ."

Amber's band was a praise band.

And that was fine. That was cool. That was one hundred percent whatever. James was right, Amber had the voice of an angel, and Carrie and Ellie were talented, too.

So why did Sam suddenly feel so weird?

Sam sat with the feeling as it squirmed its way through his brain; he wrestled and untangled it. When all the knots were gone and the buzzing slowed, he could see the source of the feeling clearly: Amber's band was a praise band, and James hadn't told him.

James was swaying back and forth from one foot to the other, the closest he ever came to dancing, really, utterly unsurprised and even giving off the appearance of a person enjoying himself, in spite of everything. Yet the James Sam knew would *not* be enjoying himself in the presence of a praise band. The James Sam knew would be catching Sam's eye right now and smirking to high heaven, two thirds of a morally superior trio in a sea of Friedman zealots and simpletons. Those were the exact words of the James Sam knew—"zealots and simpletons"—and they were not his words from that long ago, either. This new James wouldn't even look Sam's way. The swig of the flask was the only sign that this new James wasn't perfectly happy, and Sam didn't want to root for James to take another illegal sip from an illegal flask, but he couldn't very well root for a James who left him alone out at sea, either.

This new James had eyes only for Amber. This new James and Amber kept smiling at each other like they were the only two people downtown.

Now Sam was swaying, too, only it wasn't intentional. He felt dizzy, faint. Gone were the people of Friedman; everywhere he looked, there were only the faceless ones, and they were leaning into Sam, pressing against him, pressing into his lungs. He couldn't breathe. He grabbed at his throat and stumbled, falling back against something solid. Not a faceless one but a very present stranger, a brick wall of a man, who didn't so much catch Sam as he did forcefully push him back to standing.

"Hey, whoa now, watch it," the man said. Sam was mortified to realize that he'd bumped right into this guy's beer, splashing him and his girlfriend, too.

"I'm so sorry, I—I don't know what happened," Sam said.

That didn't stop the guy and his girlfriend from looking at Sam like he was a piece of gum they'd stepped in, but they didn't escalate it any further. They slunk off, presumably to grab napkins or another beer, muttering curses the whole way.

"You okay?" Delia said. She'd seen enough of what happened to come check on him. James and Denver must not have heard. Their attention was squarely on In His Name's next song.

"I think so," Sam whispered. "Just lost my balance for a second."

Delia frowned, hesitating on the verge of pressing further, before deciding to let it go. With her voice lowered so that only Sam could hear her, she said, "So, did you know that Amber's band was *rah-rah* for Jesus?"

Sam literally cackled, the surprise and relief bubbling up in him, making room for his breathing to return to normal.

That caught Denver and James's attention (not to mention the harsh stares from a few adults nearby), and they both looked back to see what was so funny.

Delia shrugged at them like she had no idea.

On the whole, it all could have been much, much worse.

They didn't stick around Main Street long after Amber's band finished their set. Everyone's drunkenness was really showing now, and the lines for food were fifteen people deep. Sam, Denver, and Amber were parked in the same general direction, and as they all headed back to their cars, a plan started forming—a plan to head either to Steak 'n Shake or Waffle House, with the majority of them wanting Waffle House because Waffle House was just better, but with James and Ellie both begging the others to do Steak 'n Shake, because James hated Waffle House for some unfathomable reason and because Ellie had had it too many times this month and needed a change. Then it came out that Denver had never been to a Waffle House, even though there were plenty of Waffle Houses in Nashville—there were no acceptable excuses—and that pretty much decided things, even if James wasn't happy about it.

Then they got to Sam's car.

It wasn't immediately apparent, because the car was parked at an angle, with cars right up next to it on either side. Everyone else was still milling about around the trunk, talking and laughing, when Sam got to the driver's side door and noticed all the glass in his seat.

"Shit!" he shouted. The talking and laughing immediately stopped.

James and Delia ran to him without hesitating, and the three of them took in the sight of his smashed windshield together, while the others peered through and around the car to get a look.

There were lots of gasps and curses. Sam paced back and forth on the sidewalk in front of his car.

"Any of y'all know how to fix broken glass?" Ellie said.

"I know a general repair spell," James replied. "But maybe there's something specific to glass we can find on the spell app?"

"For a basic crack, sure," Delia said. "But a break this big? In laminated glass? You'd probably have to pick up all the pieces out of the seat and then—"

"Hello?" Sam said, a hair shy of hysterical. "Can we please not focus on how to theoretically fix broken glass for a moment and focus instead on the fact that someone violently smashed a giant hole in my windshield?"

His mind flashed to the guy with the beer, but that didn't make sense. That guy would have no idea which car was his.

"Sam, do you think . . . I mean . . ." Denver trailed off, and when Sam looked his way, he saw that he, Amber, Carrie, and Ellie were all staring at the back of his car. Sam went around to join them, and . . . oh.

Oh, right.

The bumper sticker had been a gift from his parents—from the birthday when they'd given him the car. He hadn't been sure whether he was getting a car that year or not, because his parents had always just made noises of consternation when he'd asked. So when they'd taken him to Mo's Steakhouse and handed him a big wrapped box, the double fake out worked—he wasn't expecting the Q-Atl rainbow pride bumper sticker under the hundred layers of tissue paper, let alone the Post-it that read, "For your (practically) new (okay, it's used) car."

"Shit," Sam said again, only this time it meant something different—a word of resignation, of sadness but not surprise. Most days, he completely forgot the bumper sticker was there—it was a background fixture in his life, just like the Q-Atl meetings he periodically attended—but every once in a while, he'd see a dirty look in his rearview mirror and wonder why he hadn't taken up his parents on the offer they'd once made, in total seriousness: to move somewhere else. Find engineering and real estate jobs in Atlanta, or another state entirely. Put Sam in a school that actively supported its queer students instead of deigning to allow them. Maybe one that really valued his magicker talents, too. Sam's grandparents were gone now; they didn't need to stay for them.

"You think this was a bias incident?" Delia said, still standing at the front of the car. "It's possible that contributed, I guess, but I don't think this was a spur-of-the-moment decision."

"What do you mean?"

"Come look."

Sam rejoined her and James at the front of the car. Delia was pointing to a brick Sam hadn't noticed before, sitting in the passenger seat. There was a piece of paper folded and tied around it, and while Sam couldn't say for sure without taking it off, from what he could see, he was willing to bet the lines on it would make the shape of a lightning-bolt V when he did.

"How did those people know which car was mine?" Sam whispered urgently to James.

James didn't respond. He was staring at the brick, too, and his breathing had become deep and ragged; his hands were clenched into rocks.

"James?"

James brought his fists up to his chest, slowly, as if he were lifting heavy weights. He pushed his knuckles together, then slowly, laboriously, began to open his fingers, uniting his flat palms in a prayerful position. Sam was so entranced by James himself that he didn't think to look for the effect of his spellwork, until the rattling of glass pieces, like rain on a porch roof, brought him quickly around.

"James, don't—" Sam started to say, but too late.

The glass levitated, then hovered angrily in the empty space of the windshield, like a cloud of hornets. The glass looked like it desperately wanted to be whole again, but there was too much tension, the blunt energy too strong.

Sam saw what was coming in the second before it happened. There was barely enough time to brace for impact, but still, reflexively, his arm shot out toward James.

The windshield exploded.

Everyone screamed.

The screaming lasted just long enough to carry them into the moment when they all realized they were fine. That the windshield had shattered into the car instead of outward. They all took inventory of one another. Even one stray piece of glass, flung at that speed, could have done serious damage. But no, they were alive. They were scared but unharmed.

"I'll fix this, Sam," James said, his voice like shrapnel. "All of it. I'll show those assholes they can't mess with me and my friends like this."

Sam was too stunned to form a reply. James was talking like some kind of vigilante, like a person used to revenge. And who knew? Maybe he was. Tonight, Sam was coming up against the hard truth that there was still a lot he didn't know about James, which was a problem, not least because so much of Sam's own identity had been built on a foundation that had James in it.

"What in the world just happened?" Carrie called from the other side of the car.

"Boy genius over here tried a general repair spell without a calm mind," Delia replied. "The associations were all wrong."

"I think I need to call my parents," Sam said. "I don't think I can drive this car right now."

"I can drive you," Denver said.

"No, no," Sam said. "I mean, thank you, that's very kind, but no. I need to stay with my car. Make sure no one hotwires it away and sells the parts for a fortune."

"Well," Denver persisted, "do you want us to wait with you until your parents get here?"

Sam didn't answer that one right away. The real answer was yes, of course, there was no way he could handle being alone right now. But the other real answer was that he could see the residual fear and sadness in all their faces, the weight of a fun night disappeared, the reminder that the place where they lived could be hostile sometimes, and Sam didn't feel like sitting with that sadness. Better to be alone than to be the lightning rod for their disappointment.

"Don't worry about me," he said. "Y'all go have fun. Friday night and all that."

"Don't be stupid," Delia said. "I'm not going anywhere."

James shuffled his feet. He looked physically pained.

"James, it's okay. You can go," Sam said.

"It's just—I'm worried if I'm gone too long, my dad will catch on and notice I'm not there. And if my dad realizes I snuck out, he will actually murder me. Or worse, he'll lash out at Benji in my absence."

"You snuck out?" Amber said. She sounded equal parts horrified and flattered, and James shrugged bashfully.

"I get it," Sam said. "Seriously. You should go."

"All right," James replied, although he really did look guilty about it. "Amber, do you think you could give me a ride?"

Sam couldn't decide, as he watched them walk to Amber's car, whether he'd feel better or worse if they ended up going to Waffle House after all.

He was still working on swallowing that bitter pill when he realized that Denver wasn't leaving with the rest of them. He was taking a few tentative steps Sam's way, like Sam was a frightened cat who might swipe at any sudden moves.

"Can I please wait, too?" he said. "My mom's working tonight, and . . . at the risk of sounding creepy, I'm not sure I can just . . .

go home . . . without making sure you're okay."

Sam started to say that he was okay already, or that at least he had Delia here to look out for him. But Delia was very suddenly very interested in something on her phone, unavailable to confirm or deny Denver's redundancy.

"Plus," Denver said, "I'm still jittery myself. From the, you know, near-death experience with the glass."

"You can stay. I mean—thank you. I'm sorry tonight didn't turn out how you were expecting it to."

"I try not to have too many expectations. Just, in general."

"Okay, well, then I'm not sorry tonight turned out how you were not expecting it to."

Denver grinned.

It wasn't fair how cute his smile was. It was a cheap magic trick, mixing up Sam's brain and making it think all kinds of things he wasn't sure he was ready to think. Make comparisons he wasn't ready to make.

"You should probably call your parents now," Denver said.

"Right," Sam said. "I was getting to that."

CHAPTER 7

THE DRIVE FROM FRIEDMAN TO ATLANTA WASN'T TOO bad on a sunny day—about two hours of mostly interstate, a stretch that was rarely crowded until you passed 285 and got into the city. But today was not a sunny day—it was raining cataclysmically—and it was only because, after another night of visceral waking nightmares, Sam's exhaustion came across equally cataclysmically in all-caps texts that he was able to convince Delia to make the drive.

"I still don't understand why James couldn't join us," she said, hunched over the steering wheel and peering into the rain. Their vision was limited to the red hint of taillights on the cars in front of them and, otherwise, gray—lots and lots of gray. "Don't get me wrong, I'm happy to help. But this *is* mostly his problem. And if I can find time to go to Atlanta between work and practice, I'm pretty sure he can, too."

"You didn't see his dad last night," Sam said. "I wouldn't be surprised if James is still grounded come November. Like, I wouldn't be surprised if his dad tries to make him miss convention entirely."

"So he can sneak into the inner sanctum of a group of dark magickers, and he can sneak out to see Amber's band of Jesus freaks, but ask him to drive two hours in the rain and then it's 'Mustn't break Daddy's rules'?"

"Why does James suddenly have an English accent?"

"I don't know. Because I'm annoyed. I hate the rain."

"But I love you."

"You better. Honestly, I'm surprised your parents let *you* leave the house today. I would've thought they wouldn't let little Sam out of their sight based on how traumatized they seemed."

"With my mom, you just have to couch whatever you want to do in terms of how it will be better for your mental and emotional well-being. I said if I didn't leave, I would end up sitting in the house all day, picturing the broken windshield and getting sadder and sadder. I said spending time with you would really help me move on."

"And she couldn't see through that, with her powers?"

"See through what? None of it was a lie. That's the other trick with my mom."

"You're ridiculous."

They drove in amiable, focused silence for a few minutes, with Delia keeping her attention on the road and Sam digging around online to try to pull up more information about where they were going. James had called it "a store for magic stuff"—apparently it was some place Amber had mentioned on their drive home last night, when James hinted vaguely that he was stuck trying to find something with magic. How or why Amber knew about it was anyone's guess, and it was a sign of their collective desperation to make the visions stop that they were willing to undertake such an arduous drive based solely on her recommendation and a Google maps listing: "Findias: Retailer / Occult / Books & Crafts." Sam couldn't even find an official website or any customer reviews.

More or less out of nowhere, Delia said, "So, Denver."

"Is the capital city of Colorado? Yes, correct," Sam said.

"Is a boy who is awfully cute and awfully smitten with you, for whatever reason."

"What? No way. He's just nice."

"Please. That boy started flirting with you before he said hello. Of course, given your total lack of experience being flirted with, I can forgive you for not recognizing it when it smacks you in the face."

"People have flirted with me! I've been flirted with!"

"Online doesn't count."

"Okay, well, that seems harsh and arbitrary. Still. I think you're forgetting Eliot."

"Eliot from Q-Atl? Eliot whose mom sat with your mom two tables away while you talked about who had the higher-level character in Goblins & Gateways?"

"That counts as flirting!"

Delia sighed.

"Anyway, I've been flirted *around*. I know what flirting looks like."

"Agreed, which is why you know full well that Denver has been flirting with, around, next to, and beside you. The question is, why are you so determined right now to pretend he isn't? Are you not into him?"

"'Into him.' What is this, 'into him'?"

Delia let out an exasperated sound. Which, okay, Sam was being a little difficult.

"I don't know if I'm into him, okay?" he said. "He's sweet. It's complicated."

"Complicated? You mean because you're in love with James?"

Damn. Delia was not messing around today. But Sam didn't deny it, either.

"Sorry," she said. "You don't exactly hide it. I know it can't be easy."

"I really am fine and happy just being friends with him, you know. It's not like I'm only friends with him because I want it to be something more."

"I believe you, sort of. But if it's getting in the way of even thinking about something with Denver, maybe you're not as cool with just being friends as you think."

Sam knew she had a point. He'd come to the same conclusion himself, in the immediate aftermath of that night at the bowling alley. It was like he'd been keeping his true feelings in a soda bottle, and everything about that night had shaken the bottle and shot off the top.

"I guess part of me feels like I need to talk things out with James before I do anything else, you know? But things have been so bananas this week, and plus—"

"Plus you're afraid it will ruin your friendship forever if you say something and he doesn't like you back."

Rain beat down on the roof in sheets, the *rat-a-tat-tat* of a snare drum solo.

Sam stared out the window beside him. "I mean, we're supposed to be roommates next year."

"And that's only one of the reasons you *have* to get over him. You know you have to."

"Hold up. 'Get over him?' Why?"

He was ready for her to say that James was straight, or at least not into guys. He was ready for her to say that even if James did like guys—even if he was gay or bi or pan—Sam would be better off with a guy who wasn't closeted. He was ready for her to say that even if James did like guys, and even if he finally came out, there was still no way he'd ever be into some femme, flamboyant guy like Sam. He was ready for these arguments, because they were his own worst fears.

"Because he doesn't deserve you, Sam."

"I don't even—what?"

"You know I love him, Sam. I wouldn't be making this trip

if I didn't. But he's changed. He's not the same boy who started crying on the playground because Henry Mathis kept throwing rocks at that squirrel. He's kind of a troublemaker now. Not even kind of."

"That's where we disagree," Sam said, turning back to face her. "I think he's still exactly that boy from the playground. I think that's the whole problem."

"Sam, he went to a party hoping to do drugs with a bunch of strangers and ended up robbing them. How many more red flags can I fit into one sentence?"

"That was one time. You don't judge your friends by what they do one time."

"Okay, what about at the convention dance last year, when he left in the middle of it, and then came back drunk as a skunk with those assholes from Fayette County? I don't think I've ever been so embarrassed as when we showed up at his cousin's place at eleven o'clock at night, trying to pretend like we didn't all notice that James was slurring his words and tripping over himself."

"Wow, how do you really feel?" Sam was trying to downplay his knee-jerk defensiveness, but the truth was, he'd thought of that night often this past year—and never in a good light. He'd been so looking forward to that dance at the end of convention; the theme had been the nineties, and he'd found the baggiest pair of jeans imaginable at a thrift store, weeks in advance. Two songs in, James's disappearance had made him feel like the most deficient, boring person in the world. The jeans were so stupid, all of a sudden. He'd wanted to leave, but he and Delia couldn't until James returned.

"Listen, I agree with you, Sam. You don't judge your friends by one little thing, and James has his heart in the right place. That's why we're still friends, and why he'll probably be a fine college roommate. But I think it's pretty clear James would make a terrible boyfriend, and you can do so much better than that for your first boyfriend. Trust me."

Sam sighed, maybe a little melodramatically.

He said, "Do you remember the *other* night last year, after the senior play?"

"You mean the cast party at Adriana's house?"

"Yeah. You were off somewhere with Mark, and James and I were in Adriana's room, even though it was supposed to be off limits. And I think I said something about Adriana graduating and studying theater at UGA, I can't remember, but anyways, James said he couldn't *wait* for us to graduate and be roommates next year. And then—he was sort of laughing, but I swear, he sounded so serious, too—he said, and I quote, 'I really can't imagine next year without you, Sam.' I mean, who says that! And yeah, he's messed up, because Friedman is a not-great place to be different in any way whatsoever, and James is different in so many little ways that he hides. But he just needs to get out—get away from his dad and his church and all the bigots we go to school with. Then we can finally figure out how things should be between us."

"Sam," Delia said quietly. The rain was finally letting up a little, and Delia leaned back in her seat, the steady whir of the windshield wipers slowing to a less stressful speed. "Wasn't James drunk at that cast party, too?"

"This is why I avoid talking about this with you, Delia. It's like you *want* to believe the worst in James."

"That's not fair. Not even a little bit."

"Well, I'm sorry. That's how it feels. Now can we please talk about something else until we get there? I'm running on zero sleep and infinity caffeine. I need simple, happy topics like *Last Keeper Standing* or Kelly Clarkson."

"Okay, let's talk about Kelly Clarkson."

But they didn't talk about Kelly Clarkson, or anything else, for the remaining twenty minutes of the drive. They sat in silence, each nursing their wounds and stewing in their thoughts.

They didn't speak again until they pulled up at the address for Findias, at which point, in unison, they both said, "What the—"

Findias did not look so much like a store as it looked like a giant house.

And not just giant—it was a freaking *tower*, taller than it was wide, and at least three stories taller than the houses on either side. "At least," because it was hard to say for sure how many stories the house was. It was like a structure that a six-year-old would build out of Legos, the floors and balconies jutting out at strange angles, the walls a mixture of colors that didn't *not* go together, but that was the best you could say for them.

For all its remarkable quirks, there was nothing on the building to denote that it was a shop, and Sam and Delia might still have thought they'd pulled up to the wrong place—that James had somehow given them the wrong address—were it not for the cars double-parked in the narrow driveway, plus the cars parked all along the sides of the street. Even as they paused here, gawking, they saw a very dapper young man walk up from where he'd parked down the road and knock on the door, before he was let inside.

"I guess I'll just . . . go down here, then," Delia said, driving until she finally found an opening to parallel park.

They put up the hoods of their hoodies and walked briskly back up the sidewalk through the drizzling rain, both of them sparing a few glances into the windows of the neighboring houses, as if afraid someone might be watching them.

When they reached the front door—robin's egg blue, with an iron hand, palm outward, serving as a handle—it was clear they were both a little afraid to knock, rain or no rain.

"Executive privilege?" Sam suggested.

"I'm not the one having visions of faceless cultists," Delia said. Which, fair point.

Sam steadied his breathing and rapped his knuckles on the door.

It took almost two whole minutes before the door swung open to reveal a woman, elegantly dressed in a strapless black jumpsuit, her shoulders covered by a sheer red shawl. She was barefoot, though. Sam found that welcoming.

"Come in, come in," the woman said, ushering them in out of the rain with some urgency, ignoring their questioning looks and quickly closing the door behind them. "I can tell it can't wait."

"What can't?" Delia said.

"Whatever it is you're looking for. This isn't the sort of store people wander into aimlessly, you see. But in your case, I can see that you've arrived just in time. Thank goodness for you."

Sam wasn't sure if this was some sort of mental magic she was doing or merely a very persuasive sales strategy. Either way, it was working. Just beyond the threshold where they stood, he saw bookcases and tables teeming with objects that were neatly arranged and displayed, either for sale or else left over from a v-clip photo shoot, and he suddenly couldn't wait to go through everything in search of whatever would make the visions stop. He really hadn't slept in days. It had been a week of waking nightmares. A nightmare week.

"Is there something going on upstairs?" Delia said, not moving. Now that he listened for it, Sam could hear the steady hum of voices coming from above them. He realized there was no sign of the man they'd seen come in before in this first-floor room.

"Not just something," the woman said. "Something special. A gallery opening for my dear friend Rachel Hanover. Have you heard of her?"

Sam and Delia shook their heads.

"She's shown her art in Paris and London, and now she's gracing the walls of Findias with her work. Can you imagine? I'd say I don't know how I get so lucky, but of course I do know—I put a lot of time and effort into curating my collection."

This drew a smile from Delia, finally.

"That would explain all the cars outside," she said.

"Indeed. And I really should get back to being a good hostess. Truth be told, when you knocked, I thought you were collectors too, here for the showing. The store's technically closed today. But for you two?" She stepped back and gave them an appraising look. "For you two I can make an exception. I think I know just the thing . . ."

Sam hardly had a chance to protest that they hadn't even told her what they were looking for yet; she'd already taken three sweeping steps across the room, and now she held her hands in the air over one of the tables as if she could feel the objects on it without touching them.

Some of the objects Sam recognized in a general way. A mid-size crystal ball perched on three iron talons; geodes and pendulums and compasses that Sam knew were meant to act as spell aides, clearing the mind for strong associations and acting as a channel for the magic. There were books and tarot cards too, and the woman hovered her hands over those, as if the magic she was looking for could be in anything.

Then, she stopped.

"Here it is," she said.

Delia and Sam leaned in, both so completely under her spell that she probably could have handed them a dirty straw and called it a wand and they would have paid her everything they had for it. It wasn't a dirty straw, but it was . . .

"A bowl?" Sam said.

"A singing bowl," the woman said.

"For meditation, right?" Delia said. "Relaxation, that sort of thing."

That was the end of the spell for Sam. It felt like the lights had come on at the end of the party, telling everyone it was time to go home.

"Thank you, but I'm not sure that's what we need," he said. "I've been meditating all week, burning sage to clear the bad magic and burning sandalwood to relax. But they still . . . I mean, I'm looking for something that can help us with a finding spell. Our friend heard about this place. He lost a book that we really need to get back."

"And why isn't he here with you?" the woman said.

Again, Delia smiled.

"Anyway, it's no matter," the woman continued. "I can see that you are quite haunted. Yes, the situation seems very dire to me. But this singing bowl does not simply help with meditation, though that is one of its benefits, even for the untrained. This bowl was forged by hand and imbued with powerful magic. It won't do your finding spell for you, but it will ensure that you are unhindered in your search."

Sam shivered, as if shaken by the force of the woman's magic returning. He hadn't mentioned anything about the faceless ones spying on him last time they did a finding spell. That was all her.

"How much?" Sam said.

"Forty-five even," the woman said, and somehow her tone managed to convey both that she felt this was a steal and that she knew they were teenagers for whom any amount of money was too much. Delia sucked in a breath accordingly. But Sam pulled out his wallet, and from it the credit card his parents had given him in case of emergencies. They'd get a notification and text him about it when they did, but he'd cross that bridge when he came to it—this was a real emergency.

In one deft moment, the woman pulled out her phone, which had a small attachment for accepting credit cards; swiped Sam's card; and then handed it back to him.

"Now then," she said. "I really must be attending my other guests. You are of course welcome to come upstairs and see the art, though I'm sure you're in a hurry."

Sam assumed that Delia, who'd been so reticent to come here in the first place, would be anxious to leave as soon as possible. But even as he tried to catch her eye to confer and confirm, she said, "We'd love to see the art. Thank you so much." And she was the driver today, so that was that.

The large living space that was doubling as tonight's art gallery turned out to be the top floor of the tall house. You could see the severe angles of the roof in the cut of the ceiling, sloping to a high point in the middle, but rising and falling around turret-like peaks in at least five other places. The whole house had the feeling of a project that had been finished and then expanded many times over the years, and nowhere was that more evident than in this strange, haphazard studio space.

Sam observed two things right away when they reached the last stair and stepped smack-dab into the middle of the room:

First, that everyone else here was an adult—maybe twenty-five, thirty at the youngest? But many much older—and not just adults, but the kind of stylish, sophisticated adult you were more likely to see on TV than in real life, with outlandish jewelry and floral-print suits and dresses that made their host's outfit look subdued in comparison. They were holding champagne flutes that kept being refilled by two waiters who were circling the floor, replenishing their supply from a makeshift bar. Of everyone here, the waiters looked closest to Sam and Delia in age.

Second, that the "art" on the walls amounted to a series of canvases that had either been painted uniformly with eggshell-white paint, or else—more likely—were all completely and utterly blank.

"Um," Sam said.

"Would you like to meet the artist?" their hostess said.

"We'd love to," Delia said.

Their hostess took them through the crowd as if she were leading them in a dance, waving to guests over her shoulder, leaning forward to blow kisses, and spinning to exchange pleasantries with nearly everyone they passed on their way to the far corner of the room, where a woman with silvery hair cut in a close-cropped bob was holding court for a small circle of adoring fans.

Whatever story she'd been in the middle of telling, she brought to a natural close as soon as she caught sight of their hostess, and then, with a quick "Excuse me," she pushed out of the circle to join them. With no small amount of discomfort, Sam felt the eyes of her erstwhile audience following her, wondering who these two teenagers were to take away the woman of the hour.

"Rachel, dear, how are my guests treating you?" their hostess said, placing an arm around the artist.

"I think fewer than half of them understand the paintings, but they are all lovely conversationalists," Rachel said, smiling.

"Good, good," their hostess said, matching her smile. "I expect every last painting to be sold before the night is over."

"Who are your new friends?" Rachel said, taking a sip of champagne.

"I'm Delia, and this is Sam. We were here for the shop, but then we heard you were having a viewing up here."

Rachel and their hostess exchanged an impressed smile at that, as if they couldn't believe the manners of this articulate teenager.

"Well, Delia and Sam, why don't I talk you through one of the paintings?"

"I trust you don't need my help for that?" their hostess said— possibly just to Rachel, possibly to all of them?—and then, with a flourish of her shawl, she spun away to talk to another group.

"She doesn't waste a moment, does she?" Rachel said, as if they were all old friends. "Now, how about we start with this one." She walked them over to a large white canvas that looked to Sam like all the other white canvases. "It's called 'Firmament,' inspired by the still rather recent belief that there was a dome above our atmosphere, where lived the angels and the water that came down from the sky as rain. What do you think?"

Delia turned, in all seriousness, to regard the painting more closely, and this felt like the moment when Sam had to put his foot down on this whole charade.

"I think it's a blank canvas," he said.

Delia stared at him in horror, like he was embarrassing her.

Even Rachel frowned, a little bit.

"Is that your final assessment?" she said, her voice suddenly bored.

In a minor panic, Delia turned to stare even more intensely at the painting, and Sam did his best to join her, although he felt like a little boy being sent to time-out.

A funny thing happened as he stared at the canvas, though.

It wasn't that images appeared on the canvas, although that's how Sam was tempted to describe it at first. He knew that wasn't what was happening, because when he closed his eyes to try to clear his vision, the images were still there; if anything, they were stronger. It was more that images were pouring forth from the canvas and existing in Sam's mind. Not just existing but amplifying—images of fire and water, sea spray and clouds, crowding his vision and swirling. A few times in his life, Sam had gotten the spins—both times, it was because he'd made the mistake of switching back and forth between beer and liquor, trying to keep pace with James. The experience of this painting was like getting the spins while on a boat in the middle of a storm. It wasn't totally unpleasant, but it was totally overwhelming.

Sam struggled to re-center himself—to view the storm from outside. When he finally succeeded, gasping on a breath, it took him a moment to remember where he was. The light in here suddenly seemed garishly yellow against the gray outside the windows.

A quick glance to Delia confirmed that she was coming down from a similar experience.

Rachel smiled. Her whole face lit up, as if she'd tasted something delicious.

"I knew Vi wouldn't show favor to just any young people. Now tell me everything."

They'd started out sticking together as they made their way around the room, taking in all the paintings, from "Northern Lights" to "Songs of Innocence and Experience." But that had lasted all of five minutes, as Delia had somehow adapted to the paintings and could now experience them in about half the time it took Sam to do so. He still had a few paintings to go when he noticed she'd broken off and joined a circle of other guests, where she was now leaning in to hear something an older man in a black suit was saying. Whatever it was, it made Delia laugh uproariously, and then the man reached for two glasses of champagne before handing her one.

Sam skipped the rest of the paintings.

"How's it going over here?" he said, sidling right up next to Delia and giving the man a pointed once-over, warm but wary.

"Is this a friend of yours?" the man said.

"Yes, this is Sam. He goes to Pinnacle with me."

"Is that right?" the man said. "And what do you study, Sam?"

"Oh, I'm still figuring it out," Sam said. "Delia's the smart one. Especially at her age, you know? Our professors are always like, Gosh, Delia, you must be the smartest freshman in the class."

"Freshman?" the man said.

"I took a gap year," Delia said.

"Are you sure you'll be able to drive after that?" Sam said, nodding to the champagne.

"Excuse us," Delia said. She took Sam by the arm and led him out of hearing distance, where she said, "What's gotten into you? Are you my friend or my babysitter?"

"Sorry if I don't like to ride in the car with a tipsy driver, illegally, *during* a rainstorm. But we're clearly underdressed and underage. That dude is lying if he wants to act like he didn't know."

"*That dude* is a Keeper working for a think-tank in DC. He could be a good connection to make."

"If he's a Keeper, that only makes him more of a creep, because it means he sees right through the act and knows exactly how old you are. I saw how he was looking at you."

"Fine. Killjoy."

"Guilty as charged. Now can we please go?" Sam said.

"Let's at least say goodbye to Vi and Rachel."

They looked over together, to where Rachel was in the center of a new circle of patrons. She caught their eye and offered them a smile and a wave, then immediately went back to listening to her guests. There was no sign of Vi.

"Is that good enough for you? Come on, Delia, please. Have you forgotten why we came here? We need to find this book."

"All right, all right. Damn. Heaven forbid I make a valuable life connection when you and James are having bad dreams."

"Ouch," Sam said.

"That's not what I—oh, nevermind."

They descended the stairs back down to the shop, where Sam's singing bowl was waiting for him in a bag by the door. Or at least, it was supposed to be.

"Leaving so soon?"

It was Vi, stepping out of the shadows, holding the bag with the bowl inside.

"We were looking for you," Delia said. "We didn't want to leave without saying thank you. Really, we don't want to leave at all, but—"

"But we do have to get going," Sam said, throwing a pleading look Delia's way.

"Yes, I imagine you do," Vi said. "The mark on you is strong because the people who hunt you are strong." She handed the bag to Sam. "It is good fortune that you made it safely to my shop today. This should help you with what's ahead."

"Hunt us?" Delia said. "Is it really that bad?"

"It's what they do," Vi said. "I've seen their work before."

"Who are they?" Sam said. "Our friend took something of theirs, but we've never met them. We've only seen them through a spell."

"Best to keep it that way," Vi said. "In truth, I don't know much more than I've told you. I know them by their mark, and by the customers who come to me trying to shake it. I've seen frightened looks like yours before. I've sold charms to help people disguise themselves or disappear altogether. My advice to you is, return whatever your friend took, then put as much distance between yourselves and these people as you can. Now, I must get back to my guests. I wish you well."

She performed a gesture somewhere between a wave and a ward. Sam didn't know if it was really a spell, but it certainly made him feel better—less worried, after such worrisome news. Vi showed them to the door.

The rain had picked up again, and as soon as Sam and Delia stepped foot outside the store, they took off running, Sam clutching his singing bowl against his chest, as if the water would ruin it. As if he needed to protect it with his life.

Finally in the car, soaking wet and in mild shock, Delia and Sam turned to each other, breathing heavily from their run.

It was clear on Delia's face that she felt bad for snapping at him earlier, for underestimating the urgency, when come to find out, he was right to be alarmed. They were being *hunted*.

"Sam, I—I mean . . . if anything bad happened to you, I—"

"I thought the canvases were blank," he said.

What he meant was: it's okay. We all get it wrong sometimes.

"Well," she said, "that old Keeper was definitely flirting with me."

At the exact same moment, they burst into laughter—far more, perhaps, than the situation warranted. They were just so on edge.

They were laughing their heads off the whole way home.

CHAPTER 8

DELIA'S PARENTS WERE WATCHING TV IN THE LIVING
room when Sam and Delia crept through the back door into the
kitchen, still sopping wet, Sam hiding the singing bowl behind
his back, as if they'd have any idea what it was if they saw it.
Anyway, they didn't see it. They called out, "Delia, is that you?"
To which Delia shouted back, "Yup, and Sam," as the two of them
took off their shoes and made the short trek down the hall to
Delia's room.

"Did you tell them we were going to Atlanta?"

"Hell no," Delia said.

"What about my windshield? Did you tell them about that?"
Sam collapsed into the bean bag chair beside Delia's bed.

"Why would I?" Delia said.

"I don't know," Sam answered. He was always trying and failing to get a handle on Delia's relationship with her parents. As

the youngest of three, with an older brother and sister who were already working full time, Delia received a fraction of the parental oversight that Sam did. She always painted this like it was lucky for her, but to Sam, it seemed like her parents had meant to stop at two and now couldn't be bothered to care for their third child. It was one thing to tell your daughter you wouldn't pay for out-of-state college; it was quite another to make her buy her own clothes and gas with her paycheck, when you were fronting the down payment on your oldest's house. Again: she said it didn't bother her, so who was Sam to tell her it should? But it was one more reason to root for Delia's Pinnacle dreams to come true. "I guess I just wondered if they would be coming back here to check on us."

"Ha. You're funny, Sam. They haven't set foot in this room in ten years. Moving on. Do you have the note with you?"

Sam reached into his pocket and removed the note that had been wrapped around the brick last night—the one with the lightning-bolt V, subtext: *Bring us the book, or else.*

Delia pulled a pillow off her bed to use as a cushion, taking a seat on the floor across from Sam. Sam set the note down between them.

"Perfect. Are you ready?" She planted her hands on her knees and scooched forward until her knees were touching Sam's, forming a circle.

"How will we know if this thing is working?" Sam said, holding the singing bowl tensely, as if it were poisonous, or an active grenade.

"You know as much as I do. I guess if you start to see those faceless people, break off the spell right away."

"I will if I can," Sam said darkly.

"Are you sure you're ready to try this again?"

"I'm sure I'm ready to try *something.*"

Sam gripped the bowl in the palm of his right hand, tilting it toward the mallet that he held in his left. He rotated the mallet around the outside edge of the bowl, and right away, the sound it produced was so loud that he had to stop in surprise. He and Delia exchanged a nervous glance, and then he tried again. This time, when the sound began, he was ready for it, and he continued to rotate the mallet until the sound became steady, hypnotic, pleasing—the ringing in your ears after an excellent concert.

He and Delia closed their eyes and attempted the finding spell again, imagining the book they still hadn't seen in person, but this time with the extra associations that came from the note that lay between them. Whoever had made it wanted to find the book, too. Their urgency had left an imprint, like a bruise.

Just like last time, Sam's mind started to wander, bringing him along with it. It was impossible to pinpoint the exact moment when Sam's imagination ended and the magic began, but all at once, he realized that he was outnumbered by *details*—that his surroundings were too filled in to be the byproduct of his own mind's attempt to reconstruct them. Only, instead of the warehouse office space where Sam had expected to find himself, what he saw when he turned to take it all in was a field, the grass cut short and the dirt poking through in patches. Two beat-up soccer goals formed the field's border, and Sam stood equidistant between them, a dense forest just beyond two sides of the field, an old country road and an empty parking lot past the others.

Sam had been here before.

He would never forget it.

It was suddenly harder to convince himself that the spell was working. So vivid was his memory of the night when he'd ended up at this field, coming out of those trees to find a single, still-working spotlight in the parking lot casting an eerie yellow glow over the whole place, that he now thought maybe he *was* imagining it from the ground up, every single blade of grass and the smoke-gray sky of that night. If this was the spell, a simulacrum pulled out of his memory, it was a very cruel trick for his memory to play, bringing him here all alone, to revisit the moment without James.

Sam took a step forward, and in so doing found that his feet worked normally here.

He took another step, and another. It didn't feel right to run. Humming through the clouds was the distant sound of a bell, reverberating more than ringing, a metallic constant that beckoned him steadily toward the trees.

It was right at the border of these trees where James had thrown out his arm to stop him—"Wait. Sam." They'd been wind-sprinting through the woods for at least five minutes by then, trying to outrun that awful party, which Sam hadn't wanted to go to in the first place but which James had finally convinced him would be fun, because it was spring break, because Delia was working and there were no good movies playing at the movie theater, because what else were they going to do.

The party had not been fun.

From the moment they'd arrived, Sam could feel the weight of everyone's eyes on him. The party wasn't all that crowded, for one thing. In movies, high school parties were always filled with bodies—bodies falling out of bathrooms, sitting on counters, double-stacked on the sofa. You could crowd-surf from one end of a room to the other in a movie party. At Bridget's house that night, there were eleven people plus James and Sam. The rest of them were all sitting in a circle, on chairs and a couch and the floor, when the two boys walked in.

"'Sup," James had said, with his nonchalant up-nod. "Hey, everyone," Sam had said, somehow already sticking out before they'd even fully entered the room.

It had only gone downhill from there. Sam had known coming in that he didn't like Bridget and Bridget didn't like him—her feelings about gay people had been made clear to their whole English class in the first week, when she'd loudly objected to a book called *I'll Give You the Sun* having been on their summer reading list without a content warning. But James had assured Sam that he'd hardly have to interact with her, even if the party was at her house—that there would be at least a few Friedman people Sam liked there.

But Sam did have to interact with her. And there weren't any Friedman people Sam liked among the others. And James kept trying to leave Sam alone with them—to grab another drink, to smoke a cigarette outside, to go to the bathroom—which made it painfully obvious to everyone that Sam kept going far out of his way to stay close to James. Even if he had to stand outside the bathroom and pretend to read something on his phone.

"What do you do in that magic club anyway?"

That was a boy named Marshall, a senior at the time, two hours and countless drinks into the evening.

It was directed at Sam, in a moment of silence after James had joined a few others to smoke up on the back porch. The only things Sam knew about Marshall were that he was on the baseball team, that his dad worked the line at the Titan fulfillment center where Sam's dad was an engineer, and that he'd just asked about the "magic club" with such disdain in his voice that it was clear he was more suspicious about the answer than interested in it.

"Mostly we practice for the state convention," Sam had said. "There are all kinds of scholarships for the top teams. That sort of thing."

That hadn't satisfied Marshall.

"But like, what do you do at the state thing? Spells and shit?"

"Pretty much."

"What kind of spells? Like basic stuff?"

Here, Marshall had surprised Sam with a perfectly executed if low-level fire spell. A snap of his fingers, like flint on tinder, and there was a flame in the palm of his hand, brief but not small. No one else in the room reacted, like this was a trick they'd seen him do before. But Sam scooted forward onto the edge of his seat, intrigued and a little scared.

"Some basic stuff. Some not-so-basic stuff."

"Like what? What's the hardest spell you can do?"

"I don't know," Sam had said. "It sort of depends. There are lots of different ways to define hard."

Marshall snickered. "I bet. Sounds like bullshit to me."

The others had laughed at that—and at Sam's flush of embarrassment. His first impulse was to say, *Just wait, James will show you.* But he knew if he said that, he and James would never hear the end of it, as long as they lived in Friedman.

"Well, okay," Sam had said. "How about this?"

Sam had circled his fingers around each other, intending to show them a lesser version of the spell he had performed at convention the previous November. The task had been to craft a micro-storm of many elements; you had to include at least three distinct components for the storm to count, with bonus points awarded for every component beyond three. Sam had spent months on wind, rain, thunder, and hail, the last of which seemed a hair safer than lightning—the more popular choice. (The winner of the event had found time to summon a sandstorm and a blizzard, too, though Sam maintained that was stretching the rules.)

That night at the party, the micro-storm had gone off beyond Sam's wildest hopes; it was much more effective than it had been at convention even, which was insane, considering that Sam hadn't practiced it once since then.

The problem, of course, was that Sam was not in a fiberglass cube as he had been at convention. He was in Bridget's living room. And even at micro-levels, wind, rain, thunder, and hail had been enough to send Marshall and the other guests screaming and ducking for cover, their drinks flying and mixing in with the gallon or so of indoor precipitation, soaking everyone and everything in surprise.

Marshall hadn't wasted any time with words. As soon as he'd realized they were all safe, that the storm was over, he'd thrown the chair off his head and made a lunge straight for Sam, his eyes absolutely murderous.

And then he'd frozen in midair.

Sam's heart was beating so hard he thought he was having a heart attack, but he recognized the presence and the direction of the magic, and he whipped his head around to find James, returned from outside with Bridget and the others. Sam wasn't sure how much of the fiasco they'd seen, but he didn't have time to ask.

"Come on," James had said, grabbing Sam's hand and pushing past the others before they even knew what was happening. He threw open the back door and yanked Sam through it, and then they took off running, down the steps into the backyard, then into the woods.

James never let go of Sam's hand, and as they ran and ran, Sam started to suspect that James must be using magic even now, to keep their path clear or to keep them upright, Sam wasn't sure which. He only knew that at this speed, in these woods, he should have tripped many times by now.

Then they'd reached this field.

James had stuck out his arm to stop Sam from running forward. "Wait. Sam." He'd scanned in all directions, as if making sure the coast was clear, but then, instead of pushing ahead, James collapsed onto the ground of the forest, his body shaking with laughter that sounded deep and genuine even as it reminded Sam that James was high off his ass right now.

"You did. A storm. In Bridget's. Living room."

Which, okay, when he'd put it that way, Sam had started laughing, too, even as he'd looked behind them, squinting and trying to listen for any signs that Marshall or the others were chasing them. As far as he could tell, they were safe.

"They asked for it," Sam said.

"I'm sure they did," James said.

"No, I mean they *literally* asked for it—like, 'what's the most complicated spell you've ever done for convention'?"

"Fair enough."

James was still laughing. He spread out his limbs like he was making a snow angel in the underbrush, and then he closed his eyes and laughed some more.

"It wouldn't have happened if you hadn't left me alone in there," Sam said.

"For five minutes."

"Still."

Accepting that James wasn't getting back up any time soon, Sam sat down cross-legged on the ground beside him. It smelled earthy down here. Sam would know it was night even if his eyes were closed. His breath and his heartbeat were returning to normal.

"You could *try* to get along with them, you know," James said quietly.

"I really couldn't," Sam said. "Or at least, I couldn't try any harder than I already do."

"You were the only sober person there."

"I'm a designated driver. No idea how the rest of them are getting home. Anyway, who wants to be friends with a bunch of people who are only fun if you're drunk."

James peeled one eye open to peer at Sam, as if he was trying to gauge his own feelings, no doubt both heightened and hindered by inebriation.

"You really think it's going to be so different outside of Friedman?"

"I know so," Sam said. "Once you get out of Friedman, there are way more people like you, me, and Delia."

"Magickers?"

"For one thing. But more than that."

"Well that's good," James said. "That it's more than that. Because I can't say I've ever met someone at convention that I was dying to become friends with. They don't seem to me any better or worse than the people around here. They just cast cooler spells."

Sam started to argue that convention was the worst place to try to make new friends, not only because everyone was in competition, but also because everyone came with their own high school groups, and remained caught up in their separate dramas. He started to say that James should come with him and his mom sometime to a Q-Atl meeting—to hear queer people from all over the state, who sounded so cool in spite of the shit they were going through. But Sam was stopped short by the feeling that James had talked him down a maze, and they'd taken a wrong turn somewhere. The point for Sam wasn't that they needed to make better friends. The point for Sam was that James shouldn't leave him alone at a party—that the three of them needed to go somewhere where they would be their truest selves alone, and once they got there, the three of them would be enough.

"See, you know I'm right."

"Whatever you say, James."

Sam lay down on the ground beside him. He looked up at the sky, where he could see only a few stars through the clouds, though the stars he saw burned brightly enough for the rest of them.

Just as Sam felt himself lulled by the comfortable silence—felt himself almost persuaded by James's argument that they already had everything they needed right here—James suddenly leaned up on his elbow, his eyes open wide and mere inches from Sam's eyes. The space between them was so small, so charged with electricity, that Sam felt it ignite all the air in his lungs. His chest went rigid. His heartbeat stopped.

It was impossible to mistake the look on James's face. Sam had a never seen a look like that up close, a searching look, a look of unmasked desire. It was like the moment when Marshall had been frozen in air, his intent plain even in still life. James seemed to have been frozen, too, and for a moment, Sam wondered if he was supposed to lean forward and break the spell with a kiss, or if that would break the spell in the wrong direction.

Then James blinked, and he kept his eyes closed for a breath too long.

"Your car," he said, leaning back to a safe distance.

"What?" Sam's voice was squeaky and raspy at once.

"Your car. We need to get it before they do anything to it."

"Okay," Sam said, reorienting himself. "You think they would do something to my car?"

"I don't know. Maybe?"

"Okay."

They'd stood up in hurried unison, shaking the leaves from their clothes. Without having to discuss it, they'd both started walking in the direction of the soccer field; it hadn't felt right to go back the way they had come, through the woods. They'd followed the little road the long way around, past the old rec center that was still open but barely used, now that the new sports complex had gone up across town. In silence, they'd come back to the front of Bridget's house, where all the other cars were still parked outside; from what Sam could see through the living room windows, it looked like the party had gone back to normal.

Had they been gone even twenty minutes? It was hard to say.

Sam's car had been fine. Sam and James had been fine. Though he'd worry about it in the hallways for the last two months of the year, Sam would remain fine; after spring break, the people from the party would pretend he didn't even exist.

"James—" Sam started, as they prepared to drive away. But the word sounded strange as it left his lips, echoing and growing louder until it was no longer a word at all, but the sound of a bell. A reverberation.

Jamesjamesjamesjamesjamesjamesjamesjames

"*Sam.*"

Sam opened his eyes.

He was back in Delia's bedroom. Their knees were still touching, and Sam's hand rotated automatically around the singing bowl. His arm muscles ached. It was dark outside.

"Oh, good," Delia said. "I was worried for a second it was happening like last time."

"It was nothing like last time, for better and for worse," Sam said. "It didn't even work this time."

"What do you mean?" Delia said.

"I mean I didn't go to wherever the book is. I went . . . into a memory. Or an almost-memory. I think I might have had a dream that I actually remember? I'm not totally sure."

"Weird," Delia said. "I think it worked for me. Do you know

the old rec center? The one that looks haunted, out on Old Syc-amore Road?"

"Oh my God," Sam said. "With the soccer field?"

"Yes, exactly. That soccer field. I have no idea how or why, but I think that must be where the book is. The spell kept taking me to this one spot right at the edge by the trees, clear as day. I haven't been to that rec center since I was six years old, so no way it was a memory."

"Well, then," Sam said.

"Why? What did you see?"

"I'll tell you on the way. Come on, before it gets too dark."

"So this is your spot?" Delia said, when Sam paused just inside the trees. She raised her eyebrows suggestively.

"More or less."

"I think we need to be more exact than that."

"I don't know. It was dark then, and I wasn't *exactly* looking for landmarks."

Delia snorted. Sam could tell she was resisting the urge to say something else.

"I just don't believe it's going to be here," Sam said, even as he poked around the underbrush. There was no need for a magic light tonight. The moon was full and bathed the woods in a lustrous blue glow, more eerie than beautiful. "It feels too easy. Like if the book was here, the others could have done this spell and found it for themselves already."

"I thought about that, too, but I have a theory." Delia was looking on the ground but also up into the branches of the trees, all the way to the tops. "I think the reason they haven't been able to find it with their own magic—and the reason they tried to hijack our spell this week—is that you can't find the book without the key from James. James *created* the spell he used to teleport the book. His associations were personal—his personal safe place. And even though he didn't know it, the spell sent the book *here*. There's a reason for that. He felt safe with *you*."

"Okay, okay," Sam said. There was also a reason he hadn't told Delia or anyone else about that night before. He'd felt safe then, too. Now he felt exposed.

"Sorry, but it's important. I think the key to finding the book is in what happened here that night. You said you were both on the ground, looking up?"

"I was looking up. James had his eyes closed, until . . . until he didn't."

"Hmm . . ."

They were running out of places on the ground to check. Sam couldn't imagine how the book could be up in a tree.

"You don't think it's possible he sent it to that exact night, do you?" Delia said. "Like, back in time?"

"What? No way. That's impossible, surely?"

Delia shrugged.

"It's improbable. Especially for a spell James made up as a kid. But he's pretty powerful, Sam. I don't think he even realizes how powerful, half the time. He's not in control of it. He doesn't care about learning 'the proper way.' But it's like, for him, magic comes out of this primordial place. His associations work even when they make no sense—even when he can't explain them. And magickers used to be able to do a kind of time travel. Just think of Merlin."

"Merlin is fictional."

"As a single, literal person, sure. But as a composite of many actual Keeper-level magickers from the Middle Ages, studies suggest he is very real. At least the magic attributed to him is."

"Well, I don't see any of Merlin's Keeper-level descendants here to help us, so I think we should limit our search to what's probable. And I think what probably happened is that the book was here at some point and then—holy shit."

A cloud had swept over the moon, urged on by the chilly breeze Sam had felt right through his hoodie. In the exact moment that the woods had gone dark, something unnatural had appeared at his feet. But that wasn't quite true. What had appeared was natural enough—it was, in fact, exactly as he'd pictured it, green leather with a lightning-bolt V inlay on the cover. It was the way that it had appeared that was unnatural. One moment not there, and then, as the moonlight left the space where it lay, it had appeared in a wave.

Delia was the first to process and recalibrate. She bent down and snatched the book before the cloud had a chance to move again. Then she grabbed Sam by the shoulder and hurried them back toward her car, already muttering the words of another spell as if she were speaking them directly to the book. Sam wasn't sure if she was trying to keep the book from disappearing, or if she was trying to keep it from being found, now that it had been removed from its hiding place.

Sam couldn't think too hard about that.

"That night," Sam said. "It was cloudy that night. There were only a few stars. He sent it back in time. I don't know how, but he did."

Delia finished the words of her spell just as they reached her car.

She turned her full attention to Sam, in the exact moment before he started tearing up.

"Oh, Sam," she said. "My sweet summer child. Let me get you a Starbucks and then take you home."

CHAPTER 9

WHEN SAM GOT OUT OF BED ON SUNDAY MORNING TO find a text from Denver that read, **How are you holding up?**, his first reaction was to wonder—with much confusion and a bit of vague annoyance that bordered on hurt—just how much Delia had told him about their trip to recover the book. Did everyone know about that night in the woods now? But as he pushed through the fog of his ongoing sleeplessness and let reality catch up to him, he realized that of course Denver was asking about Friday night and the incident with his windshield.

Had that really been this same weekend?

Ha, I'm okay, he replied. **Car still in the shop.**

Do we for sure have practice tomorrow? You need a ride after school?

Sam was definitely alert now. He pictured Denver in his room, waking up early on the weekend to check on him. To be fair, it was ten o'clock, so not that early. Sam had just been beyond exhausted.

Let's check with the group, Sam said.

Sam switched over to the group text.

We still meeting tomorrow?

Yes! Delia responded right away. Wait till y'all see this book. It's insane.

What book? Denver wrote. As far as he knew, the book they'd been looking for was their old spell book, well-known to them all.

The placeholder image for an incoming text appeared, signaling that Delia was working on a response, no doubt remembering the same thing and wondering if there was any reason not to rip off the bandage and tell Denver the truth, now that the book was safely in their possession.

Her message, when it finally came, was: You'll see. It was the kind of message that really could have used a smiley-face emoji to soften the sinister.

When James finally chimed in with the ever cryptic praying hands emoji (did they really mean praying, or thank you, or what?), Sam wrote, James, is this you or your dad? Please confirm your identity. To which James responded with a middle-finger emoji and a black-heart emoji.

Identity confirmed.

All right, then, Sam wrote. My house after school. His hands hovered over the phone for a second more. Denver is giving me a ride.

It was kind of remarkable how easy it was to talk to Denver. Sam had this—in retrospect, irrational—fear that since they'd only known each other for a week, they were quickly going to run out of things to say when it was just the two of them. But it turned out that the years they hadn't known each other gave them plenty of things to say, and Denver had this genuine curiosity and delight for details that made Sam want to answer his questions in the longest, most colorful ways he could think of. They talked in an uninterrupted flow from the school parking lot all the way to Sam's basement.

"So, you're saying that little shack attached to the gas station, with a door that looks like it's made out of plywood, is actually a quality food establishment?" Denver asked.

"Mary Ellen's has the best biscuits and gravy you have ever eaten or will ever eat. It's like gravy soup with biscuit croutons. It's like a gravy landslide over biscuit city."

"I'm not sure you're convincing me by comparing the food to a natural disaster."

"It's like a natural disaster that's making way for a better civilization."

"Wow, Sam. Didn't peg you for a kill-all-humans type, but I guess we all have our dark sides. Is it better than Waffle House?"

"Depends on what you're ordering. They both have their specialties."

"Let me guess—Waffle House specializes in man-made disasters?"

"What's so funny down here?"

Sam hadn't even heard James coming down the stairs, but now he stood there, his mouth quirked into his best attempt at a smile, while the now violently purple bags under his eyes gave away the fact that he was barely hanging on.

"Sam was just telling me about the biscuits and gravy at Mary Ellen's."

"Oh," James said. He came to stand behind the couch where Sam sat, and his hands bounced in his jacket pockets, antsy, incessant. "Is Delia on her way?"

"I assume so," Sam said.

"Cool, cool. And she's bringing the book, right?"

"So she said . . ."

(And to be clear, she'd said it to both of them, but that was at lunch, and James had basically flipped out that she didn't have it with her right there, right then. She said she'd felt it would be safer at home than in her car or her locker; James had disagreed.)

Sam did his best not to take it personally now—this single-minded, sharp-edged focus James had on the book. Things would go back to normal once the book was returned. Once James and Sam both had a good night's sleep.

"So where did Delia end up finding the spell book?" Denver said.

"Oh, it was at the old rec center," Sam said, as he and James both tried to avoid each other's eyes without being obvious about it. (James hadn't been so successful at hiding his surprise and recognition when Delia first dropped the news at lunch—clearly, he'd remembered that night as well as Sam had.)

"What was it doing there?" Denver said.

"Long story," Sam said.

"You guys are not going to believe what I've found in this book," Delia said, appearing at the bottom of the stairs.

James visibly relaxed at the sight of the book in her hands, while Sam tensed up, sensitive to Denver's confusion.

"Did someone leave us a surprise in our spell book?" Sam asked, hoping Delia would get the hint and keep up the act for Denver's sake. Sam didn't want to drag Denver into their true collective nightmare if he could help it—and, if he was being honest, he didn't want to have to admit to Denver that they hadn't been honest with him last week.

Delia, it seemed, had no such moral quandaries.

"Denver," she said, "you probably already guessed this, because we're all terrible liars, but this isn't our spell book from last year. No offense."

"None taken?" Denver said, more confused than ever.

"Oh, dear," Sam said.

"We had our reasons," Delia said, half-directed at Sam, as if to suggest she had no patience for his holier-than-thou act. "But they're not important anymore. What's important is that the group that put this book together has been messing with some very serious shit. James, that spell they were doing when you were there? With the cutting and the tearing associations or whatever? I think I found it."

She and James came around to sit beside Sam on the couch, though she never took her eyes off the book, flipping quickly through the pages even as she placed it on the ottoman in front of them.

"Listen to this. 'Once the aides are in place on the points of the star, and the subjects are gathered in the inner vertices, the spell leader should direct everyone to associate rending a gap between the worlds as he'—or she, I don't see why a spell leader can't be a she, but anyway—'as he reads the incantation below.' I personally didn't recognize the language of the incantation, so I figured y'all wouldn't know it either, but I posted a picture of it on the Pinnacle Friendivist group yesterday, and somebody said that it looked like Enochian. Do y'all know it?"

The three boys shook their heads.

"Right. So, it turns out Enochian is this language that originated in the sixteenth century when these two magickers said that angels brought it to them. It's not a full language, in the sense that there are only enough words to cover what was supposedly said by these angels in the original message. But there are enough Enochian words that this language is used in all kinds of spells related to the spirits of the dead. That's what the spell was supposed to do that night, James. Open a gateway to the spirit world."

"The spirit world?" Sam said dubiously.

"Look, I'm not saying you have to believe it, but the people who made this book obviously do—that's all I'm saying. There are a bunch of spells in here that are in Enochian. Stuff that can supposedly let you talk to spirits, or at least get advice from them in signs and symbols, that sort of thing."

"So, like, evil magic," Sam said, making a joke but actually feeling a little sick.

"Not necessarily," Delia said. "What is praying if not talking to spirits? And in a lot of cultures, communing with the dead is seen as a perfectly natural thing."

"Talking *at* the dead, maybe," Sam said. "But expecting a response? Or worse, forcing one? Sounds pretty evil to me."

"Ordinarily, I'd be inclined to agree with Delia," James said, earning a hurt look from Sam. "But in this case, I think we need to remember who we're dealing with. I can't speak for everyone who was in the warehouse that night, but based on what I saw of the main group, I think it's safe to assume that if they were trying to cut a hole between our world and the spirit world, it's bad news at best and, yeah, probably evil at worst."

"And this is what you didn't want to tell me last week? When we were doing the finding spells together?" Denver was ostensibly saying this to all three of them, but he was looking squarely at Sam when he did. Sam hated to be on the receiving end of that look. It was no doubt the same look Sam had given James on the first day of school, hearing about everything he'd missed at Mike's party.

"We didn't want to drop this on you if we could help it," Sam said. "These people are dangerous. They're the same people who smashed my windshield."

"Because James stole their book," Delia added, earning a sharp response from James.

"What's that supposed to mean?" he said.

"It doesn't *mean* anything; it's a fact. And I don't doubt your word when you say that everybody was super sketch that night, but I don't think we should discount everything in this book as a result. We wouldn't discount the very powerful magic you are capable of creating just because your actions are a little questionable sometimes."

"*No offense,*" James said tersely.

Delia shrugged.

"Y'all," Sam said. "No need to fight about this. Whatever this book was before it got to us, it has only been negative since it came into our lives. The sooner we return it to those people, the sooner we can stop thinking about them and go back to worrying about our convention categories. And enjoying senior year. Remember that?"

"Or junior year, as the case may be," Denver said quietly. That touch of levity—and that gesture of forgiveness—was exactly what the moment needed. James exhaled, and Delia even smiled a little bit.

"All right," Delia said. "You're right, Sam. There are some incredible-sounding spells in here . . . but better to return this book while we can. Before those people come for us or we tear each other's hair out, whichever comes first."

"Agreed," James said. "The only question is, how? I don't exactly want to walk up to that warehouse and leave it at their front door if I can help it."

"Are they really that dangerous?" Denver asked.

"Based on the nightmares they've quite literally caused me in the past week, I'd say yes," James said, and Sam shivered, remembering his own visions, which had single-handedly turned him off wanting to remember his dreams, perhaps for good.

Delia said, "I'd say yes, too, based on this book. But the good news is, there's a spell in here that seems tailor-made for this moment."

"What does it do?" James said.

Delia started flipping toward the front of the book. It was a little unnerving to Sam that after only one day, she seemed to have such a thorough knowledge of the book's contents, but then again, that wasn't *that* unusual for her. She had helped him prepare for countless tests over the years, and always, she had a better grasp of the material than he did—even when she wasn't in whatever class Sam needed help with.

"Here," she said. "A Spell of Conveyance. For transporting light objects across long distances."

"Surely we can do better than that?" James said. "Sam, what about the spell you did for convention sophomore year?"

"The switching spell?"

"Yeah."

"You have to be able to see both objects for that to work. Or at least I did. Plus, I never made it beyond switching two cinder blocks. The guy who came in first made a trash can switch places with a table."

"Well," James said, "this book probably doesn't weigh more than a cinder block."

Sam frowned. He hated when anyone, but especially James, made him say no to the same thing twice.

"I just don't see why we would choose some great-sounding spell we don't know over an imperfect spell we do know," James continued, and Sam tried not to read into that. "It seems like we're asking for trouble."

"Well, learning new spells is always a little dangerous," Delia said. "But I'm with Sam—no way the switching spell is strong enough for what we need. So either we try this spell, or we look up another spell on one of the apps. But as someone who spends a lot of time studying what's on the apps, I can tell you right now I've never seen another spell that could get the book from here to there—at least not a spell that's within our ability level. Meanwhile, this spell of conveyance seems pretty damn achievable. So as club president, I am officially putting this to a vote. All those in favor of trying this spell?"

She raised her hand immediately, and Denver raised his shortly thereafter. She made a compelling case. That was why she was club president.

Sam was more hesitant, if only to protect James's feelings. But honestly, he was persuaded.

"All right then, no need for another vote. Three to one, it's decided."

This spell, it turned out, was not written in Enochian. It was written in English. There were no special implements or ingredients required, but the instructions did say that it got easier the more magickers participated—Merlin's Law was a common refrain in this spell book, according to Delia—and it also said it was easier if everyone involved could visualize the object's full trajectory, more a literal conveyance than an associative one. So Delia pulled up her maps app on her phone and dropped a pin on the gray square they finally agreed was the right building, and then she translated that location into a list of directions.

Denver said, "Am I sabotaging this spell if I can't picture these places like y'all can, or am I still helping it by adding my magic to the group's?"

"Just grab Sam's hand, please," Delia said.

"Yes, ma'am!"

"Wait," Sam said, standing up quickly. He didn't know why he felt so nervous. The spell would work or it wouldn't. "I want to get one thing first." He ran upstairs to his room, took a deep breath, and then returned with the singing bowl. "It worked well last time," he said to Delia. "It's supposed to stop interference from other magickers," he explained to James and Denver.

"Good idea," Delia said.

The singing bowl also meant that Sam's hands were fully occupied, so the four of them touched knees as they sat in a circle on the floor, and then they began the work of reciting the words to the spell, and preparing to visualize the steps of the directions, while not becoming distracted by the high-pitched hum of the bowl. Which—sure thing, spell! Nothing to it!

For all the reasons the spell could have gone wrong, it didn't.

Hardly had the four of them finished the last word of the incantation when the book snapped closed and leaped into the air, flying so fast up the stairs that Sam would have thought it was a frightened bird or a bat if he didn't know better. He heard the crash of a first-floor window breaking a split second later, and he and Denver both jumped, losing their concentration, but the spell kept going, anchored by James's and Delia's cooler minds.

The book was flying so fast, it was hard to know when he was focusing on the right part of the course map and when his brain was really miles behind, but the wildest part was, he swore he could *feel* the book's movement, like he was holding the remote control to a car and had to account for the resistance of the tires as the car turned. His stomach dropped whenever the book lost altitude, and it went up in his throat when the book flew higher to avoid some obstacle. When the book finally slammed into one of the boarded-up windows of the warehouse with such velocity that it broke right through, Sam felt the spell's release crashing into him like the ground at the end of a long fall.

They all gasped.

"I think . . . I think it worked," Denver finally said, still catching his breath.

"You think?" Delia said, sarcastically but not unkindly.

Sam put down the singing bowl in the middle of the circle. "I guess the book was legit."

James frowned.

"You disagree?" Sam asked.

"I don't like it," James admitted. "What if the spell had unseen consequences? What if these people trace the spell back to us?"

"Then it will be no different from where we were, when they came after Sam's car," Delia said. "They already know who we are. At least now we don't owe them anything."

James didn't have anything to say to that, though Sam wished he did—wished James had a better defense for his own part in getting them into this mess.

But the mess was gone, right? The book was out of their lives. It was over. It had to be.

"Seems kind of weird, thinking about everyday old convention spells after that," Denver said brightly, breaking the broody silence. "I almost wish we'd taken photos or something of *all* of the pages."

Delia smirked.

"And miss out on the chance to stumble your way through spells way above your experience level to middling results at convention?" Sam said. "Like a true Fascinator? I think not."

They all laughed, but Denver's words proved prophetic—the four of them had a hard time getting in the groove of practicing after that, their conversation returning again and again to what might be happening with the book at the warehouse at that very moment. What other spells might have been in there.

The book itself had been easy enough to get rid of. But their glimpse into another life, a few miles from their own and yet a world away, seemed like it might be a different story.

CHAPTER 10

WHEN THE BOOK CRASHED THROUGH THE WOODEN slats over the window, Liv thought it was the sound of a gun going off—that they'd finally been caught. That someone was looking out for her after all.

She and Isaac were standing in the center of the common room, frozen in mid-fight, the shock of the explosion jolting him enough that he'd dropped his grip on her arm and jumped back, his survivor's instincts kicking in. If that book had arrived even a minute later, there was no telling what Isaac might have done in that time. She knew their secret, and he was furious.

Now, they both turned to where the book simply lay there, right at their feet. She had a pretty good idea what he was thinking—that this couldn't be real. That after all the magic and the shouting and the fear of the last two weeks, all of it fruitless, there was no way the book could simply turn up so easily.

"Don't move," he said to her, as if he could sense that she was readying herself to bolt. Or maybe he was trying to protect her from the book, suspecting it was a trap; maybe he was still capable of that kindness, although after what she'd learned this week, she seriously doubted it.

He crept over to the book and waved his hand over it searchingly. He knelt down beside it, put his face at floor level, examining the book from every angle. Finally satisfied, he picked it up slowly, carefully, and that was the moment Mr. Grender, Grace, Alex, and Alex came running out of their rooms to join them.

If Liv needed one more reason to leave at the next chance she got, the fact that they'd come now, so quickly, after ignoring the sounds of her fight with Isaac, was it.

"Give it to me," Mr. Grender said hungrily.

Isaac handed it over, almost quivering from the honor of delivering it and from the hope that it would finally put things back to normal at the compound. Two weeks of tightening the screws on the thief and his friends, and ironically, the first person to crack under the pressure had been one of their own. Carl's breakdown had been a sight to behold; his unhinged wailing—and his explosive accusations against Mr. Grender and Grace—still echoed in Liv's brain two days later. Liv didn't want to believe the things he'd said—the things they'd *done*—but none of the rest of them had tried to deny his account. They'd absorbed his episode as if they were museumgoers observing a strange bit of performance art—a piece that ended with Carl getting in his car and driving off into the night. Down a seventh member, they hadn't met as a group since.

Mr. Grender flipped through the pages of the book, one at a time, and as he did, the creases of worry on his face gave way to relief, unsettling to behold. It was all there, intact.

"I think your messages may have finally gotten through," Mr. Grender said to Grace, as he continued to flip through the book. "Now we can get back to focusing our efforts where they truly belong."

"They still could have made copies," Alex said.

"What if they go to the Keepers?" said other Alex.

Mr. Grender had reached the middle of the book, and it lay open in his hands, revealing a piece of paper that had been torn out of a spiral notebook, folded into fourths, and stuck in between the pages. Cradling the book in one arm, he unfolded the paper, and Liv craned her neck to get a better look at the jagged V that seemed to be the only thing on it. However the paper had gotten there, Isaac appeared to recognize it, and he started to speak, but Mr. Grender held up a hand for silence, passing the paper to Grace. Grace closed her eyes and ran her fingers over the symbol, and when she opened her eyes again, she had a smile so bright it lit up her whole face.

"I don't think they'll be going to the Keepers," Mr. Grender said, some silent communication passing between him, Grace, and Isaac. "In fact, if this little message she's left us is any indication, I think we may have found a new ally. Isaac?"

"I'm on it," Isaac said.

"But you make a good point," Mr. Grender said to Alex. "Reproductions may have been made. Isaac, keep an eye on the others. See what they know, and what they plan to do with it."

Isaac nodded.

That seemed to be their cue to go back to their separate corners, though Grace followed Mr. Grender to his room; no doubt they had some secret errand, related to whatever Grace had seen on that piece of paper—or *in* it, perhaps, since it apparently contained some message Liv couldn't see.

She'd been so naive to think that living among other magickers would make her a better magicker. These people were parasites. That was what Carl said. They'd burned through the boy in her room before her, and now they'd burned through Carl. If she stayed here any longer, they'd burn through her, too.

"This conversation isn't over," Isaac said. "When I get back, we're going to discuss how to get you back on the right track. You've lost your way, Liv. You're forgetting all the things we've done for you, when no one else would."

She nodded without speaking. She looked down at her wrist, at her grandmother's watch.

How far could she run without needing a break? How many miles was it from the compound to the nearest house?

By the time Isaac got back, she would be long gone.

CHAPTER 11

ON WEDNESDAY MORNING, SAM GOT A TEXT FROM HIS mom that his car was ready at the shop, and she could pick him up and take him between showings of a new house if he could wait until three forty-five. This kindness felt like progress. They'd been sniping at each other all week following the discovery of a second broken window, this one in their house, which Sam swore wasn't a result of practice, though it was obvious to her that it was. That was a small price to pay, though, for having finally gotten the book off their hands. He was sleeping again. The visions were gone.

Thank you! He wrote now. **No need to miss work. I'll get a ride from one of my friends.**

"Sorry, I have to work today," Delia said at lunch. "The youth group crowd always comes to eat early on Wednesday nights."

"You could drop me off on the way?" Sam suggested.

"But it's not on the way."

Sam turned to James.

"My mom's got the car today. I'm taking the bus home."

Sam sighed.

"Why don't you ask Denver?" Delia said.

"I don't know him that well yet. Asking for a ride to an auto shop is like a best-friend level request."

"I don't know. What better way to get closer to someone than to endure an onerous errand with that someone? You could kill two birds with one stone and offer to buy him a Frosty on the way there, to say thank you and I'm sorry. Who doesn't love a Frosty? Maybe if you're really lucky, he'll invite you on another date, and this one won't be so disastrous."

"What date?" James said.

"There was no date," Sam said, throwing her a warning look. "There was a group outing. You were there."

"Oh, that," James said, and unless Sam was imagining it, he seemed relieved.

"That was partly what made it a disaster," Delia said. "Though there were other disastrous parts, too. A Frosty would make up for them."

"All right, I'll ask him. But only because I really do need a ride. Not because I want a . . . a Frosty."

Delia cackled. This was exactly why he hadn't told her about the night by the soccer field for so long. Why he still hadn't told her about what happened at the bowling alley. Delia could be a loose cannon. She balanced her own moral scales.

Denver responded to Sam's text right away, saying he would be happy to take Sam to the auto shop.

I'm right by the entrance of the lower parking lot.

Better than Uber! Sam wrote.

SO much better than Uber ;) Denver replied. Which, Sam supposed he had opened the door for that one.

"How did you know Frosties are my favorite?" Denver said that afternoon.

"*Lucky* guess."

"Ah, I see what you did there. But you didn't have to do that. Buy me something, I mean. It's not like I had anything else going on today."

"Gosh, when you put it that way, I feel so honored."

"No, I mean—I'm happy to help. I just—never mind."

"I'm only giving you a hard time," Sam said.

"Oh. Right." Denver smiled. Whatever was in the water in Nashville that made a person's smile look like that, with dimples for days, Sam wished more of it would make its way down here. "Actually, I was glad you texted, because I wanted to ask you if you might be free this Friday to go to a play in Atlanta."

"A play?"

"Yeah. It's at the Fox Theatre. It's called *Celestine.* It's supposed to have a lot of magic in it, and I happen to have an extra ticket."

"Oh yeah?" Sam said, gulping. "And why would you 'happen' to have an extra ticket?"

"Honestly? Well, I bought two tickets because my boyfriend,

Arjun, was supposed to be visiting me this weekend."

"Oh."

Oh!

"But then Arjun went and broke up with me right before school started, because he said he couldn't handle long distance. Which, ironically, is why I had this grand, romantic weekend planned, to convince him that long distance would work. Perfect timing, huh?"

Sam's brain was in hyperdrive.

"So, wait. That was . . . two weeks ago? How long had you two been together?"

"Well, we sort of started talking on the DL in eighth grade. On the DL because he wasn't sure how his family would take him being gay, but then he came out to them last year and it went way better than either of us was expecting. We were officially boyfriends most of last year."

"Wow," Sam said. "Three years, and it just ended?"

"Pretty shitty, huh?"

"Very shitty."

It was, in fact, shitty in a way that Sam was struggling to articulate. Yes, it was shitty for Denver, but this new revelation about what Denver was going through didn't make Sam feel great about himself, either. It pointed to a reading of Denver's recent interest in him that required words like "rebound," "hookup," "utter delusion." Or maybe it had never been "interest" at all. Maybe Denver really was just looking for a friend—a fellow queer magicker in a town where either of those things was rare but both of them together was like a rainbow-spewing unicorn. Maybe Sam was the delusional one.

And Sam *knew* he was experiencing a double standard here. That it wasn't fair to resent any caveats to Denver's feelings, when Sam's own feelings came with a giant James-shaped caveat of their own. He also *knew* that there wasn't some requirement that said people could only date one person at once—he'd heard plenty of people his age at Q-Atl meetings describe playing the field, limited though that field may be. But even before he realized he might want to be more than friends with James, Sam had never felt like *he* would be the type to act on feelings for multiple people at the same time. There was a tiny part of him that felt like he was *cheating* on James somehow, just being in this car, enjoying Denver's company.

Still, this news about Arjun hit him like a loss.

It had been so nice to feel like a first choice for a change.

"So, the play?" Denver said. "I know it's last minute. You probably already have plans."

"I don't have plans," Sam said. "I'll check with my parents, but I'm sure they'll be cool with it."

"Cool," Denver said, pulling into the parking lot of the auto shop. "If we leave right after school, maybe we can even go to the Varsity for dinner. Have you been? I read that it's famous."

"Oh yeah, always happy to make a trip to the Varsity," Sam said. "'What'll ya have, what'll ya have.' Definitely worth experiencing." He paused. "Was that part of the plan too? With Arjun?"

Denver raised an eyebrow, like he sensed there was a question underneath the question, but he wasn't sure what it was exactly.

"It was the part I was most excited about," he said.

"Well, then," Sam said. "I wouldn't want to disappoint you."

Delia was delighted at lunch the next day.

"I knew the Frosty trick would work."

"Trick? How was it a trick?"

"So wait," James cut in, "does that mean you two are for real going on a date?"

"No, no, nothing like that," Sam said. "We're friends. We're hanging out. Anyway, turns out Denver got out of a long-term relationship less than two weeks ago. He just didn't want the ticket to go to waste."

"Right," Delia said, rolling her eyes. "It's not a date, and we're going to win convention this year."

"I know you're making a joke," Sam said, "but you know, I really don't see any reason why we couldn't win convention this year, or at least place. I've been thinking about it this week, in fact, ever since . . . since we did the spell from the book. *The Spell of Conveyance.* We're freaking talented, y'all. What do those Atlanta schools have that we don't have?"

"More time?" Delia said.

"Full teams?" James added.

"Okay, yeah, that makes it harder. But what if this year—now that we have four members—we really went for it? What if Denver and I each did two categories, and you two each did three? There's nothing in the rules that says the same team member can't do more than one category."

"Except we'd be running around from one end of the convention center to the other," James said. "And each event we do would probably suffer as a result."

But Delia looked intrigued, Sam could tell.

"We *do* always end up placing in our individual events . . . ," she said.

"Exactly. And I bet it would really impress Pinnacle if you placed in not one but *three* individual events. Plus, I just think . . . I think we need this. I think if we don't do it, we'll always wonder what we might have been capable of, if—if we'd had more opportunities."

What Sam wasn't saying—what he didn't have to say—was what he meant by "more opportunities." For the past three years, the bougie Atlanta schools at convention had been the stand-in for everything they didn't have in Friedman, but always in such a way that it remained a point of pride for them, how well they were doing without those same privileges. In Delia's case, they were also the fuel to her fire—the reminder that their nice clothes and nice cars, their vast circles of magicker friends, were only theirs because of a happy accident of location, and they could all be Delia's, when she finally got out of here.

That had changed this past week, since they'd done the spell from the book. Their fixed point of comparison had faltered. Their guiding light had flickered in the sky. There was powerful magic right here, almost within their reach.

All three of them could feel it.

It had been four days since they'd returned the book, and so far, no one had even attempted to schedule another practice.

The gap had widened between what they had and what they could have, just a little bit. Or at least their awareness of that gap.

Maybe, Sam thought, if they spent more time practicing between now and November, it would get their minds back on track. Close the gap. Bring things back to normal.

(Because sidebar: the lack of practices had also meant a lack of opportunities for Sam to talk to James, and the longer they went without talking about what had happened at the bowling alley, the harder it was getting to imagine broaching the subject, period. Sam needed things to be easy and fun between them again, or the conversation would land like a lead balloon, if it happened at all.)

"I guess, as club president, I could get behind this idea," Delia said agreeably. "Operation Win Convention. Win-convention mode."

"I guess, as vice president, I am compelled to get in line," James said. "But if we're going to take on all these extra categories on such short notice, we're going to need way more practice time. More weekend study sessions, less hanging out at the Fox Theatre."

"Wow. Jealous much?" Delia said, only half under her breath.

But Sam just blushed. He was seriously wondering the same thing.

Celestine, it turned out, was not a play, but a musical. It did, as Denver promised, have a lot of magic in it.

"You hate it," Denver said at intermission, when the lights had come up and people were standing in the aisles or making their way to the restrooms.

"What? Not at all. I'm really enjoying it."

"You've had a scowl on your face for the last twenty minutes. It's the singing—admit it. You're not a musical guy."

"No, no, it's not that. I love musicals. Okay, I do think it's borderline homophobic that the prince seems like he is going to save the princess from this evil witch who *absolutely* also has a crush on the princess, but I'm willing to be surprised in act two. What about you? You can't be watching the play too closely if you're noticing my facial expression."

"Honestly, I'm not really a musical guy. But it's fun. This theater is gorgeous."

It was true, the inside of the Fox Theatre was a place to behold. Their seats were close enough that they were under the starry-night ceiling right in front of the stage, but they hadn't gotten a great look at everything on the way in because they'd been running late, and the lights had already been down. It had taken longer to get through traffic than they'd anticipated, and then, after an extra-rushed dinner at the Varsity, all the closest parking lots to the theater had been full. They'd ended up having to shell out thirty dollars to park a few blocks away, and that meant Denver had sheepishly been forced to accept a twenty from Sam. But Sam had been glad for the chance to make this feel that much less like a date. Even if Sam *were* to go on a date—because honestly, it's not like he'd gone on many . . . okay, *any* . . . real dates before this (those chaperoned hangouts with Eliot really didn't count)—he'd still want to pay for half of everything himself. Lord, why did his mind keep going to hypothetical dates and whether or not this, hypothetically, was one?

"Everything okay?" Denver said.

"What? Oh, yeah."

Sam had been momentarily distracted, looking up at the balcony, by the face of another boy looking down at him. It wasn't anyone Sam knew—at least, Sam didn't *think* he knew this guy—but the guy was definitely staring right at him, not even bothering to look away when Sam's gaze stopped on him and they locked eyes. Finally, Sam broke contact, a little unnerved, and as Denver started to turn to see what Sam had been looking at, Sam said, "No, don't. Give it a second. There's a guy staring right at us."

"I don't see him," Denver said, because of course he'd charged ahead with gawking before Sam could stop him.

"Right at our one o'clock," Sam said, but as Denver continued to scan the crowd, Sam looked up and realized that the guy wasn't there anymore after all. "Never mind. That was weird."

"What did he look like?"

"I don't know. Our age? Maybe a little older? Buzz cut? Looked like a football player."

"Did you give him my number?"

"*Har har*," Sam said. But the joke broke the tension enough that he was able to shake the unease in his brain.

When the curtain went up and the play resumed, Sam was even able to focus on the story again, scooting forward to the edge of his seat and balling his hands into fists as the subtext became more anti-queer instead of less, with the evil witch masquerading as a prince to try to fend off the competition, only for the princess to see right through the disguise. Hard pass.

At one point, Denver took Sam's fist in both of his hands, and when Sam flinched just a little bit—mostly out of surprise—he managed to play it off as a funny attempt to make Sam realize how worked up he was getting. Sam spent the rest of the performance looking for a natural moment to return the gesture—to show Denver that the flinch was an accident, and he was as funny and flirty as Denver was, *ha ha look, we're holding hands*. But the problem was, it didn't really feel like either of them was kidding; he sincerely wanted to hold Denver's hand. And that was very inconvenient indeed, since what Sam was *really* still looking for was the most natural moment to break the ice with James.

"Well, the magic was cool, at least," Denver said as they made their way out of the theater at the end.

"That's true. I really want to know the spell that the witch used to make herself look like a tree at the end. I read in the program that the actress was a Keeper. The tree looked so real. I wonder if it was."

They walked out the doors into the night air, pressed into the throng of fellow audience members. As limited as his line of sight was, Sam didn't notice until it was too late that he was walking right into a person who seemed to be going in the opposite direction, or else had just been standing there.

"Excuse me, I'm sorry," he said, looking up and realizing with a jolt that it was the boy from the balcony.

The boy didn't respond. Only stared at Sam with his intense, football player glower.

Sam broke away and rejoined Denver in the flow of the crowd, already looking over his shoulder to confirm that the boy wasn't following them.

"That was the boy from before. Who was staring at me," he whispered to Denver.

Once again, Denver turned immediately. This time, at least, he saw the guy, confirming Sam hadn't lost his mind.

"Oh, he *is* cute," Denver said, frowning. "Should we go back and talk to him?"

"*No,*" Sam said immediately.

"Sorry, sorry. Kidding. I didn't realize he upset you that much."

"Let's just get to the car," Sam said, hurrying them along the blocks back to the parking lot, looking over his shoulder every few feet. A couple times he could swear that he saw the boy again, never actually moving—always standing stock-still.

Back in Denver's car, Sam didn't waste a second before locking the doors.

He only fully exhaled when they were back on I-20, headed east toward Friedman.

"You want to talk about it?" Denver said.

"I don't know. Maybe? Maybe that would help? I just . . . between everything with that book, and my windshield, and the vision last week. I don't know. It all has me pretty shook."

"Understandable," Denver said.

"Yeah? That's good. I'm glad you can understand. Because I've been feeling a little mental lately."

"No, Sam, seriously. I get it. Being with Arjun for two years before he was out, every time we were in a public place was this, like, constant game of peekaboo from hell. Okay, you can laugh, but seriously, that was at the time the best way I could think of to describe it. One second I was looking at the real Arjun, the next second, he would see someone from school or someone who *looked* like a homophobe, and suddenly it was like he was hiding behind his own face. At first, I'd get kind of impatient with him about it, cause it felt like he was ashamed to be with me. But then we had some friends of ours get gaybashed at a Vanderbilt party. Vanderbilt! Which is super liberal! And then honestly, I started getting as self-conscious as Arjun was. I even made us learn some pretty high-level self-defense spells, just in case. The fear never really goes away."

"You know," Sam said, "I think that truly is part of it. Peekaboo from hell. I mean, this guy had this *look* about him. Like there was something about me he *hated*, even though he didn't even know me." Sam shivered. "Lord, it was creepy."

"Well, my mom's working another nightshift, if you're worried about having nightmares . . ."

"Oh, I don't have nightmares. Or dreams." This seemed like a safer avenue than responding to the part where Denver had invited him over to his place. As close as he'd come to grabbing Denver's hand in the theater, he really didn't trust himself to be alone with him in his room. Denver's reaction to his confession went exactly as he'd have guessed.

"Wait, what? What do you mean, you don't have dreams?"

"Exactly that. I mean, I've been told that I probably *have* dreams, but I've never remembered one, so it's hard to say."

"Never ever?"

"Never ever."

"Damn. That must make it harder to do magic."

"How do you mean?"

"I don't know. I guess I think of dreams as being the same kind of associations I have to do when I'm casting a spell. But then again, it's not like I use my dreams in any active way. I just imagine the two processes as coming from the same part of my brain. The part of my brain that makes something imaginary real. If that makes sense."

"Well, James always says I'm good at associations, but I figured that's his way of keeping my spirits up, like handing out a trophy for 'most improved.'"

Denver laughed, but when Sam didn't, he tried to act like he'd been clearing his throat.

"So, um, sorry about before. I mean, I was kidding about you coming over, mostly. Your mom made it pretty clear she would vaporize me if I didn't bring you straight home."

"I hope that's okay."

"Sam. Of course it's okay. Sorry, I shouldn't have said it at all. I have this bad habit of saying the exact wrong thing when I get nervous. I guess talking about that guy had me more freaked out than I realized."

"I do the same thing—joke when I get scared. Don't worry about it."

"Phew. Okay. Thought I'd made things weird for a second there."

"Weird*er*, you mean?"

"Ha! Fair enough."

The rest of the drive home could have been awkward after that, but somehow, it wasn't. They talked right over the speed bump, and by the time Denver pulled into Sam's driveway, Sam was genuinely smiling, all thoughts of the creepy guy from the Fox and the will-we-or-won't-we tension forgotten.

"Thanks for coming with me," Denver said.

"Thanks for inviting me."

Sam could tell there was something more Denver wanted to

say before he got out, and sure enough, Denver kicked off with that most ominous of conversation starters: "Can I ask you something?"

"Okay," Sam said, drawing out the word to signal his reservation.

"I know it's not my place, but—you and James. Is there something there?"

It was so not what Sam was expecting him to ask that he kind of spluttered even trying to form the words of a simple no. Maybe it was that Denver was so charming, or disarming, or whatever, that Sam didn't have his usual armor up, prepared with a lie. Denver waited patiently for Sam to find the words he wanted, but based on the look on his face, it was clear that this speechless disaster was already answer enough.

"Is it really that obvious?" Sam finally said.

"I mean, as a guy who dated another guy on the DL for two years? Yeah, kind of."

If anything, this came as a relief to Sam. One of his greatest fears with James was that he was reading too much into something that wasn't there. The idea that whatever it was between them could be obvious to an outsider—that whatever it was could be compared to a real relationship—felt like the best possible affirmation.

"So, what—are you guys hooking up? Boyfriends? All of the above?"

"None of the above," Sam said. "It's more like we're friends with a long history of confusing moments. Almosts. Sort ofs. But I'm determined that one day soon, we will finally get everything out in the open and figure out what this thing is between us."

"Oh," Denver said, and there was a whole paragraph in that one sound.

"You won't say anything to him until then, will you?" Sam said. "I mean, it's not exactly a secret, but I'm waiting for the right moment, and with everything that's been going on the last couple weeks, it has most definitely not been the right moment."

"No, don't worry, I won't say anything." Denver then added a very awkward thumbs-up, the universal symbol for powering through discomfort. "I just hope you're not getting your hopes up for nothing."

"Same," Sam said. "That would be the worst."

CHAPTER 12

IN A GROUP MESSAGE INITIATED BY SAM, THEY SET THEIR next practice for Monday afternoon, and other than that text chain, Sam didn't hear from any of his friends for the rest of the weekend. He kept starting separate messages to all of them and then changing his mind. He really did have enough homework that he needed to spend a good chunk of the weekend doing it, and after everything that had happened, he was sort of glad that his downtime came in the form of watching TV on the couch with his parents.

Still.

A school-year weekend in which they didn't have plans, for no clear reason, felt like one more sign that things had taken a wrong turn somewhere.

When practice finally rolled around, Sam was ready with a document of all ten briefs for this year's convention categories, having decided that he wouldn't leave everything for Delia to do for a change.

Denver and Delia arrived at the same time, with Delia getting Denver's full report of the play on their way in, no doubt comparing it to what she'd heard from Sam at lunch.

When the upstairs door opened again, signaling James's arrival, Sam was surprised to hear the sound of more than one voice echoing down the stairs.

Delia and Denver noticed it, too, and stopped talking. They all exchanged a worried look, their minds going to the same anxious place—that James had been followed. That the faceless ones hadn't been satisfied by the return of their book.

But the additional voice turned out to belong to Amber.

That was enough to make Delia and Denver relax. Sam's body stayed tense.

"Hey, everybody," James said, like he was a coach gathering up his team for a pep talk, "look who I brought."

They all smiled and waved hello.

"I thought Amber could help us out, now that we're planning to run the full gamut and make a play for this thing."

"Ah," Delia said.

"Wait, help us out how?" Sam said.

"By competing in one of the categories," Amber said, like it was both obvious and a surprise she'd been looking forward to delivering. "James explained it all at church yesterday. Now he won't have to be in two places at once."

"I thought you had soccer?" Sam said.

"I do. But only twice a week until the spring. And James told me y'all haven't been meeting as often this semester."

"I thought we were planning to change that?" Sam said, with just enough of a question in his voice that no one picked up on how adamantly he was trying to resist this.

"Now we don't have to," James said. Which, ouch.

"Which competition category were you thinking?" Delia asked Amber. "I already penciled in the new ones I thought each of us should take on, based on our strengths."

"And I'm betting you penciled me in for the Elements of Empathy trial," James said, "which Amber would be even better at."

"You have empath skills?" Delia asked her.

Amber nodded.

Sam crossed his arms over his chest. "Prove it," he said.

"Are you joking?" James said, while Amber looked at James in confusion. This probably hadn't been part of the plan they'd discussed at church.

"I mean, Denver had to do the tryout two short weeks ago," Sam said. "I'm sure we're all happy for the help at convention, but it doesn't seem like it would be fair to let Amber in without passing the same tryout, especially since she could almost definitely do it using the empath magic she'll have to do at convention pretty soon."

"Sam," James said, with a warning in his voice.

Denver jumped in to defuse the tension. "I'm sure Sam isn't

saying Amber has to pass the tryout right here, right now—just that she has to be able to pass it at some point before convention. Right, Sam? That's what you mean?"

"Yes, as club president, I'm okay with the tryout if we add that caveat," Delia said, adding her own look of reproach to the dour glances already directed Sam's way.

That wasn't what he'd meant, and Denver knew it. But Denver was trying to keep him from doing something he would regret, something that would make him a person he didn't want to be, and with the slight step back afforded from that intervention, Sam recognized that giving Amber such a harsh ultimatum really was something he'd regret.

"Yeah, sure," he said. "That's what I meant. That you have to be able to do it at some point before convention. Preferably using empath magic."

"Oh, okay then," Amber said, her smile returning. "What's the tryout then?"

"You have to figure out how much money Sam has in his wallet," Denver said.

"Oh," Amber said. "I'm pretty sure that's something I can do right now anyway." She turned to Sam, scrunching her face up, as if she was really taking him in—as if he were a magical painting hiding inside a blank canvas. The longer she stared at him, the more bothered she looked. Sam was just starting to feel a sick sliver of triumph when Amber said, "I'm getting the vibe that you've been through a recent loss, that you're a little low, that you're out of reserves. I'm not entirely sure that it's money-related, but it's the best I've got, so I'm going to have to say zero dollars. Am I right?"

"More than you know," Sam said. Whatever triumph he'd felt was gone.

Alone in his bedroom that night, Sam fell into a spiral of looking through old photos, even dredging up some rarer ones he'd never posted on social media, ones that he stored on the cloud.

Here, on his v-clips, was one of him, James, Delia, and Ms. Berry at their freshman magicker conference, posing with Delia's and James's medals above their heads like they were checks for a million dollars.

Here, from the cloud, was one of James and Delia, smiling across from Sam at a booth in Mary Ellen's, with presents wrapped on the table in front of them because they were there to celebrate Sam's sixteenth birthday, when he could finally drive them himself.

Here was a candid photo of James alone, definitely not posted, from when James had come with Sam's family on a weekend trip to Jekyll Island. He hadn't even known Sam was taking a picture, and he was staring out at the ocean as if he wanted to be on the other side of it, as if he were much older than fifteen. On that same trip, James had said to Sam's parents, "I wish I could be part of *your* family," quote unquote.

What would it mean if all these moments, these memories, didn't end up building to something more than friendship? What if Sam said nothing while Amber and James became a couple right under his nose? What if this was exactly how James was feeling, watching Sam get close to Denver?

Too long, he'd ignored his mom's advice to put it all out there—talk to James about his feelings. Too long, he'd been worried about screwing up the group dynamic of the Fascinators, because without the Fascinators, he didn't know who he was.

Now, the group dynamic was screwing itself up just fine on its own, and it seemed like having a real conversation with James might be the only way to get it back on track.

The opportunity seemed to present itself in the form of—of all things—a house party.

Sam hated house parties. Even before the catastrophic one at Bridget's house last spring break, he'd suffered through plenty of endless nights watching people play beer pong or King's Cup or whatever else could make getting drunk on cheap beer seem like a fun game instead of a sad diversion. And the worst part was always watching James drink faster than anyone, because it made Sam feel like his company was one of the things James needed to be diverted from.

But—guilty as he felt for even letting his mind go there—Sam was hoping that this time, like that night by the soccer field, his company might be one of the things drunken James was diverted *to*.

Because tonight, the house party was for some brainy sophomore named Kevin in Sam's economics class who'd boldly invited all the juniors and seniors in their class even though he didn't seem to be real friends with any of them. His address was in one of Friedman's two super-rich subdivisions, which was all the explanation Sam needed. The kid was probably used to getting whatever he asked for.

James had seemed dubious.

Will I know anyone there? he'd responded to Sam's text the night before.

You'll know me. And I'll know the host. Nice kid. Knows his opportunity costs.

Not sure you're using that term correctly.

Was a joke! ;)

Since when have you wanted to go to a party on a Saturday night anyway? James had said after a long pause, at which point Sam was disheartened to realize that James was pretty clearly not feeling this.

Since you told me I should try to make other Friedman friends, Sam ventured. He took James's lack of a response to mean he knew exactly when Sam had meant, and had probably been remembering that night a lot too since they'd found the spell book in those moonless woods.

You know I'm sort of still grounded, right?

Since when has being grounded kept you from going to a party on a Saturday night?

See you at eight on the corner at the end of my street.

At first, the party had played out exactly as it was supposed to.

Kevin had looked pleasantly shocked to see them, opening the front door and then welcoming them in way too quickly, explaining that his parents were out of town and he'd managed to get a twenty-four pack of PBR from his older cousin and would Sam and James like some—all before Sam and James had even said hello.

Sam and James had grabbed beers and then moved to a far corner of Kevin's back porch, where more wide-eyed underclassmen were looking way too giddy to be here.

"Well, here we are," James had said, quirking an eyebrow at Sam as if he might actually suspect that Sam had an ulterior motive for inviting him on this dubious outing.

"Parties, am I right? I'd better stick to this one," Sam had said, motioning to his beer. "Designated driver and all that. But you feel free to go wild. I can't believe you've been grounded for two whole weeks."

"My dad is . . . He's been . . . Well, it's been worse than usual."

"Is Benji okay?"

"I think so?" James said. "I guess in Sunday school last week, they covered Noah's Ark and the flood, and he got really freaked out, thinking it was a story of a current event. He was still crying when I picked him up from his class, and my dad and I ended up having words because he told Benji he couldn't cry like that in public."

"Lesson learned: do not tell apocalypse stories to first graders," Sam said.

"I think the lesson is that my dad is an asshole."

"No, I know," Sam said. "It's good Benji has you there for another year."

This was apparently not the right thing to say, because James frowned and then finished off his first beer in a single long gulp.

But the night had quickly gotten worse from there, because Sam and his econ classmates weren't the only upperclassman who'd caught wind of the fact that a rich sophomore with a huge house and no chaperones was hosting a party, and waves of people kept coming out the back door onto the porch, until it really was starting to look like one of those legendary movie parties, with enough people Sam didn't know at all that they could have just as easily been extras as Friedmanites.

During one such wave of people, about thirty minutes after the boys' arrival, a deep, bro-ey voice called out "James!" and Sam had looked up with dread to find two guys and a girl, all three of whom he only vaguely recognized, making their way right toward them.

"How's it hanging, man?" the original speaker said. He was wearing a pink polo shirt whose front half was tucked into a pair of khakis. A bro-ey ensemble if ever there was one.

"I'm good, I'm good," James said. Then he gestured to Sam, who tried his best to look these strangers straight in the face and appear at ease, like he belonged here. "Sam, you remember Brad, and this is Ben and Kayla. They graduated last year. They all go to Friedman Baptist."

"Ah, yeah. That's right. Hey, y'all," Sam said. He did remember them, sort of. Not from any specific moment, although he was pretty sure he'd seen Brad play football or maybe baseball, possibly both. But in the four months since graduation, it looked like the three of them had aged a thousand years. On the other hand, if they were still in Friedman, and still showing up at an underclassman's party, they couldn't have progressed that much.

"We're friends with Kevin's cousin," Ben said, as if he could read Sam's mind. "We promised him we'd step outside and make sure y'all kids weren't going too crazy out here." He eyed the beers in Sam's and James's hands. "You know, not doing anything we wouldn't want to admit in front of everybody tomorrow morning."

It took Sam a second to catch on to what Ben meant, and when he did, he was hard-pressed to fight a smile, even though Ben definitely wasn't kidding.

"You don't go to church with us, do you?" Kayla said, catching his smile right away. "I don't think I've seen you there before."

"Oh, no, I don't."

"Where do you go?" she pressed.

"I don't really go to church. My parents go to First Methodist, but they've always said I'm free to believe or not believe whatever I want, and . . . and yeah, I don't really go to church," he repeated inanely.

Now it was their turn for the acid smiles, and Sam suspected he knew why—his lisp always slipped out on "First Methodist," without fail. As soon as he started saying it, he'd felt his tongue betraying him and seen this reaction coming, as it often did.

"Gotcha," Ben said, like that was all they needed to know about that.

"You be good, James," Brad added, with this insinuating look between the two boys that made Sam feel judged and gross.

Then the three of them left to check on and/or harass more innocent high schoolers, leaving Sam and James in an awkward silence until finally Sam said, "Assholes."

Which was once again not the right thing to say, apparently. James folded his arms across his chest and said, "They're usually nice to me."

"Well, you go to their church. They're contractually obligated to be nice to you."

"That's not true."

"Gee, sorry for implying that people at your church are nice to each other. Won't make that mistake again."

"Sam, lay off my church, all right? I don't attack you for your beliefs or lack thereof. Please don't generalize me or put me in some idiot box because of mine."

"You think I—what?" Sam wanted to cry. This seemed like something James had been prepared to say, like maybe it was something he'd been thinking about for a while. Was this Amber's doing? Had she put these thoughts into his head? "James, I don't think you're an idiot. You know that."

"Do I?" James said. "Cause I'm pretty sure you and Delia both think I'm this, like, party animal who only wants to get drunk and high on the weekends."

Sam was at a loss for words. He wasn't even sure where this was coming from, but with so many random underclassmen around, just out of earshot, now didn't feel like the right time for whatever emotional reckoning James was trying to have with him. It certainly seemed to be the complete opposite of the emotional reckoning Sam had been hoping to have tonight.

"Wait, what the hell?" James said. He wasn't looking at Sam, though. He was looking over Sam's shoulder, at something out in the backyard, down the porch steps.

"What?" Sam said.

James was already heading in the direction of the stairs, and Sam followed him instinctively, sensing something serious was up.

"Remember the three guys I told you about? Who took me to that warehouse party in the first place?"

"Yeah?" Sam said.

"That's them." James nodded at three guys who were smoking cigarettes in Kevin's yard.

"Wait, James—"

"Hey, assholes," James said, his tone somewhere between confrontational and casual, so that the three guys looked up, not sure if the person approaching them was being funny but friendly or if he was seriously about to throw down.

Sam wasn't sure, either.

"Hey, I recognize you," the guy in the middle said.

"You think?" the guy on the right said, squaring his shoulders, his whole body tensing. "This is the shithead who got us kicked out of True Light."

"Holy shit, you're right. It is him. Dude, what the fuck?"

"Dude, what the fuck is right," James said. "You three told me it was a party, not some cult initiation."

"It *was* a party," the guy on the left said, flicking out his cigarette and stomping on it. "Till you went and stole Mr. Grender's book. He was so pissed at us when he found out we were the ones who invited you. Biggest mistake of our fucking lives."

"Well, it wasn't a high point for me either," James said, but he sounded a little less righteous in his anger now, as if it came as a surprise to him that his actions had had consequences for them, too. "I know what that spell was supposed to do, by the way."

"Oh yeah?" the guy on the right said.

"Yeah. We found it in 'Mr. Grender's book.' Cutting a hole into the spirit world? That's your idea of a party?"

This seemed to come as news to two of the guys, although they tried to hide it—and probably wanted to believe James was lying. But the guy in the middle didn't flinch. He was paying more attention to James's use of the word "we," taking in Sam's existence for the first time with an ugly smirk.

"Come on, let's just go," Sam said. He reached out to tug on James's sleeve but thought better of it at the last second.

"I do remember you now," the guy in the middle said to James. "That night, it was a girl telling you what to do. I guess you swing whatever way you can find someone willing to boss you around."

Sam could tell without looking—his face had gone red as a beet.

"I guess I do," James said, unfazed. "Why, are you interested? You seem like the type who likes to do the bossing."

"You're sick," the guy said.

"Better sick than stupid."

The guy let out a joyless laugh and shared an eye roll with his buddies, and for a moment, Sam entertained the hope that that was the end of that. But it turned out to be only the silence before the storm, as with hardly a second's warning, the guy lunged at James in a full-body tackle.

The fight was fast and mean, the two boys scrabbling on the ground like snakes let out of a bag.

Sam shouted for help, which only made the people up on the porch run to the railing to get a better look. The guy's friends tried to reach in to break up the fight, but the tangle of arms and legs was too kinetic for them; they kept getting punched.

Somehow, in a terrifying burst of aggression, the guy managed to bring his body around so that his knees were on James's chest and his hands were on his neck.

James was choking, struggling to breathe.

Again, the guy's friends tried to pull him off, but it looked like the guy had gone fully berserk, his killer instinct taking over.

Why was no one else coming to help?

In the exact second before Sam threw his body at the guy, James emitted a roar like an old boulder coming to life. It was a terrifying sound, panic and rage in one. *Primordial* had been the word Delia used for his magic, and it was primordial magic that Sam was feeling now, the very ground beneath their feet quaking until it ruptured, sending spikes of earth shooting from the dirt all around James. The guy who'd moments ago had him in a death grip suddenly went flying, flung by the peaks in the yard, his body twisting as it fell. Both the guy's friends were thrown off their feet, too.

Sam heard screams from behind him, as people up on the porch gripped onto the railing, fearing another quake.

James scrambled to his feet, his breathing ragged and heavy. There was something about him in that moment that seemed decidedly unhuman; Sam was reminded of the actress in *Celestine*—the one who became a tree.

James was a force of nature, and he walked right over to where his attacker's body lay at a painful angle. He kicked the guy once, twice, again. The guy let out a groan of tremendous pain.

"James! Enough!" Sam cried. His voice was shrill, hysterical. He'd heard and felt each kick as if it were landing on him, too.

James relented but didn't budge from where he stood, until finally Sam forced himself to move, coming around and grabbing his friend by the arms, pulling him back away, rounding the side of Kevin's house and running them straight to the street, where at least twelve cars were parked in a conspicuous line.

James half-resisted Sam the whole way, and they could still hear one of the guy's friends shouting, "We're gonna kill you! We're gonna find you and fucking kill you!" But as Sam put more distance between the two of them and the party, the fight went out of James.

They made it to Sam's car, where Sam opened the passenger side door and literally placed James in his seat. It was like the reality of the situation was setting in, and James was sinking back into the ancient stone from which he'd burst forth moments ago.

Sam put the car into drive and peeled out of there. He waited until they were safely out of the subdivision, always glancing behind him, expecting the headlights of another car, but none appeared.

Finally, when they were back on a main road, Sam let loose.

"What were you thinking? Causing an earthquake like that? Getting into a *fight* like that? Calling him stupid? You only had two beers! You can't tell me you were drunk. I mean, Lord, do you know what it would do to your UGA application if you got suspended? Or went to jail? You'd end up working on roofs with your dad forever. You'd never get out of here. Shit. If those guys don't come after you for what you did to them, Kevin might come after you for property damage. Are you going to say anything, or are you going to sit there in silence the whole way home?"

Still, James said nothing.

"Why did you go to that warehouse party in the first place, James? Why did you stay there when it was obviously not a party? Why did you take their book?"

"Are you done yelling at me now?" James said, his voice frighteningly monotone.

Sam gripped the steering wheel until his knuckles turned white, but he forced himself not to respond.

Finally, after an unbearably long silence, James said, "I went to the warehouse party for the same reason I said yes to tonight: because I thought it would be fun. Turns out I was wrong."

Then he switched on the radio, not bothering to change the station when happy pop music flooded the car, letting it fill the space between them with how wrong it felt.

"Let me out at the corner?" James said when they reached his block.

And so Sam did, and then he made the drive home.

Once, in the days before Sam came out to his parents, when it seemed like every little thing could set off a yelling match and often did (moody silences, not enough cereal in the morning, perfectly reasonable knocks on his door that Sam would call invasions of privacy), Sam had looked at his mom and said, "Why do you have to fight with me all the time?" And, rather than pointing out that Sam was fighting with her just as much and as often as she was fighting with him, his mom had very calmly said, "Sometimes, Sam, we fight with people because we care about them too much to give up on them."

Sam had thought the line was utter bullshit at the time. And things with his parents had been so good for so long since he came out; clearly, there wasn't some corollary where caring about someone meant you *had* to fight with them.

But right about now, Sam found himself remembering those

words of his mom's and hoping they were true. Because either Sam and James cared about each other so much that the dam had finally burst tonight and their feelings had rushed out faster than they could control them, or else Sam and James had just had an apocalyptic falling out, the fire and the flood.

CHAPTER 13

SAM HAD GAINED ONE THING, THOUGH, IN THAT TOTAL disaster losing streak of a night, and that thing was a name. "True Light," the guy had called them. He'd been "kicked out of True Light" for bringing James to their spirit party.

Unfortunately, True Light was a hard phrase to look up online. There were countless results, ranging from various unrelated churches to actual LED light companies. Sam was momentarily distracted by a random fan page dedicated entirely to the aurora borealis.

But he wasn't seeing anything about a True Light near Friedman, Georgia. Not until he decided to check a fringe forum site for magickers that he almost never visited, given its reputation for hate-speech, conspiracy theorists, doxing, and worse. It was the site Sam always imagined as being populated by child predators, actual children, and no one in between. He hated even typing in the URL.

On this site, a search for "True Light" once again turned up plenty of results, less about church and light bulbs and more of the spell-casting variety, with the top post being a spell that promised a handheld but narrow light beam that would shine brightly as far as you could see, piercing fog and other elements that gave other light spells trouble. Based on the likes and responses, this spell seemed like a real winner, easy to replicate—and of course, here was Sam getting distracted again.

He went down deeper into the results, passing spells that were less about light and more about lie detection, passing rituals that required the light of the aurora borealis to function, passing stupid memes that had very long strings of words in them, two of which just happened to be *true* and *light*, until finally, when he was on the verge of giving up, he found a post that didn't even have "True Light" in the subject line. The match appeared in the body of the post; the subject line was "Mr. Grender."

Sam felt chills crawling up his arm. Mr. Grender. That was another name those guys had said tonight.

The post was recent—only six days old. It had zero likes and zero comments, and Sam read it with an increasing sense of recognition—and dread.

39 yo male here, looking for help w/ advanced protection spell. Don't know where else to turn. Cops don't believe me. Keepers won't even respond to emails. This is re: group called True Light, led by Albert Grender ("Mr. Grender"). I lived with True Light for seven months after friend in rehab told me about it. Started out good. A place to live and meet people. Cheaper than rehab. Then shit got weird. Won't go into specifics but point is now I have these visions, like nightmares. Some stuff I saw when I was there, but some new stuff—definitely a spell. I've tried wards, sleeping spells, cloaking spells, all of it. Nothing works. And these people are DANGEROUS. Have been getting away with shit for a long time. Serious commenters only. Thanks in advance. —Carl

Sam didn't know what to do. He was tempted to respond with a link to Findias—maybe Vi could give this Carl person something to protect him. But maybe getting mixed up with him would be asking for trouble. Even if Sam believed him, the guy had lived with True Light for seven months. Surely that made him a little dangerous, too.

"Everything okay in here?" Sam's mom said at his doorway, and her sudden appearance made him jump back with a little yelp.

"Jeez, Mom, you scared me."

"Sorry. You're back from the party sooner than I was expecting. No fun?"

"Really no fun. Like, the least fun."

"You want to talk about it?"

"Maybe later? I'm still kind of processing."

His mom gave him a good, long stare—the kind that he knew had magic in it.

"Okay," she said. "But I'm going to hold you to that."

All night, Sam tossed and turned. He wasn't sure when he finally fell asleep, but when he got out of bed at noon on Sunday, he distinctly recalled seeing 4:03 a.m., 5:11 a.m., and 6:14 a.m. on his phone.

He texted Delia that he needed to talk to her right away, but when she didn't respond, he remembered that she was working the after-church shift at Chili's today, and decided that it couldn't wait. His parents were still at church themselves, so he wouldn't be missed.

Sam didn't often visit Delia at work, because she was too much of a rule follower to get him free food beyond the occasional skillet cookie "for his birthday," and also because she was usually too busy to hang out anyway.

Today, Sam took a seat at one of the tall tables for two and ordered a Coke. There were so many families here dressed for church. He may have been imagining it, but it seemed like people kept looking his way, wondering what a teenager in a T-shirt and jeans was doing by himself on a Sunday afternoon. All it would take was one person from Friedman High recognizing him as the gay magicker, and who knew what choice words their parents would have to say to him on their way out. That's how it always happened in Sam's imagination, at least. He was always expecting the hammer to fall, because it did fall, constantly.

Finally, Delia came over to his table.

"What's going on?" she said, smiling but under no illusion that Sam had come here just to say hello.

"Hey, sorry to bother you at work," Sam said. "I couldn't really sleep. It was kind of a rough night."

"How so?

"Long story. I know you're busy. But the short version is, James and I ran into some people from the warehouse compound whatever party. They call themselves True Light. And then I found this post online that is about the same people. I think this True Light group has been around for a while."

"Oh, yeah. I sort of figured that," Delia said.

"You did?"

"Yeah. There were a few things in the book that made it seem that way. A lot of the spells were handwritten, with corrections and additions and stuff, which made me think one person had written the original entries and others had added to them over the years. I think that's why they were so hell-bent on getting their book back."

"Okay," Sam said, drawing the word out in a question. "Were you planning to mention that at any point?"

Delia shrugged. "It seemed like you didn't want to talk about the book any more after we sent it back. I got the impression you only wanted to move on."

"I mean, I do—"

"How's it going over here?"

It was Bob, Delia's shift manager. A nice enough guy, but he always called his employees his "Chili's family," and he was a bit overzealous with awarding "employee of the week," as if he really loved his job. Delia hated him.

"Everything's great," Delia said. "Sam was asking me about those new corn fritters, and I was telling him that they're the best thing I've ever eaten."

"That's right. I think I'm going to order some."

"Well, that does sound good," Bob said. "I'll put in that order with your section waitress. In the meantime, Delia, I think I saw one of your tables waiting for their appetizers?"

"Getting right on it," Delia said, walking off with a big smile on her face that morphed into a grimace for Sam when Bob wasn't looking.

Which, yes, that was funny. But Sam was still stuck on the other thing. What else did Delia know that she wasn't telling him?

Unfortunately, the crowd never really died down, and after Sam finished his corn fritters and two refills on his Coke, he had to accept that Delia didn't have time to come back. They would have to pick up this conversation later.

Sam tried to test the waters with James over text message, thinking ahead to how awkward it would be to see him at lunch on Monday if they hadn't made up. But James's one-word responses gave nothing away, because that was often the way James responded to text messages, even when he wasn't mad. Sam was used to this feeling, of wanting to read between the lines of every little thing but forcing himself not to, to accept James at face value. Maybe the reason things felt different now was not that James had changed, but that Sam had.

Neither option felt good.

The Fascinators' practice on Monday felt worse.

James and Amber showed up as a unit again, this time before Delia and Denver arrived. Sam kept trying to participate in the conversation, but Amber and James had this dense, impenetrable way of talking, predicated on references and inside jokes that may have started at church but now went beyond it, and neither of them made much of an effort to give Sam the necessary annotations. James was avoiding Sam's eyes entirely, as if their fight from the weekend was as fresh in James's mind as it was in Sam's.

When Delia and Denver got there, practice hardly became more inclusive; instead, they fractured into two distinct groups, with Amber and James working together and Sam and Denver working together, as Delia went back and forth to offer help, having already made such confident strides in her own categories that she felt her time would be better spent on everyone else.

It was the first Fascinators practice Sam could ever remember wanting to end before it was over.

The magic, as it were, was gone.

It almost came as a relief when, at the end, Denver said, "Random idea, take it or leave it, but I wonder if we'd feel like we had more room to spread out and really work on some of these hands-on spells if we were in a bigger space, like the Friedman gym? I still feel kind of bad about breaking your window last week, Sam."

"I guess two extra people really does change the way we take up space," Sam said.

"Actually, this sort of goes right into something I was going to suggest," Delia said, her usual presidential confidence giving way to something more unsure—something nervous. Instantly, she had the room's attention. "I've been so busy lately, between work and Pinnacle application stuff. And, like, I really am happy to practice with the group sometimes, but I'm sort of feeling like the usual after-school hours are getting harder for me, which is going to make scheduling a regular meeting difficult. Even today, Mr. Eckels was saying people could come by after school for extra credit in AP Chem, and I can already tell I'm going to need it. And Friday, I'm supposed to help my sister move a hoarder's worth of belongings from one apartment to another."

"So, what?" Sam said. "You're saying we have to meet even less often than we already are?"

"I'm saying that instead of the whole group text thing, maybe we should put a standing meeting or two on the calendar, and whoever can make it can make it, and whoever can't, can't."

"That makes sense to me," Amber said—super unhelpfully, Sam thought. "That's how we do it in soccer."

"Yeah, but if you miss a soccer practice, don't you have to run wind sprints or something the next day?" Sam said.

"Sure."

"But we don't have a coach to answer to," Denver said. "And Delia does already seem to have her convention categories down, so it's not like the group will suffer if she misses a practice or two."

"Except that Delia is our best teacher," Sam said, trying and failing to not sound like he was whining—to sound instead like he was paying Delia a compliment and not fighting her in front of everyone.

"What do you think, James?" Delia said. "You've been pretty busy, too."

"Yeah. I mean, whatever the rest of the group wants. I can go either way."

"Two practices a week would actually be more than we've had the past couple weeks, and I definitely need more practice in my categories," Denver said.

Delia looked pleased. "All right, then. It's settled. If we want to say Tuesdays and Thursdays, I should be able to do at least one of those days next week."

"Same," James said. "The rest of this week is out for me, too."

"Let's start next week, then," Amber said, all chipper-like, as if it wasn't obvious she was saying she didn't want to meet with Denver and Sam alone later this week.

Which, to be clear, was fine by Sam. He wouldn't have met just the three of them, either.

What would be the point?

It wouldn't be a Fascinators practice.

CHAPTER 14

WITHOUT FASCINATORS PRACTICES TO LOOK FORWARD to, Sam's days at school started to feel—put politely—like a miserable slog. Lunches were awkward, with Amber now joining them every day and dividing their conversations in two just like she had their practice. Kevin had told the whole sophomore class about the seismic fight at his house party, and somehow Sam was implicated in the assholery along with James, so he felt even more non grata as a persona in his classes than he normally did.

Worst of all, the big worries of senior year suddenly seemed much bigger. Did he definitely still want to go to UGA if it wasn't to be James's roommate, or should he be seriously considering all these emails from other colleges, weighing his options? Would these other schools require SAT scores higher than the eleven eighty he'd gotten last year, and if so, would he need to find a tutor who could help him improve?

In his vision of how this year was supposed to go, this was the time when he and James would get to gloat about having their lives already sorted, while everyone around them freaked the eff out. Admittedly, that's where the vision ended, but Sam had never doubted that with James in his corner, other visions would just sort of follow very organically from there.

Now, with that vision in jeopardy, Sam found himself trying to pay more attention in his classes, giving each assignment the additional weight of wondering whether it represented something he could do for the rest of his life. There were only so many careers in which a person could get by on magic and magic alone, and Sam had never kidded himself that he was good enough at magic to do any of them.

Maybe he would become a real estate agent. Pick up the business from his mom. Live in Friedman forever.

Die alone.

On Friday afternoon, bored and depressed at the prospect of another weekend with nothing but homework to look forward to, Sam texted Denver during his last period class to ask if he wanted to go see a movie that night.

Oh! Sorry, already have plans.

Of course Denver had plans tonight. Denver was outgoing, funny, charming. Three months into living in Friedman, he probably had so many friends that he had more plans than he knew what to do with. For some reason, he'd liked Sam, but Sam may have totally screwed that up, too.

No worries! Sam replied. **I'm around all weekend if you want to hang.**

Cool, Denver texted. Then, the three dots of a further reply kept appearing and disappearing, like maybe he was typing with his phone under his desk or else thinking hard about what to say. It turned out to be the latter. **Actually, Arjun is visiting this weekend. Long story. But definitely another time!**

No worries! Sam replied again, realizing too late that it was exactly what he'd responded last time. To mix things up, he tried to find the perfect emoji to show that it was all good and no big deal at all that Denver's ex was in town, but after staring at each individual emoji and deciding that he hated all of them, Sam finally gave up and let the conversation go.

He texted Delia.

Hey! Know you're busy today, but text me if you have any free time and want to hang out this weekend.

He added the man-doing-cartwheel emoji. Maybe that one wasn't so bad.

Sorry, Delia replied after a few minutes. **My brother's got so much stuff! Will probably take all weekend.**

Um. What?

Thought it was your sister?

Again, Sam stared at the text window as the three dots of doom appeared and disappeared. Did Delia have an ex in town, too? Or maybe she was planning to be the third wheel for Denver and Arjun?

My sister's the one moving. But my brother has a lot of his stuff at her place, because he has no storage at his apt. So we have to move it with the rest of her stuff. So much stuff!

Delia added a smiley-cry emoji and a skull emoji, and those, more than any of the rest of her overly detailed explanation, proved to Sam that she was hiding something.

So much stuff indeed.

Good luck with the move! I hope you've picked out some good spells to make things easier.

You know me, Delia said.

Sam gave it an hour after he got home, halfway pretending to do other things, before hopping back into his car and driving over to Delia's sister's apartment.

Sam was fully prepared to find Delia there, packing up a storm, loading a U-Haul. If that was the case, he was also fully prepared to say that he'd been so bored at home that he wanted to come help with the move, even if that meant he would actually have to follow through with the offer.

He halfway expected to find no one home, in which case he would drop these dark thoughts, assume that the family was already en route with a load of furniture, and gladly go home, never to speak of this again.

What he truly, sincerely did not want to happen was exactly what happened when he got to Katherine's door. Namely, Katherine opened the door, looking very surprised to see Sam, and revealing behind her an apartment that showed no signs of going anywhere soon.

"Everything okay?" Katherine said suspiciously. "Haven't seen you in a while, Sam."

"Oh, yeah, sorry," Sam said. "I thought Delia said she was coming over to your place to help you move, but now that I think about it, she actually said it was your brother who was moving."

Katherine sized him up, a look of pity on her face.

"Far be it from me to get my sister in trouble, but Tom finished his move two weekends ago. I'd been storing a lot of my stuff at his old place, so now my apartment's a bit of a mess, or I'd invite you in."

"My bad, my bad," Sam said. He couldn't believe it. Delia had cared enough to make the story 49 percent true, but as he'd feared, she was 51 percent lying. "That must be what she said. I left my cell phone at school, or I would text her."

"Right," Katherine said. "Well, tell her hello from me when you see her."

She closed the door.

Sam felt winded. Felt sick to his stomach.

It was like the time he got food poisoning from a gas station hot dog, and then, instead of waiting it out, he had tried a spell he found online that was supposed to cure food poisoning, but actually seemed to have the effect of tripling food poisoning.

One of his best friends had lied to him.

Had possibly been lying to him on an ongoing basis.

In the span of a second, his mind went to all the dark places he worked hard not to let it go. The places where he wasn't talented enough to deserve Delia's friendship. The places where James wanted so badly to reciprocate Sam's feelings, but he couldn't, because at the end of the day, Sam wasn't whatever enough. (Masculine? Cute? Religious? What?)

These places looked like memories, except they were his memories from the perspectives of others. They looked like hypothetical parties where everyone was having the best time without him—maybe *all* of them were somewhere together right this moment, uncovering the true secret of magic and the spirit world, now that he finally wasn't weighing them down.

Without even really thinking about what he was doing, he got in his car and drove over to Delia's neighborhood. He parked on the corner where he could see her house, turned off his car, and waited.

And waited.

And waited.

Until finally, a little after seven, Delia pulled up and rolled into her driveway, and Sam got out of his car and started walking toward her.

"Delia!" he called out before she reached her front door. She turned around on the stoop with a bewildered expression on her face.

"Sam? Are you okay? You look terrible."

He paused in the driveway, beside her car.

"Where were you?"

"I just came back from my sister's. We finished the first load in record time."

Sam scoffed, but it came out sounding more like a choked sob.

"Sam, what's wrong?"

"*I* was just at your sister's, Delia. She said to tell you hello."

Delia's face drained of color.

"You . . . what? I mean, why? Are you spying on me?"

"You're the only person in the world who's as bad of a liar as I am," Sam said.

The color quickly returned to Delia's face, until it flushed a bright, angry red.

"You *did* spy on me!"

"I don't exactly feel good about it, let me tell you."

"Oh, that makes me feel a hundred percent better, thank you so much."

"Delia, where were you? Were you ditching me?"

Delia sighed and rubbed her temples, but Sam refused to be deterred.

"Were you?"

"No, Sam, I was not ditching you. Not everything is about you, you know."

"And what is that supposed to mean?"

"I was at the warehouse, Sam. There. Are you happy?"

"The warehouse? But those people are horrible, Delia. What were you doing there?"

"They're not horrible," Delia said immediately. "They're powerful."

"They threw a brick through my window."

"Only because James stole their book."

"They literally invaded our brains."

"Because they wanted their book back. Tell me, Sam, have you had a single vision since we gave them back their book?"

"Oh, yes, that's very fair of them. Very generous."

"You don't get it, Sam. How could you? You've never had to work a day in your life. Your parents give you everything you want, as soon as you want it, and they never make you do anything you don't want to do. Shit. They have a college fund saved so you can keep on doing whatever you want to do for a long time."

"Not go to Pinnacle. I couldn't get in there with all the money in the world."

"These people can get me into Pinnacle, Sam. Hell, with these people, I hardly need to go to Pinnacle at all. That's how powerful they are. They know things that the undergrads at Pinnacle only *wish* they were learning."

Sam couldn't believe what he was hearing. It was her choice if she wanted to go to college or not, of course, but Pinnacle had been the next step in Delia's dream life for years. Every dollar she earned, every test she aced, it had been Pinnacle, Pinnacle, Pinnacle. It would have to take some powerful magic indeed to push her off that track—and so suddenly. If it were anyone else, Sam might have expected the work of some legit mind-control magic. But not Delia. Delia was far too strong-willed to have anyone else make up her mind for her.

"I don't think James is going to like the fact that you're hanging out with these creeps."

"If you tell James or anyone else about where I was, I will tell James that you're madly in love with him."

"You wouldn't."

"I'm serious, Sam. If you tell *anyone*, our friendship is officially over."

Sam didn't know what he'd expected to happen, waiting in his car for this confrontation. But it wasn't this. Never in a million years or with a million spells would he have seen this coming.

"Okay, I won't," he said. "Jeez. Will you at least tell me what you've been doing there?"

Delia paused to consider.

"I'm sorry. But I can't."

"Oh."

"And even if I could, I wouldn't, because you spied on me. And that's a dick thing to do, Sam."

"Yeah, but—okay."

"Anyway, I can't."

"Okay."

"Bye, Sam."

And then Sam went back to his car, and drove home, and cried.

CHAPTER 15

ON SUNDAY MORNING, WHEN THEY GOT BACK FROM church, Sam's parents could tell right away that he was still in the funk that had been following him all weekend. He was curled up on the couch, wrapped in a blanket so that only his face and his feet were peeking out. The TV show he'd been streaming had paused at some point in the indeterminate past to ask if he was still watching, and it was one of the rare times when he wasn't, really.

His mom stood over him and looked him in the eye.

"I think I know what you need. Come on, go take a shower and get dressed. We're going to *Qatl*."

"Oh my God, no."

"Yes. I'm not asking. You haven't been in two months, and I can tell. You are officially spiraling. It's coming off you in waves."

It was true—she looked like the waves of his mood were

actually rocking her on her feet. Feeling things this way was the price she paid for being an empath—it was the reason, she said, that she could never be a therapist.

"None of my friends will be there. They're all in college now."

"You can make new friends. That's the whole point of *Qatl*."

"Can we please stop saying *Qatl*?"

"What? That's what it's called."

"It's called Q-Atl. Queer Atlanta. When you say 'Qatl' it always sounds like 'coddle,' and that only makes it feel more like a daycare than it already does."

But even as he was saying it, Sam got off the couch and headed for the shower. The truth was, he was already happy that his mom had made the strong suggestion. Sam had been going to Q-Atl meetings off and on since sixth grade, having come out right around when the group was forming. His mom had even helped the director with the paperwork to buy their building after an early online fundraiser had gone viral. The group was almost like a family at this point.

As with family, spending time with them sometimes felt like an obligation. Sam hardly brought up the desire to go anymore unless his mom expressed a desire to go first. Unlike in sixth grade, he had close friends at home now, and Q-Atl wasn't really a great place to meet a boyfriend, although Sam had tried it once. (This had amounted to the few awkward dates freshman year with Eliot from North Georgia—dates that included their moms, sitting on the other side of a FroYo place, then on the other side of an Applebee's, then on the other side of a movie theater. The mom thing aside, it was just hard to get anything off the ground with a shy guy who lived that far away—all texting, no chemistry. It didn't help that, at the time, Sam had already begun falling for James. The two of them *definitely* had chemistry.)

Today, the parking lot for the Q-Atl building was surprisingly crowded.

"Must be the back-to-school crowd," his mom said.

"You'd think we'd have found a way to cut down on the bullying by now, after all these years."

Sam's mom put the car in park and turned to look at him.

"You're not dealing with that kind of thing anymore, are you?"

"I mean . . ."

"Truly? Still?"

"I think people at Friedman view me as some kind of weird bird that could attack them at any moment. If they can keep me in a cage, it makes them feel safer."

"Cage?"

"It's not the best metaphor. I just mean I don't get outright bullied, but I still don't feel welcome."

"That Denver seems nice and welcoming."

"All right, time to go in," Sam said, climbing out of the car and leading them into the building, while his mom tried to act like she had no idea what she'd done to cause him to blush like this.

The Q-Atl building—the "head-queerters," as Sam lovingly called it—was a two-story townhouse, though that was maybe putting it generously, as the buildings on either side were a cell phone store and a Hungry Henry's. Hanging from the second-story window was a rainbow flag, which had been replaced twice in the years that Sam had been coming here, after the first flag had been stolen and the second one had been vandalized.

The Q-Atl director, Emma, was there in the entryway to greet them. Emma was a white trans woman from Portland with a hearty laugh and a wicked sense of humor, and she personally oversaw the teen group because her background was in counseling homeless youth.

"Sam. Leslie. I haven't seen you in a while."

"Blame senior year," Sam said with a shrug.

"I had to roll this one off the couch this morning," his mom added.

"Ah, yes, sleeping in. I remember what that was like. Well, I'm happy to have you back. You know the drill. Adult group in the back, teens upstairs, and I think the coffee might actually be hot today if you're still feeling tired."

Sam smiled and parted ways with his mom, heading upstairs to a room where six teens he didn't know were already arranged in little cliques—a group of two, a group of three, and a girl by herself whom Sam sat next to, because she wasn't just alone, she looked positively miserable.

"I'm Sam," he said, taking the chair a couple seats down from her.

The girl looked up as if she was surprised and a little wary of being spoken to.

"Hey," she said.

"Is this your first time coming?"

"Yeah."

"It's probably my . . . fiftieth meeting? Can that be right? I think so, which is insane."

"Ha."

Sam had met enough people like this at Q-Atl over the years—people who gave one-word answers, never revealing much about themselves—to know that it was best to let them come out of their shells in their own time, only if they wanted to. Half the people came here looking to forget what was happening at home or at school.

But when Emma walked into the room a few moments later, she said, "Ah, Sam, I see you've already met Liv. I was hoping you two would chat. Sam, Liv could give you a real run for your money in the micro-storms department."

"Oh, yeah?" Sam said, turning to include Liv in the conversation, but her eyes were on the floor again.

Emma moved on from the moment without missing a beat, having the teens circle up and introduce themselves with their name, preferred pronouns, and favorite movie. They were off to the races, and as the conversation started turning to their daily lives, from the microaggressions they were facing to the ups and downs of dating, Sam instantly remembered why he'd loved coming to Q-Atl in the early days. Delia and James understood the part of him that loved learning a new spell and feeling the magic click into place inside him, but these would-be strangers understood the part of him that lived in constant fear of being jumped if he stared too hard at a guy's arms. The part of him that wasn't sure what to believe vis a vis God and religion, because he'd never felt welcome enough in a church—or by the people in that church—to figure it out.

The forty-five-minute meeting flew by, and as everyone started gathering their stuff to go, Sam tried one more time to reach out to Liv, hoping she'd gotten as much out of today as he had. She'd stayed awfully quiet on nearly every topic, but based on the few things she'd said, Sam got the impression she wasn't living with her parents.

"So, where do you go to school?" Sam said. "Are you in your school's magic club? Sorry, two-parter."

"I'm not really in school at the moment," Liv said.

"Oh. Shit, I'm sorry."

"It's okay. I mean, it's not okay. But Emma's helping me out."

"Emma's good people. Way back when, she helped my mom see it was okay for me to be out and agnostic, even if everybody else in Friedman might think that means I'm going to hell."

"Wait, you live in Friedman?"

They were almost to the door that led back downstairs, where Sam's mom would be waiting, but Liv had stopped cold.

"Yeah?" Sam said.

"And are you, like, in any magic clubs?"

"Yeah, I'm in my school's club. I'm the treasurer, pulling double-duty as secretary, but I'm easily the weak link . . . Why do you ask?"

"I was lucky to get out of a group down there. Not in Friedman, but right by it."

Sam was confused. "You mean Lakeside High?" It was the only other high school Sam knew about within a thirty-minute drive of Friedman High. But Lakeside hadn't even fielded a magic club team for convention last year.

"No, not a school group. More like a cult."

Sam felt his mouth go dry and his arm hair prickle.

"Wait . . . you don't mean True Light, do you?"

"That's fucking exactly who I mean," Liv said, her face coming alive, but not lighting up—in fact, her face did the opposite of lighting up. "You know them?"

"I know enough to know they're horrible people," Sam said quickly, because it seemed like his even knowing about them was enough to make Liv want to hurt him.

"That's the fucking understatement of the century."

The floodgates had been opened. No more one-word answers for Liv. Her hands were balled into fists.

"How so?"

"What do you know about them already?" Liv said, searching his face. Beneath the hard veneer of anger, Liv was obviously scared. It seemed like she didn't trust Sam, which he could understand and forgive, in light of the circumstances.

"I know that they have a book that's all about trying to break the barrier into the spirit world. And I know that my friend kind of stole that book, which meant that the good people of

True Light kind of threw a rock through my car window, which means that I kind of want to find them and punch them in their collective face, if I can't punch each of them individually in the face."

"Your car window?" Liv said, as if he'd just said his golden spoon had a crack in it. "These people are psychotic. If your friend's who I think he is, you're lucky you're alive."

Sam took a step back into the wall. They were the only two people left in the room. Sam's mom was probably watching the stairs right now, wondering why he wasn't coming down. Any moment, she would come up here to check on him. "Do you know what they're really trying to do at True Light?" Liv pressed. "With all the spells in that *book* about the *spirit world?*"

Sam shook his head but didn't say a word. He could hardly breathe. Liv was all the way in his face. She was articulating each word with a jab to his chest with her pointer finger.

"They're stealing magic from other people. They're like giant fucking mosquitos, sucking it out until it's gone. Why do you think they're camped out in the middle of Bumblefuck, Georgia? Why do you think they handpick abandoned losers like me to join? Because I'm good at little storms? Hell no. It's because no one would give a shit if something happened to me. You ever heard of a person alive who didn't have magic?"

Sam shook his head as much as he could in the limited space.

"No, you haven't, because it isn't possible. Your magic is right up there with your brain or your soul. Ignore it all you want to, but you can't live without it. I only barely got away myself, not that anyone cares."

Sam wanted to say something to reassure Liv that this was ridiculous. That of course people would miss her. That she was probably *exceptional* at little storms, and she shouldn't count herself out in that regard. But such reassurances were so woefully beside the point of what he was hearing, so worthless in the face of these frightening details and Liv's own frightening anger, that saying them was only likely to get *him* punched in the face.

"Well," Sam said finally, because Liv was still leaning into him, waiting for some kind of response. "I guess it's a good thing you got out."

"Did I, though?" Liv said, but she took a step back. Whatever she was seeing behind her eyes, it was haunting enough to overshadow the fight that had been building inside her.

"Have you told Emma about any of this?" Sam said.

"There's nothing she can do. She would want to go right to the police or whoever and get it all sorted, but it wouldn't work. It would only put her in danger."

"How do you know? I mean, that the police couldn't do anything about it. I'll bet there are some Keepers on the Atlanta police force. Are there really that many True Light people, that it wouldn't be enough?"

"It's not a number thing," Liv said impatiently. "It's a power thing. It's an *idea*. The head of True Light says an *angel* brought them this secret of magic. So, when you see their magic in action—and when they let you in on a spell to suck all the magic out of some unsuspecting newbie—you start to think, hey, maybe these people are onto something. I don't know about an angel, but maybe this magic of theirs is really something, you know? That kind of thinking, combined with that kind of power? It's like a virus. And the only reason it hasn't spread wider is because they don't want it to—they're keeping it to themselves, denying anyone who tries to speak against them until they're ready, and then, when they're ready—"

"How's it going in here?" Emma had reappeared at the door. She was leaning against the doorframe, looking friendly as ever.

"All good," Sam said, when it was clear that Liv wasn't planning to respond. She'd sunken back into herself, her face expressionless, eyes hollow.

"Okay, well, your mom's all finished up in the adult group. You're welcome to hang around a little longer if you want, but I have a feeling your mom wants to get you back home before dinnertime. I hope you won't be a stranger, though. Liv and I would love to see you again next month, isn't that right, Liv?"

Liv nodded, and Emma smiled sadly.

Emma had no idea.

"Thanks for—for talking," Sam said. "Do you maybe want to exchange numbers? Or are you on Friendivist?"

"I don't have a phone right now," Liv said, "and I'm never getting on Friendivist again."

She gave him one last defiant look for the road.

"Okay, then," Sam said.

Sam headed downstairs, where his mom was waiting by the front door.

"Everything all right?" she said.

"I'd tell you it was, but you'd know I was lying."

On a hunch, Sam checked the magicker forum again that night, and while he clicked obsessively through one thread after another, he couldn't find the post about Mr. Grender anywhere. It was just gone.

It was like Liv had said—these True Light people weren't ready to have their secrets shared, and they were powerful enough to see to it that they weren't.

The question was, how much of what Liv had said did Delia know?

Was Delia hoping she would be one of the anointed inner circle whose powers would increase at the expense of some poor nobody? Or did True Light think she was some poor nobody herself?

If they knew her parents were laissez-faire-going-on-neglectful, maybe they'd see her as an opportunity. Maybe they'd take her magic and leave some forged note with her parents about how she'd run away.

Oh . . .

Can you talk? he texted her. **It's kind of important.**

At least she didn't wait long to respond—not bothering with

a text, but calling him directly. He'd worried she might still be too mad at him after Friday.

"Hey," Sam said.

"What's up?" She sounded uninterested. Busy. Maybe she was still mad at him after all.

"So, I went to a Q-Atl meeting today, and I met this girl, and I swear I didn't bring it up myself, but she was telling me some stuff about True Light that has me seriously concerned for you."

"Are you freaking kidding me with this right now?"

"Um, no?"

"This is why I didn't tell you in the first place, you know. I knew you would do your judgy thing and tell me all the reasons why, after much over-analysis and moral grandstanding, you'd decided that this was not the right thing for me. I didn't think you would stalk my movements or make up some fake new girl to try to get me to go along."

"I'm not making this up, you weirdo. I'm trying to prevent you from getting killed."

"Oh, right, you're *protecting* me. Because I am just a weak, helpless girl who doesn't know what she's doing."

"Actually, I wish you *were* a helpless girl who didn't know what she was doing. It's scarier to me to think that you might know what you're doing with those people yet you're doing it anyway. Do you know what Liv said? That's the girl I met today—Liv. She said that the spell James interrupted that night wasn't trying to break through to the spirit world at all. It was trying to steal the magic from half the people in the room for the leaders. This is some serious cult shit, Delia."

"You don't know what you're talking about, Sam, and it's clear that this girl Liv didn't either. Anyway, one person's cult is another person's extracurricular. Why don't you go talk to James about cults, huh? He and Amber seem to be going to church an awful lot at this point. Who knows what they're getting up to, right? Maybe you should put a camera in James's room so you can find out."

Sam flung his phone across the room. It hit the wall with a sickening *crunch*.

CHAPTER 16

HE STAYED HOME SICK FROM SCHOOL THE NEXT DAY.

He didn't even have to pretend. After a night of no sleep spent worrying that his two best friends in the world no longer liked him, he tried to stand up at seven thirty and felt dizzy and hollow.

His mom said she would call the school for him.

Around lunchtime, when he was feeling more anxious in bed than he would out of it, he got up and made himself a Hot Pocket, then went to work gathering everything he needed for the most complicated spell he had ever attempted.

He'd torn this spell out of a magazine sophomore year—one of the sensationalist tabloids that he always saw at the check-out aisle of the grocery store—and he'd stuffed the page into the back of his sock drawer as if it was something obscene, because, on some level, it had the potential to be.

It was a soothsaying spell.

It promised to show you the future.

Even for expert magickers, the best of the best, divination magic was a tricky business. Soothsaying spells were, more than anything, like scientific hypotheses without the data. They represented an attempt to wade through the noise-that-is-everything and emerge with a clear and persuasive grasp of the way things were, which, in turn, would make a case for the way things were headed.

But since no one could ever agree on the way things were, interpretations of the way things were going varied wildly. And when a prediction failed to come true, it was usually impossible to tell whether that meant the spell hadn't worked, or whether the spell had worked but the interpretations of its findings had been wrong.

None of that, however, prevented this magazine from boldly proclaiming that its unique combination of scrying, dowsing, and symbological techniques was guaranteed to hit you with the kind of out-of-body revelation that was too real to be a memory. Too vivid to be bullshit.

The reason Sam hadn't tried this spell before was that he was always happy enough with the way things were. The temptation had always been there—to peek into five years later, see if James and Delia were still in his life, and if so, in what capacity. But greater than the temptation was the fear. The fear that Sam wouldn't like his five years later. The fear that James and Delia wouldn't be in it at all.

Now, Sam was coming to terms with the fact that he might never have had a clear grasp on the way things were, like he'd thought he had.

Maybe he hadn't wanted to, really, because the truth was too hard to bear.

Whatever.

Things were different now. Things had officially gone to hell in a handbasket, and his friends were in danger. James was being reckless with a powerful enemy, and Delia was courting that enemy's friendship.

Sam didn't care if this spell was bullshit.

He needed to know what was coming—in case he needed to stop it.

He grabbed a hand mirror from his parents' bedroom. He filled his bathtub all the way up to the rim, then placed the hand mirror faceup on the bottom, so that it reflected the ceiling at weird angles. He grabbed his tarot deck, painfully aware that it was a gift from Delia that he didn't use very much, and then shuffled it and placed it on the ledge of the tub. He rooted around in his closet until he found the Y-shaped copper wire he used even less often than the tarot cards—a dowsing rod he'd made for freshman-year convention, when his category challenge was to find a way to detect and eliminate toxins from drinking water. Finally, he lit a stick of sandalwood incense, not expressly required by the spell but always helpful for this very intense, introspective magic.

All his implements gathered, Sam sat down on the bathroom floor, facing the tub, and read carefully through the steps of the spell one more time.

It was the kind of spell where it seemed like it would help to have four hands and as many eyes. He was supposed to do a three-card spread from the deck, at the same time that he was supposed to read the incantation, channel energy into the dowsing rod, and keep a "passive eye" on the mirror, whatever that meant.

It was a dexterity challenge as much as a magical one.

Sam gave himself a mental *on your mark, get set, go*, then flipped the top three cards—flip, flip, flip. Three of Cups, Seven of Swords, Death.

Party, theft, death.

He read the incantation, a series of nonsense syllables the writer claimed was a mix of languages, whose roots and meanings went unexplained.

He gripped the two arms of the dowsing rod, feeling it guide him left—no, right—no, left—well, sort of left, yes, there.

And though he kept his face forward, following the guidelines of the spell, he left his peripheral vision open to the mirror, feeling a little silly because of course it was still just reflecting the ceiling, at slightly different—

Wait.

He snapped his head to stare at the mirror, but there was nothing there when he looked right at it. Instead, he felt the dowsing rod tugging him, left—no, right—no, left again, until he was facing the same direction—until he was sure he saw the same thing in the corner of his eye.

It was glass against water, which made it confusing, but it wasn't the mirror in the tub—it was something else. Some*where* else. It was a building, familiar. It made Sam think of the Savannah Convention Center, but only if you were somehow standing at the bottom of the Savannah River and looking up at it through the water. He couldn't say why that's where his mind went, but the inclination was as strong and real as the tug of the dowsing rod.

He scrambled to his feet, accidentally knocking the tarot cards and the incense into the tub in the process. He cursed.

The Savannah Convention Center was the site of the magic convention.

The Three of Cups, which Sam had been quick to read as a party, could really be any kind of celebration or gathering. The Seven of Swords, which Sam had read as theft, could, more generally, be deception, trickery. Their combination had an infinite range of possible meanings, but none of them seemed like good news for November.

The Death card had a range of meanings, too. It pointed to transitions and endings, and in relation to Sam's very last magic convention of high school, it could—optimistically—be a redundant reminder.

But sometimes Death just meant death.

Sometimes the spells you found in a magazine just worked.

And sometimes, seeing the future out of the corner of your eye didn't mean that you could change it, because when you faced it head-on, it was only water and glass.

CHAPTER 17

THE FRONT STEPS OF FRIEDMAN HIGH SCHOOL TURNED
out to be a totally acceptable place to eat lunch. If anyone missed
Sam at their usual table, well—they certainly weren't texting him
to say so. (And the shattered screen on his cell phone felt like
a fresh slap in the face every time he checked.) No doubt James
and Delia both thought they were the reason for Sam's continued
absence, but whether they actually gave a shit about it was anyone's
guess. Thanks to Delia's disingenuous scheduling maneuver—the
come-if-you-can plan that in retrospect was clearly about freeing
up her time for more powerful magickers—Sam didn't even have
to tell anyone that he wasn't coming today.

When Denver finally texted him from practice to ask where
he was, Sam responded—carefully avoiding the cracks in the
glass—Still not feeling great. Going home.

He thought that was the end of that.

Right as he and his parents were finishing dinner and a TV show, there was a knock at their front door. The three of them looked at one another in confusion.

"Are you expecting anyone?" his mom asked his dad.

"I'm not. Are you?" his dad asked Sam.

Sam shook his head and shrugged.

Sam's mom hit pause and went over to the door, peering through the peephole they almost never used but that seemed like a good feature at the moment. Then she stood up beaming, giving Sam a mischievous look before she opened the door.

"Well, hi there, Denver from Nashville. Come on in."

"Hi, Mrs. Fisher," Denver said, coming on in.

Sam's dad stood up and brushed the crumbs off his shirt, clearing his throat and going over for a handshake as if Denver were the Archduke of a country he'd never heard of and not a junior at Friedman High. Denver loved that. "You must be Sam's new friend I've heard so much about. Welcome, welcome," Mr. Fisher said.

Sam shot his mom a look. If his dad had been hearing a lot about Denver, it most certainly had not been from him.

"Thanks. Nice to meet you, sir," Denver said. "I came to check on Sam. He said he was sick."

Denver held up two Wendy's cups by way of an explanation. "Sorry, I only thought to get two. They're a little melty anyway, after the drive."

"You brought Frosties," Sam's mom said, with a significant

look to Sam as if Denver wasn't standing right there where he could see said look.

"Okay, why don't we head back to my room," Sam said. "We'll keep the door open," he rushed to add, before one of his parents could humiliate him further with that request.

Denver followed Sam back to his room. He was definitely blushing.

"So, this is where the magic happens," Sam deadpanned—a defense mechanism more than anything, because now that Denver was actually in his room, Sam was realizing that he was blushing a little bit himself.

"Wow. I didn't know they made posters of Lady Gaga that big."

"Yes, well, you have to remember, I only experienced culture for the first time in my life at the Fox Theatre a week ago, so it's going to take some time before I've gotten rid of all proof of my basic upbringing."

"You seem like you're feeling a little better," Denver said lightly, handing Sam a Frosty.

"Turns out all I needed was a nice long nap."

"Right."

The face-off lasted a half second longer than either of them meant it to, until Sam was forced to turn away and pretend that it was to clear some space on his bed for Denver to sit.

"Thank you for this," he said, taking a bite of his Frosty.

"What happened here?" Denver said, eyeing the tarot cards spread out to dry on Sam's dresser, warped and waterlogged.

"Only the world's worst weather forecast."

Denver laughed, clearly not believing Sam in the slightest but accepting that Sam wasn't going to offer any further explanation.

"So, how was your visit with Arjun this weekend? Did you take him to Mary Ellen's?"

"No," Denver said, drawing out the word so that it had two distinct, long syllables.

"Just hanging around at home, then?"

"Listen, Sam, that's part of why I wanted to come over tonight. I know this is probably awkward of me to say, and I could be way off base, but I was thinking—I got the feeling that maybe I had made Fascinators practice weird for you? By mentioning Arjun's visit?"

"Oh, no, Denver, you don't have to—"

"No, it's okay. I want to make sure you know that we're just friends."

"Who's just friends?"

"Sorry, God. I'm making this worse. I mean, me and Arjun. He and I are just friends. It wasn't, like, a getting-back-together visit. But we'd been together for so long. We were boyfriends and also best friends, you know? And after cancelling the first trip I had planned, I think he felt bad about it, and he reached out last week asking if he could visit as a friend. I didn't tell you this before, but when he broke up with me? It was over text. Yeah. After three years."

"And you forgave him for that?"

"Well . . . yeah. I mean, it sucked, but losing my best friend of three years altogether would have been worse. Don't get me wrong, it was a little awkward, having him in the apartment, sleeping on our couch. But I think we're going to be okay now."

"That's . . . that's great, Denver."

"Yeah. So anyway, I wanted to tell you that. In person. Not in a text. Sorry, now you're looking at me like I'm crazy. I should probably go."

"No, wait—"

Sam had reached out to stop Denver before he knew what he was doing, and he'd grabbed Denver's hand, which was warm and solid and real.

He dropped it almost as quickly, but judging by the O of surprise Denver's mouth was making, he'd felt the sparks, too.

"I'm glad you told me," Sam said. "And I'm glad you and Arjun are just friends. I mean, I'm glad you're still friends. But you didn't make practice awkward. Delia and James saw to that well enough between the two of them."

"Oh yeah? Delia wasn't at practice today, either. Is something going on?"

"Yes, something is very much going on. Possibly more than one something, depending on how you're counting. I'm sort of fighting with Delia and James? And I'm worried about them, but I sort of promised not to say why?"

"Oh. Damn. Sorry, Sam. That sounds awful."

"Well, I'm sorry, too. You came over from a magic club that

placed eighth in the state, and now you're in one that can't even meet twice a week."

"Don't worry about that. There are way more important things than practicing magic, and friends are pretty high up there. I guess I'm just surprised. You, James, and Delia seemed like such a tight-knit circle."

"I'm as surprised as you are. I guess this is the problem, right, when your friendships are based around what you do instead of who you are? Or maybe it's the problem of being friends with anybody for as long as I've been friends with Delia and James."

"What's the problem?"

"You're not allowed to change."

"Oh," Denver said. He stared into his cup.

"Damn, I'm sorry. Here you were incredibly kind and brought me this Frosty, and now I'm making us both depressed. You know, if it's not too dramatic for you, maybe you and I should branch off and form our own Fascinators sub-committee to practice for convention."

"You think convention will still happen if we're not meeting as a full group?"

Sam thought of the Three of Cups, which he'd started to imagine had meant him, James, and Delia for better or worse, but could just as easily have meant nothing at all.

Still.

"I think so. James would never admit it, but the individual medals he's won at the last three are some of his proudest achievements. And I can't imagine Delia would give up her best chance to show Pinnacle that she's not some Georgia bumpkin." *Assuming she's actually still applying.* "Not to mention, we've got you this year. You and your luck magic."

"Aw, shucks. Well, much as I hate conflict of any kind, if I have to choose between practicing with James and Amber or practicing with you, it's an easy choice. It takes some considerable magic to even get them to notice when I'm in a room with them."

Sam smiled, even though it hurt.

"Okay, well, I'll let you get back to napping or whatever."

He turned again to leave.

"Denver?"

"Yeah?"

"Do you think you could teach me some of your self-defense magic?"

"I guess so. Why?"

"Not sure if you heard about what happened at Kevin's party the other night?"

"With James and the earthquake?"

"That's the one."

"And you want to be able to protect yourself against James next time?" He was teasing, sort of, but he was really asking, too.

"I've just been feeling more helpless than usual lately. And I don't want to fight fire with fire or anything like that. But I don't want to get burned, either."

"Gotcha. Yeah, I can teach you what I know."

"Thank you."

Denver smiled. If it was possible, his smile only got better the more times Sam saw it, as if its charm had a cumulative effect, carrying with it all the smiles that came before.

"See you on Thursday, Sam."

"Not if I see you first."

CHAPTER 18

ONCE, WHEN DELIA WAS IN SIXTH GRADE, HER MOM forgot to pick her up from her clarinet lesson. That her mom forgot to pick her up wasn't really the notable thing, though. At eleven years old, Delia had already collected a long trail of being-forgotten memories, the excuses from both her parents becoming no less hurtful over time for their increasing mundanity. Getting lost in the shuffle because your mom is working late while your dad is at the doctor is one thing; finding out that your parents simply lost track of time watching their favorite TV show is another. At least when it happened at school, Delia could get a ride home with Sam, whose parents were always right on time, like they couldn't wait to see him. It had happened enough that they would sit in their car for a few minutes, calling Delia's parents when it seemed she'd been forgotten. Again.

No, what made that day after her clarinet practice notable was that, for once, instead of waiting and calling and waiting some more, Delia decided to walk home. She told her clarinet teacher, Ms. Eldicott, that she saw her mom's car outside, and then, while the next student after her provided an easy distraction, she made a dash for the corner. It was at least five miles from Ms. Eldicott's house to hers, along the winding back roads of Friedman—roads that had been carved right out of the woods and had shoulders so narrow she often had to walk in a lane.

She still had three miles to go when the rain started coming down.

Her first instinct was to start running faster, but at the sound of an oncoming car, so close she could feel its tailwind, Delia all but dove into the woods, not even feeling the branches as they scratched her.

When she at last found a patch of land that was covered enough to provide a dry spot to stand in, she took stock of her surroundings, and started to let the dread sink in. Her choices were either to wait out the rain and then walk three miles—soaking wet, possibly after dark—or else find a house nearby from which she could call her parents.

No sooner had she made her decision than a house appeared, not forty yards ahead. It was a small house, and it really was raining hard, and those were the only two excuses she could come up with for why she hadn't noticed the house right away. She would decide only later that her gut had been right; that the house hadn't been there, and then it had.

The lights were on inside, and when Delia knocked on the door, it took only a moment before a very tall girl answered it. She hardly looked older than Delia's older sister, who was three months shy of graduating from Friedman High.

"What in the ever-loving world?" the girl said, her eyes going wide with alarm. Delia was drenched and shivering. "How did you find your way here? You know what, get inside, tell me what's going on."

Delia obliged, entering into a house that on the inside looked to be one big room, with a sink and a countertop stove against the wall to her right and a single bed against the wall to her left. For this girl's sake, Delia was relieved to see a small bathroom peeking through a half-closed pocket door.

"I got caught in the rain," Delia said.

"That much I can see," the girl replied.

"Can I use your phone?"

The girl nodded. "Course. Let me get you a towel first." She went into her bathroom and returned with an old towel that hardly looked dry itself. Not wanting to appear rude, Delia took it and dabbed at her arms. To her surprise, she began to see results right away. Not only her arms, either. Even her clothes, her hair, her *shoes*, started to dry as she spread the towel around, until it was like she had never been in the rain at all.

She looked dubiously at the girl.

"Just so you know, I can do magic," Delia said.

"Is that right?" the girl said, already taking back the towel and handing Delia a cordless landline.

"Yeah. Me and a couple of my friends. Some of the teachers and parents at my school say we shouldn't be allowed to do it around the other kids, but my parents told me I can do whatever I want."

"And where are your parents now?"

"They forgot me at clarinet practice. So, can you do magic? Was that what happened with the towel?"

"You're not shy, are you, knocking on a stranger's door and asking them all kinds of personal stuff?" The girl was smiling, but she wasn't answering Delia's question.

"I have an older sister and an older brother. My sister and me have the same room. You can't be shy at my house."

Now the girl's smile fell.

"Well," she said, "in my experience, a little personal space is about the best thing you can ask for. A place you can run off to and not have to explain yourself to anybody. A place you can do whatever you want, sure. But being forgotten? Now that's a different story." The girl put her hands on her hips. "Tell you what, after you talk to your parents, why don't you pass me the phone, and let me say hello."

So, Delia called her mom on her cell and found that she was still running errands. She was totally shocked to hear that Delia had left her lesson without waiting. *Serves her right*, Delia thought, before passing the girl the phone.

The girl calmly explained how Delia's mom could find her house, and then, just as calmly, she explained how relieved she was to have found Delia before something awful happened to her; how someone had died in a car accident the other day on the exact stretch of road by her house; how she'd even heard some of the deer around her property had rabies. She was laying it on thick without ever raising her voice or overtly chastising, and Delia could already tell—she wasn't going to be forgotten again by her parents any time soon.

"Now," the girl said, after she'd hung up the phone, "it's going to take your mom about twenty minutes to get out here, so why don't we make some hot chocolate, and you can tell me more about what those other parents and teachers are saying at your school. It is totally within your rights to practice magic at school, you know. Even in Georgia—it's the law."

It was like Delia had stepped into a fairy tale, only—instead of feeding her candy and stuffing her into a cage—the witch in the woods was setting her free. Giving her what she needed. Her own guardian angel.

Delia never caught her name, and she never saw her again, but even years later, when she started winning medals at convention and attracting attention from out-of-state schools, it was never her parents she hoped were proud of her—it was Ms. Berry, who told her she could be a Keeper one day, and it was that girl in the woods, who'd shown her how.

So, yes, James had been the one to come up with the name "the Fascinators," but Delia wasn't club president because she was the bossiest or the most organized or some shit like that. She was club president because the club was *her idea*. Because she needed magic to breathe. Because it wasn't enough to be okay—to have this little thing she could do. People who were okay got forgotten. Delia wanted to be the *best*.

And you know what? Sure, Sam and James had never left her in the rain, and yes, they'd been as committed to the club over the years as anyone could reasonably expect them to be, but did they really see Delia as an equal? Did they value her company as much as they valued each other's?

How many times over the years had Delia caught wind of some party the two of them had gone to over the weekend without inviting her? Even before her job provided a convenient excuse for them to assume she was busy, there were always the plans she'd only hear about later, or the pictures she'd see online, like when James went with Sam's family to Jekyll Island. So what if Sam seemed to be a little bit in love with James, no matter how many times he mentioned Eliot or whatever guy he was talking to online that month? Didn't that make it even weirder for Sam and James to be so close, forcing her to be a third wheel?

If Sam and James couldn't see how much it had hurt her to be so consistently forgotten, what did she owe them anyway, in the face of this new opportunity? This new group, who hadn't ended up with Delia by an accident of geography, but had picked her, quite intentionally, because of what she could do?

✶✶✶

Practicing with Isaac and the others felt nothing like practicing with the Fascinators. Delia didn't have to teach these people anything. For once, Delia got to be the learner.

The leaders of the group, Grace and Mr. Grender, seriously knew their stuff, and they were pushing the boundaries of magic, especially Grace. She never spoke, which Delia had finally brought herself to ask Isaac about, and Isaac had said that this was a matter of choice. That she had other, magical ways of communicating. Even that seemed badass to Delia—someone who was so magical, she didn't even have to *speak*.

It had felt a little weird at first, showing up at the dilapidated warehouse she'd given James so much shit for visiting, then sitting in a room that looked like an office from the seventies doing group spells with a bunch of adults. Another guy, Hank, joined the group only a little after she did, and he looked like he must have been thirty or so.

But she was eighteen-going-on-thirty herself, and besides, Isaac was practically her age.

And after the second time meeting with them, the physical space felt irrelevant anyway, as it always did when you were lost in the magic. Existing out of space and time, thinking of incantations and associations while you were waitressing tables, while you were staring out the window during calc, while you were walking through the halls of Friedman High School, not seeing all the faces of the people who didn't get it.

It had been a little tempting, really, when Isaac had mentioned the open room. When he'd said that the girl who'd lived there before had gone totally crazy—had left them with her rent to pay on not even a day's notice, and Grace had told Isaac specifically that Delia seemed like she'd fit right in with the group . . .

No way would her parents allow that, though. They were hands-off, but they weren't *that* hands-off.

Today it was chilly, mid-October. Mr. Grender was getting frustrated because the spell he most wanted to work on—the spell that they'd attempted that night with James, the one that would open the door to the spirit world—required the magic of a lot of people. Isaac had explained it was like a pulley system, person to person, and while seven was something of a magic number for most group spells, for spells like this one, a bigger pulley was required.

"Why can't we just throw another party?" said one of the Alexes.

"Yeah. It's seriously starting to get lonely around here," said the other. "All this space and no one to fill it with."

"You know why we can't throw another party," Isaac said. "Keepers have been sniffing around ever since Carl lost it and started sending out distress calls. We need to lie low for a little while, until they accept that he's nothing more than a bitter alcoholic and move on."

That was another thing that had been weird at first—hearing the way these people talked about Keepers, when for years now,

Delia had had her sights on becoming one. To hear them tell it, Keepers weren't called Keepers because they possessed the most magic; or at least, that wasn't the only reason. They were the Keepers because they kept the rest of the world's magic in check; they made *sure* they possessed the most magic by putting a cap on everyone else's.

"Do the other magickers have to *participate* for the spell to work?" That was Hank. He seemed normal enough. A little quiet, maybe. A little on the thin side, and he always wore the same red plaid shirt. He lived in Carl's old room.

"What do you mean?" Isaac said. "Of course they have to be there for the spell to work."

"But do they have to *participate*?" Hank repeated. "Willingly, I mean. Or is it enough for them to be present?"

Grace and Mr. Grender exchanged a look.

"Technically, no," Mr. Grender said. "It's not enough. Being in the presence of other strong magickers does make your magic stronger, sure. It has a cumulative effect like that. But the spell . . . well, it takes something out of you. It's like giving blood. Nothing you don't get back, mind you," he rushed to add, perhaps in response to the look of shock that Delia, Alex, and Alex shared. Isaac seemed to have heard this already, and Hank didn't seem to be unsettled by anything. "That's why we always ask for volunteers at the parties. We don't want anybody giving anything unwillingly."

"What does it matter, if they get it back anyway?" Hank said, as calmly as if he were asking about the weather.

"It's a moot point," Isaac said. "You're never going to find a room full of strong enough magickers who would also sit there and let you finish the spell. Either you invite them to help, or you don't get them together at all."

"Really?" Hank said. "You can't think of a single place where a group of magickers might fit the bill?"

Later, Delia would think back on this moment and wonder what had motivated her exactly. If it was some need to prove herself useful to this new group of powerful magickers, whom she desperately wanted to impress. Or maybe she'd just gotten caught up in the brainstorming, like an improv game that demanded jokes faster than you could process them. Or did she already know, on some level, that this was a spell that had the power to undo, and was she motivated, even a little bit, by the desire to undo the greatest symbol of her best friends' shared goals?

"There is," she said, "always the state magic convention. It happens in a few weeks in Savannah. There are tons of magickers there."

The seven of them had exchanged looks around the table. This was the opposite of what it normally felt like, offering suggestions as club president. Here, Delia was the lowliest member, the unproven initiate. It felt like a lot was hanging in the balance of their response.

Mr. Grender said, "It could work."

And they started to plan.

CHAPTER 19

SAVANNAH WAS THE OLDEST CITY IN GEORGIA, AND, depending on your definition, it was the most magical, too. If you defined a city's magic in terms of its population in the aggregate, Atlanta would probably have it beat. If you counted in terms of magic per capita, Savannah, with its density of old-money families in ancestral homes, had the edge.

And if you were thinking instead of the magic built into the bones of the city itself—if you were the kind of person who believed in an afterlife, where the magic of the departed lingered on just out of sight—then there was no contest.

Whatever you believed, however you counted, there was no denying that here in Savannah, all your spells were a whisper more powerful. Your associations came more easily. The effects lasted longer.

Which was why every year, bewildered high schoolers at the

state magic convention found themselves performing feats of which they did not think themselves capable.

Like Sam, for example. Who knew that he could pull off the high-level feat of self-delusion it took to walk into the Savannah Convention Center for perhaps the last time ever with only one other member of his magic club, acting like everything was going to be okay?

"Hey, you all right?" Denver said, catching the nauseated look on Sam's face.

"Me? Oh, I'm fine. I'm great."

"Boys! Sam and Denver! Over here."

It was their perpetually frazzled but always still-smiling sponsor and chaperone, Ms. Berry, wearing a purple pantsuit and a giant dragonfly brooch.

"I picked up our registration packet at the sponsor meeting," she said. "Here are your name tags and category room assignments, plus a map for you, Denver, and . . . Where's the rest of the team?"

"They got a late start at the continental breakfast. We figured we'd head over and let them catch up."

"Well, they'd better get here in the next ten minutes. James has one of the first times in the Lunar Tides Challenge. He does realize that, right?"

Sam shrugged.

"Honestly, I'm happy to support you all really going for it this year, but this is exactly the kind of logistical headache I was hoping to avoid when I convinced the school to book us the hotel rooms."

He may have been imagining it, but Sam thought she was looking at him in a particular way when she said that last bit. Probably because in the end, Denver's grand fundraising dreams for their club had turned into Sam going into Ms. Berry's office and asking her to please beg the school for more money, because with two more members, at least one of whom was possibly dating an existing member, there was no way they could all fit on a family couch and an air mattress. It still wasn't clear how much of the four hotel rooms had been paid for by the school district and how much had been paid by Ms. Berry as a graduation gift. It was clear she wanted them to place in the overall category as much as they did, if not more.

"I'm sure they'll be here soon," Denver said. "Come on, Sam. Let's go find our first rooms."

The convention center was an absolute madhouse, as it always was—a mix of a few familiar faces Sam recognized from the categories and podiums of previous years, but far more so, a sea of excited young magickers he didn't know. He remembered being a freshman in this exact same hallway, looking around in awe, wondering what it would feel like to be one of the cool in-the-know seniors who had it all figured out, and not some bumpkin also-ran.

Now that he was actually here, Sam had to face the fact that the ability to figure things out—to feel in control, to take decisive action—wasn't one that simply came with age. Possibly, it was an ability that Sam just didn't have and never would. You could take the boy out of Friedman . . .

"At the Tennessee convention, your time slots were determined by your school's rank from the year before. If your team came in last place the year before, you had to go first, and the first-place school got to sleep in. In theory, that meant the competitors in each category got better and better as the day went on, but it also meant that the expectations got more intense. Defending champions got dethroned left and right because somebody choked under the pressure of going last."

"I can relate to the choking under pressure part," Sam said. "Not so much the expectations."

"Oh, I totally expect you to do well in *both* your categories today. You've been amazing at practice."

It was true, this past month Sam had come closer to mastering Illusions of Grandeur, his original category, than he had in the whole last year of practices with James and Delia. Even in his second category, the Pit and the Pendulum, which he'd picked up relatively last minute, he'd made enough progress that he wasn't afraid of embarrassing himself today. It was something about the energy when it was him and Denver alone. It was like, now that he wasn't the worst of his practice group, he couldn't fall back on that as an excuse for not trying harder than his hardest. And okay, maybe he was partly motivated by a desire to show Delia what she was missing—that they weren't powerless nobodies, dragging her down.

But he was equally motivated by the fear that he needed to

be ready when his prediction came true.

Because after all this time, he still hadn't figured out what True Light might be planning that would result in the prediction he saw, let alone found a way to stop it. A few times he'd thought about going through Emma to reach out to that girl from Q-Atl, Liv, but it had seemed so clear that day that she was ready to put True Light behind her; Sam didn't want to re-traumatize her on a hunch.

That fear extended to Delia, too. He refused to believe that she was complicit in whatever True Light was up to, but all these weeks later, she still hadn't apologized to Sam and he still hadn't apologized to her. They were barely speaking at all, to the point where it had been impossible to miss during the convention logistics meeting last week, causing Ms. Berry to ask what was up with them anyway (answer: "nothing").

Sam almost *hoped* something would happen this weekend, if only so that he knew where he stood with his friends. All this waiting around, reading between the lines of their Friendivist and v-clip posts, and feeling hurt by everyone could have been enough to warrant the Death card on its own.

"I think this is your first room," Denver said, stopping at room 106. "I'm upstairs in the morning, and then it looks like we're both in exhibit hall A this afternoon. Maybe whoever's done first can text the other one and we'll meet at the entrance to go find lunch?"

"Sure, yeah, I like that plan."

"Oh my gosh, you sound so nervous. I didn't peg you for the stage fright type."

"I'd say what I'm feeling goes a little beyond stage fright."

"Well, I won't tell you how to feel. But all I will say is, this fight between you, James, and Delia? Winning your categories won't make it go away."

"This is supposed to make me feel less anxious?"

"I mean, yeah. Whether you win or totally bomb in there, you are deserving of their friendship, and if they can't see that, that's on them. It's not all on you to suddenly have to change who you are and be a better person. That's not how friendship works."

Sam couldn't find the words of a reply right then. He was afraid if he spoke he would just start crying. But he smiled and gave Denver a very awkward shoulder pat, which would have to do. And then he headed into the room to show off his illusions.

Denver's encouraging words ended up being their own prophecy of a kind. Sam didn't totally bomb, but in his humble opinion, he clearly didn't win either, especially with that kid from Clayton County putting on a master class of a fireworks show, which wasn't fair at all, since the guy also looked like an all-American athlete, with cheekbones chiseled from stone. You were supposed to get one or the other, but not both.

When the thirty magickers competing in Illusions of Grandeur all finished up, Sam had no new messages from Denver, which meant the Temporal Magic category was somehow taking even longer. As he exited the room back into the sunlit hallway, typing out a text to say he was heading to the entrance now, Sam was so preoccupied with his phone that he walked face-first into someone without realizing it, and only saw when they both took a step back in a mutual flurry of curses and apologies that it was Amber.

"Oh! Amber! Hi!" he said, his voice shooting up into a register that should not have been detectable to the human ear.

"Sam! How are you? All finished? How did it go? This was illusions, right? How did it go?"

At the same time, they both seemed to realize how ridiculous they sounded, and mercifully, they both took a deep breath and managed to laugh it off.

"Illusions, yeah," Sam said more calmly. "It went okay. Not great, but okay."

"It can't have been worse than me at Elements of Empathy," Amber said. "When it got to the part where I was supposed to detect how the judges were feeling behind a closed curtain, I guessed disappointed, and that's one of the few I actually got right."

"The first convention's the hardest. The nerves are killer."

"Right? I never get nervous playing soccer, and we've made the playoffs before. I guess the difference is that soccer's a team sport. If I'm ever having an off day, I know my teammates can step in and pick up the slack."

"That must be nice."

"Yeah."

"So, listen, I was about to go meet Denver for lunch, so . . .

Good luck this afternoon, I guess? No wait, sorry, you only had the one category, duh. So, if you're going to watch James or Delia, I guess wish them good luck?"

"Sam."

"Hm?"

"This doesn't feel good, does it?"

"What doesn't?"

"You know what I mean."

"Oh. That."

"I know it's not really my place, because I'm new to the group and I don't know all the history and stuff, but you know what I think?"

"What do you think?"

"I think James really needs you right now. He's just too proud to say it."

"Come again?"

"I know he hasn't told you this for some bizarre reason that I can only assume is because boys are dumb sometimes, but I first heard it at church, when we were all told to pray for him, and . . . Anyway, his dad actually lost his job, and things have been pretty rocky at home for him ever since."

"Oh yeah?" Sam said, trying to keep up the stoic act, though this news really did come as a surprise to him. "Since when?"

"Since July."

"Seriously?"

"Seriously. And apparently, it was after he hit on some woman whose roof he was working on, so he hasn't been eligible for unemployment. He's been working odd jobs here and there, and James has been helping him out, but without the company's clients, it has been really tough. I think your opinion means a lot to James, and he doesn't want you to think less of him."

"Think less of *him*? Because his *dad* got fired for harassment?"

"I mean, no offense, Sam, but even the way you just said that sort of proves him right."

"Wow. Okay, sorry, it's just a lot to take in, especially since it's not even coming from James."

"I get the sense he wanted to wait to tell you in case things turned around. The way things stand right now, it's not looking good for him going to college at all next year, let alone sticking to your roommate plan. He doesn't want to leave Benji home alone until he knows there's a steady income. And his mom's been talking about finding work, but . . ." She shrugged.

"Well, don't I feel like an asshole now," Sam said.

"No, don't," Amber said. "Seriously, Sam, I'm not telling you to make you feel bad. I just hate to stand by and watch your friendship fall apart over nothing."

Sam bristled a little at that. It wasn't *nothing*. Did Amber know that Sam had been in love with James, even when he'd tried so hard not to be? Did James and the church ask her to pray about that, too, and did he ask her not to tell Sam? Was he telling her about all the times when it had been so painfully obvious to him that Sam had a crush on him? Sharing an air mattress last year?

That night outside the bowling alley? Or in the woods?

That's when it hit Sam.

July.

The book. Maybe this was why James had snuck in to look at it in the first place, at such a great risk. Maybe he thought there was some spell in there that could make his family rich. Maybe he was *planning* to steal the book, to hold it for ransom. Maybe the need to do something, anything, had felt so great, he'd acted without a clear plan at all. Maybe his desperation had made planning impossible.

Sam could relate.

His phone buzzed in his pocket. It was a message from Denver.

At the entrance. Where are you?

"I have to go," Sam said. "But . . . thank you. For telling me this. It doesn't fix everything, but it explains a lot."

"I really think if you can be the bigger person and apologize, it will all be forgiven."

"Duly noted. Are you three planning to come to the dance tonight?"

"I'm not sure. Delia and James didn't bring costumes, so I don't think they are. They said it's usually boring."

"But you brought a costume?"

She nodded.

"Good for you. Don't listen to them. It's only boring because James always gets drunk, and neither of them ever dances. Denver and I will be there, though. If you can convince James to join you, maybe I'll see what I can say."

Amber smiled. She had a nice smile, too, warm and inviting like Denver's. Who knew what their little magicker chapter could have accomplished, if they'd had all five of them from the beginning and none of this mess with True Light?

It was a shame they'd never know.

CHAPTER 20

SAM WAS UNDER NO ILLUSIONS THAT THE CHATHAM Ballroom was the lap of luxury. But with a full wall of windows looking out onto a gorgeous sunset, and with a decorating committee that had used the full extent of their magic to bring the Modern Fairy Tale theme to life, the room—as it was set for the convention-ending dance—cast an undeniable spell.

It was possible that Sam was still riding high from their coup at the podium that afternoon.

When all the judges' decisions had been handed in, and all the scores had been tallied, the Friedman High Fascinators had come out with a fifth-place overall finish, on the strength of three category firsts for Delia, a first and a third for James, and even a third apiece for Sam and Denver. The fact that they had scores at all in the rest of the categories meant that those exceptional individual results were enough to catapult them to right behind the elite Atlanta schools. They'd even placed ahead of Savannah Country Academy, sending a shockwave among all the students gathered in the auditorium.

It should have been a unilaterally triumphant moment, but of course, it wasn't. They'd accepted their trophy as two distinct groups occupying the same space on the stage, and even Ms. Berry—when she finally finished her ecstatic whoops of joy—was forced to acknowledge that Sam, James, and Delia were not celebrating with one another, or talking at all for that matter.

Whatever.

The others could stay at the hotel looking for a room party, or they could make the drive back tonight for all Sam cared.

He and Denver were going to enjoy this dance. They were going to post lots of pictures in their modern fairy-tale costumes, and they were going to send off this four-year chapter in Sam's life in style.

"Puck?" Denver had said, meeting Sam in the hotel lobby. They'd agreed not to tell each other their costumes ahead of time, and Sam had been looking forward to showing off his revealing vest and vines—not to mention the pointy prosthetic ears—more than he'd been looking forward to anything else this weekend.

Which he'd realized was silly when he'd turned around and seen Denver. That's what he should have been looking forward to the most.

"Oh. My. God."

"Can you guess who I am?"

"The Swan Prince?"

"I was going for the Swan Princess, but close enough."

From the fitted shirt of white feathers, intricately arranged, to the opalescent blush accenting his cheekbones—all the way to the silver diadem nestled in his curls that really was rather feminine now that he said it (though in Sam's defense, Denver was wearing black pants)—Denver had arrived like an absolute vision. Sam had felt the eyes of all the other hotel guests on them as they stood there appraising each other. Puck and the Swan Princess then headed over to the convention center for a dance where their attention to detail fit right in.

Even the music tonight had an otherworldly air. Sam recognized the vocals from pop songs he knew, but whoever they'd gotten to DJ the event was remixing everything to have a more elegant cadence. Not that anyone here had any idea of the best way to dance to such music. But it was nice to see all these eccentric souls whirring about the room at their own pace, in their own styles, instead of breaking off into heteronormative pairs and pantomiming reproduction, as had been the case at the last Friedman High homecoming dance Sam attended.

"So now we just . . . dance," Sam said, still mostly on a high but feeling a little self-conscious about his bare shoulders among so many strangers.

Denver moved his whole body in sync to the rhythm, as if that was just something humans knew how to do. "That's right, Puck—master of revelry, dabbler in mischief. We dance."

They eventually glommed on to another group of misfits, and they danced in one of those circles that required brave souls to show off their moves in the middle.

It was all so fun—or it would have been, except . . . except that Sam kept wondering what James and Delia were doing. Kept wondering what it had looked like when Amber had asked James to consider going to the dance, *if* Amber had asked James to consider going to the dance. They hadn't talked about it again since this morning.

Not to mention, Sam was still on high alert, thinking about his prediction. Everyone who looked at him funny seemed as if they were getting ready to attack, and Sam would tense, preparing the one self-defense spell from Denver he'd managed to master, only to realize that it was some random kid in a costume, looking past him on their way to rejoin their friends.

Denver kept noticing Sam in these moments, and he'd offer a crooked smile to remind Sam that he should smile, too—which of course was easy to do when Denver reminded him.

"Are you having a good time?" he finally said, dancing in front of, around, and beside Sam.

"Sure," Sam said.

"Sure?"

"I mean, yes."

"I see. Missing Delia and James, then?"

"Not even," Sam said too quickly. "I've tried to have a good time at this thing all four years, and all four years, they've ruined it."

"And yet . . ."

"I just don't know how people turn off their brains and have fun, you know?"

"Are you calling me brainless?" Denver teased.

"No, sorry, that's not what I'm trying to say. What I mean is, I thought the point of dancing was to *not* think about every little thing, but I keep noticing how awkward my hands are, and I keep thinking of how Delia and James probably hate me, and I keep imagining that all these other groups around us are doing it differently, doing it better, because they aren't weirdoes back in their own hometown, and—"

"Here," Denver said, taking both of Sam's hands in his. "Try this."

The music didn't slow down—not exactly. But it suddenly seemed as if it had, as Denver placed Sam's left hand on his shoulder, cupped his own right hand on Sam's back, and held Sam's free hand in his free hand—a waltz position, though Denver wasn't leading him in a waltz. He led them in more of a freestyle sway, in rhythm with the music.

Denver's shoulder was surprisingly warm, or maybe it was just that Sam's whole body was suddenly warmer.

"Is this okay?" Denver said.

"Yes," Sam said.

"What are you thinking now?"

"Nothing."

"Then it's working."

"Denver," Sam said, even though he wasn't even sure how he planned to finish that sentence. Anyway, he didn't have to, because many things happened at once to interrupt him, in that moment when time was already slowed.

Six erstwhile dancers—five along the room's edges, and one dead center—all began a complex and synchronized choreography that, together with their matching masks, revealed them to be part of some crew. An innocent flash mob, perhaps, forming the points and the center of a pentagram. Except that . . .

A man all in black, in a seventh matching mask, stepped right through the rippling wall of windows, as if it were water, not glass. He carried a book, opened to a page in the middle, and it looked like he was reading it aloud as he came. *The Seven of Swords.* Sam had been so fixated on the symbolism of the card during his spell—deception, theft—that he'd hardly given much thought to its more literal reading. But now the seven swords of True Light were here, and there was no joy in having seen the future coming, nor time to do anything about its arrival, because in that same moment . . .

James—in a plain T-shirt and dark jeans, his only nod to a modern fairy tale being the glittering blue lipstick he wore—stopped short in the main entrance, first taking in the sight of Denver and Sam dancing together with an unreadable expression, then taking in the sight of the seven masked figures, recognizing them immediately for what they truly were, because of course he knew the spell—had felt the associations in action once before. Which was why . . .

Before Sam had even processed the reality of these simultaneous developments—before he could even prepare his meager self-defense spell, which would have been useless in any case—the seven swords of True Light completed the precise motions of their collective spell, and James screamed the guttural sounds of a spell of his own, and those parallel but opposing forces met like a blinding supernova giving way to a black hole.

Sam was thrown clean off his feet.

It was only because he was holding on to Denver, and Denver was flung in a perpendicular direction, that they didn't go farther. Plenty of the other partygoers weren't so lucky; they were hurled into the air like bowling pins caught in a strike, and they landed on top of one another with cries of pain.

Everyone's vision was recovering from the flash.

Mixed in with the clear sounds of injury were as many clear sounds of fear. Sam frantically blinked the stars out of his eyes, feeling around for Denver, who was moaning in pain.

"Denver, we have to get out of here. Denver, are you all right?"

"My leg . . ."

Sam willed his vision to return. As it finally began to clear up, what came into view was Denver's right leg bent at a horrible angle.

"My leg . . ." Denver repeated.

Sam tried not to throw up.

"Don't move. I'm going to get you help. Stay right there."

All around him, people were clutching at sore limbs or rubbing their eyes. Everyone was shaken but getting their bearings, and a few people with stronger survival instincts than Sam's were quick to stumble for the entrance, aware that the danger hadn't fully passed.

The swords of True Light were still in the room. Four of them, including the leader with the book, were still down, and a fifth was standing over the leader, trying to shake him awake.

The other two were—

Oh no.

They were standing over James. James wasn't moving.

Sam pushed through the haze and charged at them like a bull, screaming at the top of his lungs and leaping over anyone who got in his way.

His brain was too white-hot with panic to produce any spells. He wasn't like James, who could exhale magic like it was carbon dioxide. Even the self-defense spell Denver had taught him was useless in this moment.

The only weapon he had was himself, but that would have to do. He body-slammed the masked figure closer to James, jack-knifing to take out the other with his feet, and the force and the element of surprise were enough to send them all rolling into the wall with an *oomph.*

That lasted only a moment before he was full-on wrestling with them both. Lashing and kicking out like he was some sort of rabid animal, while the two of them struggled to contain him, one focusing on his arms, the other on his legs.

A lucky kick connected with a stomach, and it was almost enough to give him the upper hand. He might have gone through with throttling them. There was no telling what he was capable of in that moment.

Except that without so much as a word of warning, Sam felt his body freeze up, and looked over to see the figure from before, who'd been checking on the leader. An older woman, from what Sam could see behind the mask. The figure now held the book under her arm, and with a flick of her wrist, she'd frozen Sam in place.

As she approached them, one of the boys Sam had been fighting—a guy with a football player's build—turned to her and said, "Sorry, we're hurrying," even though Sam hadn't heard her speak.

The other guy—the one Sam had kicked in the stomach—now struggled to stand, but when he finally did, he didn't waste a moment landing a quick kick to Sam's ribs. The pain was excruciating, but still Sam couldn't move.

"Stop it, you dumbass," the first guy said, running an anxious hand over his military buzz cut, balling the other hand into a fist. Sam had a flashback to something, though he couldn't place it. Meanwhile, the woman flipped through the book, searching for something specific, until finally, she found whatever it was and started moving her free hand in the motions of a spell.

Out of the corner of his eye, through the entrance to the ballroom, Sam could see a group of adults sprinting toward them. One of them looked to be a police officer, and there were two paramedics, but everyone else appeared to be teachers. Ms. Berry was among them. Someone must have had the good sense to call for backup, instead of running headfirst into the assailants like Sam had, violating nearly every emergency drill he'd ever learned in school.

"Hurry up!" the muscular guy called again, this time to a fourth masked figure who was shuffling their way. At first Sam thought the figure was limping, but no—they were just moving reluctantly, wringing their hands. Finally, they came to the side of the woman with the book and placed a hand on her shoulder, and Sam saw that it was a girl's hand. A girl's hand that Sam would recognize anywhere, because of the friendship bracelet.

The two guys placed their hands on the leader, too, and then, in the millisecond before all the adults made it into the room, the four swords vanished—there, and then gone.

Sam felt control of his movements returning instantly—felt the agony intensify. He rolled to his unhurt side, groaning from the pain in his ribs.

The adults swarmed the room, running with a purpose that confirmed Sam's theory—they knew what they were looking for. With the help of the police officer, a few of them were quickly conjuring a binding spell to detain the three swords left, which didn't look to be too hard, given their own injuries.

Ms. Berry ran straight for Sam.

"Oh my God, oh my God," she said. "Sam, can you hear me? Can you talk? Can you breathe?"

"Yes, yes, and ow," Sam said, trying his best to sit up. "It was all so sudden. They came out of nowhere."

"Don't worry about that now," Ms. Berry said. "You're okay. You're safe."

She'd already moved on to James, now that Sam was talking.

"Help!" she screamed, when James didn't respond to her attempts to wake him.

"He stopped them, Ms. Berry. He came in, and he saw what they were going to do, and he stopped them." Sam was babbling now. He was absolutely losing it.

One of the paramedics ran over to them, hearing the panic in Ms. Berry's voice, and as soon as he saw James, he spoke into a radio comm on his shoulder, before leaning down to James's side to check for a pulse.

"He's breathing," the paramedic said. "Back up, please."

Ms. Berry complied, but she had to pull Sam away.

"Where's Denver?" she said.

"Over there. I think he broke his leg pretty bad. He needs a doctor, too."

"We'll get him one. Oh my God, oh my God."

They both stared at the paramedic as he ministered to James, attempting a series of spells that seemed to have little to no effect.

Ms. Berry spoke in a frantic stream, the words pouring out of her. "He told me he was coming over here, and I almost joined him, because there'd be three of the five of you here, instead of two. But then he promised Amber he would come right back, and I thought, I'd better stay here—a chaperone needs to stay at the hotel, too. Who knows what they'll get up to if I leave. I should have come with him."

Sam said nothing.

"We have to tell them," Ms. Berry said. "One of us has to tell them on our way to the hospital. Otherwise Amber and Delia won't know what happened to us. They'll be worried sick."

"Oh, I think Delia already knows," Sam said bitterly, all the anger that had been trapped behind a precarious dam of necessity now spilling over and out, flooding his vision with red, red, red.

"What do you mean? How could Delia know?"

"She's one of the ones who did this. She just escaped with their spell book."

Ms. Berry gasped.

"No," she said immediately, but it wasn't an expression of disbelief. It was an expression of exactly the kind of self-loathing Sam was feeling, too—a realization that their inability to read the signs right in front of them had led to this moment. In Ms. Berry's case, it was a far more innocent claim to blame—a reluctance to wade into an all-too-typical fight among teenagers, to ask them what all the drama was about. As if they would have told her anyway.

Not so for Sam. Sam had had all the pieces. It had been so obvious—Delia's allegiances so clear.

But Sam hadn't done a damn thing about it. Hadn't wanted to accept the truth.

Now James was lying there, alive but unconscious, and with all his healing spells exhausted, the only thing the paramedic could do for him was call into his radio comm with increasing urgency.

And it was all Sam's fault.

CHAPTER 21

"YOU TOLD ME IT WAS HARMLESS. LIKE GIVING BLOOD!"

Delia's head was swimming. Her breaths were coming quick and shallow. She'd never teleported such a long distance before—had no idea it was even possible—and the version of herself that had appeared back at the compound felt like it was more than a few pieces shy of complete.

"I never said that," Isaac said, his mask up over his head as he paced around the office, muttering curses under his breath. Grace had been forced to lie down immediately upon arrival, the effort required for the teleportation spell taking nearly all she had to give. Hank had run to the bathroom, presumably to throw up, and Delia had a feeling she might be doing the same very soon.

"Mr. Grender said it, then, and you agreed," Delia said. "I trusted you. You said we weren't going to hurt anyone."

"And we wouldn't have, either, if your little friend hadn't

gotten in the way. It was his spell that hurt everyone. Don't you see? What the hell was that, anyway? How did he know how to do that?"

"He didn't," Delia said, exasperated, sad. "He's like Grace. It all comes from him. He, like, wills it into being."

"That's not how Grace's magic works," Isaac said, and for all the contempt in his voice, he may as well have said, *You don't know anything.*

And maybe she didn't.

Oh God, what had she done?

What had she done to *James*?

She'd told them about convention. She'd helped them with the planning. She'd helped with the spell. And all for what? Because she wanted to be powerful? Because she wanted to be the best?

Delia may have had a lifetime of being forgotten, but this was not how she wanted to be remembered.

"There's no coming back from this, you know," Isaac said. "The police will be after us. The Keepers will be after us. We're in it now. Our only way out is through."

With a loud, harsh *bang*, the door behind them flew open, and Hank barged into the office, his normally placid face twisted up with almost ecstatic glee. There were trails of magic coming off his fingers, rising up like ten tendrils of electricity, each a different color. Stranger still, he was six inches off the ground, hovering there like some kind of angel decked in plaid.

"It worked!" he shouted. "It worked! It worked!"

CHAPTER 22

WHEN SAM WAS THIRTEEN, HIS GRANDPARENTS HAD passed away within a week of each other—his grandmother from lung cancer, and his grandfather, seven days later, from heartbreak. That was actually what the doctor said at the time—that the official cause of death was a broken heart, although he had a longer name to go with it, to make it sound more official.

That week had been one of the worst in Sam's life, especially because his mother, as an empath, had felt the death of her parents so acutely that her grief had been like a contagious disease, overwhelming for all in her vicinity. Sam would never forget the sight of her, sobbing over her father's deathbed in the Friedman Hospital ICU. He would never be able to dissociate that memory from the antiseptic smell of the floor; he thought of it sometimes when he washed his hands.

The Savannah Memorial Hospital smelled even stronger than

the Friedman Hospital, which wasn't surprising, since it was so sprawling and high tech in comparison. What was surprising was how immediate and visceral Sam's reaction had been when he entered the hospital, running right past the automatic doors, followed closely by Amber. He'd broken down before he even made it through the lobby. Amber had been forced to pull him up by the shoulders and drag him the rest of the way to the receptionist's desk.

Thank goodness for Amber.

While Sam hadn't been able to get two words out, Amber had not only figured out how to get to the emergency room where the paramedics had taken James and Denver, she'd convinced the receptionist that she and Sam should be allowed security clearance to go find them. It helped that the hospital was utterly upside down, flooded with injuries mostly related to freak falls but some of them from strange residual magic.

"Can you hold yourself up from here?" Amber asked.

"Yes, sorry."

They found Denver quickly, because Denver was sitting up straight on the edge of a gurney, along the wall closest to the entrance. He looked dazed but all right. Sam was relieved to see that his leg was no longer bent at an irregular angle.

Before Denver even registered their approach, Sam enveloped him in a hug, careful to avoid his leg.

"I'm so relieved you're okay."

"It still tingles where the doctor worked his magic. They said they want me to stay here for a little bit longer so they can be sure the bone is setting properly. Mostly I'm worried about what my mom's going to do to me when she gets here."

"How could your mom possibly be angry at you about this?"

"It's more that I'm afraid she's going to break more bones when she hugs me. She was in a panic on the phone. It sounds like this is on the Atlanta news."

"I can imagine," Amber said. "Our parents are on their way, too. Hey, did you see where they took James? The receptionist said a room in the back corner, but this place has multiple back corners."

Solemnly, Denver pointed to a room clear on the other side of the operations desk. "I think it's that one. I didn't see them take him in, but doctors have been going in and out. It has to be him."

Amber immediately took off for the room, and with an apologetic look back to Denver, Sam followed her. They got all the way up to the door—through which they could see James lying on a bed, hooked up to a frightening number of machines—before a nurse came running around the desk to stop them.

"Hey! Can I help you?" he said, in a tone of voice that made it clear he was less concerned with helping them than he was with keeping them out.

"We're friends of his," Amber said.

"Sorry, but it's medical professionals only for now. For his safety as much as anyone's."

"What's wrong with him?" Sam said.

The nurse chewed his lower lip, like he knew more than he was allowed to share.

"We're still trying to figure it out for sure."

"Does he still have his magic?"

The nurse narrowed his eyes.

"What makes you ask that?"

"I think I know the people who did this to him. At least, I know what they were trying to do."

"Wait right there," the nurse said. "I'm going to get a doctor, and you can tell them all about it."

The nurse took off in a brisk, hospital-friendly speed-walk, fast enough to confirm Sam's fears that whatever was afflicting James had them seriously concerned.

Sam and Amber exchanged terrified glances.

"I still can't believe Delia," Amber said. Back at the hotel, Sam had frantically explained as much as he could to her and Ms. Berry. He'd followed Ms. Berry back to gather Amber and all their things, figuring that whatever happened tonight, they'd probably have to leave straight from the hospital. He'd had to tell them both why they shouldn't waste their time knocking on doors, looking for Delia.

"The problem is, I *can* believe it. I just don't want to."

"Why did their spell only affect James like this, though? That's what I don't understand."

"My theory is, whatever spell he did protected the rest of us, but it left him vulnerable. I guess it's also possible their spell didn't work at all, and James's spell did all the damage. But that's not how it *felt* in there. It felt like we were caught up in an undertow, flowing against the main current."

"That's awfully poetic," Amber said, and for a second, Sam thought she was taking a dig at him. But then she added, "James says that's why you're so good at magic. Your associations are so strong."

Sam felt his heart flip over. James was a good friend. Maybe Amber was, too.

"He's going to get better," Sam said, though he was picturing Death.

"I hope so."

The nurse came back with not one but three doctors, and Sam explained everything he knew and felt. They treated him like a case they were studying, asking probing questions from a cool distance, curious but almost uncaring, wanting to know more about these True Light people than anything.

"How is this going to help James?" Sam finally asked, growing exasperated.

"We're not sure yet," one of the doctors said. "But this helps point us in the right direction for a counter curse. His symptoms are consistent with those of someone suffering from a diabetic coma, which supports your theory in a way—his body needs magic. Unfortunately, *magic* is not something we can supply like insulin. If it's true what you say, that these people have a spell to transfuse magic like blood, they may be the only people on the planet who do."

Which was exactly what Sam was afraid of.

While the doctors went back to call their colleagues and search their databases for anything that might help them, Sam turned to social media, to see what the world was saying about what had happened in the Chatham Ballroom tonight.

Right away, he found reports that the three people he'd seen apprehended had since been arrested and named, though no one had gotten a motive out of them yet. In the mug shot associated with all the stories, the leader of the pack had a name Sam recognized—Albert Grender. So maybe that was a silver lining. Mr. Grender was in custody. He couldn't hurt anyone else.

But reading about the four fugitives police were seeking, and knowing that one of those fugitives was Delia, was about as far from a silver lining as it got. It was a horror for which there was no metaphor.

Sam was still caught up in the spiral of news stories and random comment threads when two very loud voices erupted through the doors of the emergency room, announcing the arrival of James's parents.

"—and if I have to ask one more time, you're all going to be sorry."

That was James's dad.

"Where's my son? Where is he?"

That was James's mom.

Benji trailed behind and between them, looking miserable and scared. Sam tried to keep his focus on him when, at almost exactly the same time, like two predators catching a scent, James's parents looked up and spotted Sam and Amber standing outside their son's room.

With curt nods and nothing more, James's parents brushed past their son's closest friends and went to stand beside James's bed. The nurse who'd tried to stop Sam and Amber started to speak, to issue them the same warning, but James's dad barked out, "We're his family," in such a scary voice that there was no arguing with it. Benji was openly crying beside James's bed, and that sight, even more than the smell, was bringing back all of Sam's memories of his mom and his grandparents.

"What's wrong with him?" Benji said between tears.

"We don't know yet, sweetie. The doctors are still trying to figure it out."

"'Course we know," Mr. Dawson said. "It was magic that did this to him, like we always said it would."

That only made Benji cry harder, and it made Sam's blood boil, too. It wasn't untrue, strictly speaking, but it didn't feel fair, either.

"You mark my words, Benji. Ain't nothing good can come out of getting mixed up in the stuff. This is why we don't let you run around with those kids from the rec center. It's to protect you. So you don't end up in a hospital bed like your brother."

"Just so you know," Sam said, stepping into the room and trying his best to keep his voice from shaking, "James saved a lot of people tonight. With magic."

"Is that so?" Mr. Dawson said, and it was clear he didn't like being challenged. Amber put a hand on Sam's arm, trying to pull him back out into the hall. "So, what, magic doesn't hurt people—people hurt people? The only way to fight magic is with magic?"

"What? No."

"Yeah, I didn't think you'd feel that way. A boy like yourself. So why don't you mind your own business?"

"Tom—" Mrs. Dawson said in warning.

"No, Sandy, I am sick of standing by and pretending that our son isn't putting his life in danger every time he tries to bend his spirit around some blasphemous act. Far be it from me to tell other people's children what a life of piety looks like, but no, ma'am, our son will not be forsaking God any more if he wakes up from this."

Sam could feel Amber tense beside him. Clearly, they each took this as a personal dig.

"Your son will be eighteen in less than two months," Sam said. "*When* he wakes up, you won't be able to control him forever."

Mr. Dawson's jaw actually dropped and stayed there. Mrs. Dawson said, "You've said your piece. Now we'd like some time alone with our son, if you don't mind."

And what was Sam supposed to say to that?

Sam barely remembered the trip back to Friedman. Denver's words proved prophetic, and not only for him. All of their parents, when they arrived, wrapped them up in such violent hugs that they nearly required the services of the ER doctors.

The news reports must have been very dire indeed.

Apparently, Sam's parents went back to see James's before leaving, and somewhere along the way home, they asked him about Delia. But Sam only put that together based on what they said the next day—as it was happening, he registered their movements and questions with the kind of sleepy, confused distance he'd always imagined he would experience in a dream.

He'd barely come out of his trancelike state when he found himself driving to the True Light compound on Sunday evening.

With their leader and two acolytes arrested, Sam wasn't sure if anyone would even still be there. If they were, he wasn't sure if he was planning to beg for their help curing James or to get revenge in the most spectacular way he could think of on the spot. He figured he could decide when he got there.

There was one problem, though. Getting there was turning out to be more difficult than it should've been.

He'd reached the road James had shown them that first day, and he drove along it exactly as he had before. But even though he kept his eyes trained out his passenger side window, he wasn't seeing the open field or the compound at all, and before he knew it, he had reached the turnoff to the fairy-tale forest where they'd looked for the book as a group. That was odd . . .

Sam turned around and made the drive in the opposite direction. Again, he drove right past where he remembered seeing the compound, and again, there was nothing. He made it back to the main road a full minute before he expected to.

The compound—and the land it sat on—had simply disap-peared.

As soon as he got home, he texted Amber and Denver, strongly requesting—begging for, really—an emergency meeting of the Fascinators.

They responded right away, without hesitation. It was like they'd been waiting for just such a rallying cry. When they showed up at his house, it was clear Sam's mom thought they were all there to work through the trauma together, and in a way, that was true—Sam's mom must have felt it.

"I'll put some pizza bagels in the oven," she said with a wor-ried frown.

Sam, Amber, and Denver trudged down the steps to the basement in silence. Sam considered his first words carefully, determined to put up a calm, leaderly front. The club's line of succession left him as acting president, after all.

He took a deep breath.

And another.

And another.

Amber spoke tentatively. "Our pastor said this morning that they'll be moving James to Friedman Hospital sometime this week. Sounds like whatever counter curse those Savannah doctors tried didn't work, and so they're saying he might as well try to get better at home."

"Do you know what they're going to try next?" Denver said.

"I don't. It didn't really seem right to ask questions, since everybody was staring at me like I was the devil just for having been down there, too."

"I have an idea," Sam said. He held up a thick stack of papers. "The first week of school, Delia gave us this syllabus she picked up from a class at Pinnacle. Applied Magics. I don't think she thought I would actually read it. Maybe she did. Who knows. Anyway, a lot of what's on here is incomprehensible, but not all of it. And there's a thing here, something she thought we could use to find the book, that says if you know the words, components, and associations of a spell, you can work out a counter spell."

"Arnauld's Axiom," Denver said.

"Wait, how do you know that?" Sam said.

"It was one of the Tennessee convention categories last year."

"All right, then. Anyway, I'm betting this is what the doctors in Savannah were trying to figure out, only they didn't know the spell that the True Light people had done."

"And you do?" Amber said, a hint of excitement creeping into her voice.

"Not exactly. But I know who does."

"Delia, you mean? President Traitor?"

Sam grimaced. Even if he was thinking the same thing, and even if this hardly made sense, he wasn't sure Denver had earned the right to be mad at her.

"Do you even know where Delia is?" Amber asked. "I thought you said she disappeared."

"I'm willing to bet anything that they're back at their dank warehouse, planning their next steps. But here's the thing. I tried to go by there earlier, and their compound is *gone*. Like, vanished-without-a-trace gone."

"You think it was some kind of spell?"

"I do. But it would have to be a very advanced one. To make not only a whole building but the land it was on disappear? I didn't believe Delia when she said they were more powerful than the Keepers, but maybe I should have."

"What if it's still there, but hidden?" Denver said.

"What do you mean?"

"I mean, I agree—I've never heard of magic that could make a whole tract of land just not exist. But I have heard of plenty of cloaking spells. Spells that make something functionally invisible, by drawing the eye away. A sleight of hand on a major scale. It's still complex magic, but not impossible."

"Maybe we should let some adults handle it from here," Amber said. "Tell Ms. Berry, or better yet, the police, that the four fugitives they've been looking for are hiding behind a cloaking spell in Friedman."

"No, we can't do that," Sam said. "Negotiation 101. If they're arrested, they'll never tell us the spell they used on James."

"Not even Delia?" Amber said, horrified.

"Especially not Delia. She learned her negotiation skills from my mom, same as I did."

"Cool, cool," Amber said. "So, the plan is literally to negotiate with terrorists. What could go wrong?"

"What choice do we have?" Sam said.

Amber shifted uncomfortably but said nothing.

Finally, Denver said, "Well, I'm not sure what sort of spell we need to break through a cloaking device, but if it would mean saving James, I'm all in."

"Thank you, Denver. I appreciate that show of solidarity. I know the group hasn't exactly been a happy family for a minute."

"I'm doing it for you as much as anything. If James doesn't wake up, you'll never get over it. You'll compare every guy you ever date to him, and wonder what you could've had, if things had gone that way with James."

Now Sam stared at him bug-eyed, shocked that he would say this in front of Amber. But Amber was looking at everything else in the room *but* Sam right then. It couldn't be clearer: this wasn't news to her. It dawned on Sam that it wasn't news to anyone. He'd only wanted to think that it would be news to James, because that was better than the alternative.

Nevertheless, Denver was right. Whatever the truth of James's feelings, Sam needed to hear it from James. He hated that it took his friend being in a magic-induced coma for Sam to finally feel up to the task of talking to him about it.

"I have an idea of where to get some help," Sam said. "Are you two free to come with me to Atlanta after school tomorrow?"

Emma was thrilled to see him again for the second time in two months—especially with new friends—even if she could tell right away from the looks on their faces that they weren't there for Monday movie night.

"Is Liv here, actually?" Sam said, after making a round of very quick introductions.

"She is. She's upstairs. Why?" Emma looked suspicious and even a little protective, like maybe Liv had opened up to her about some of the things she'd mentioned to Sam last time, and now Emma was hoping this wasn't the reason Sam was here. Sam had seen her go into Momma Bear mode before, and he didn't want to get on the wrong side of it, ever.

"It's about our friend, James. He's in a bit of trouble, and we think Liv might know some magic that could help him."

"I don't suppose you mean her knack for storms," Emma said, frowning.

"We wouldn't ask if it weren't really important," Amber said.

Emma eyed Sam carefully, until finally she seemed satisfied by what she saw, and stepped aside to let the three of them upstairs.

Just like last time, Liv was sitting off by herself, oblivious to the four younger kids huddled in front of a horror movie projected onto the far wall. She didn't even look up when Sam, Amber, and Denver walked in, but she said, "I knew you'd come back, sooner or later."

"The warehouse," Sam said, cutting right to the chase. "We think it's covered by some kind of cloaking spell."

"You're quicker on the uptake than most, aren't you?" Liv said. "Though if you were really smart, you'd stay the hell away from there."

"That we can't do," Sam said. "Our friend's life depends on us getting in there."

"Must be some friend," Liv said darkly.

"He really is," Sam replied.

"Well, I saw on the news you put Mr. Grender behind bars, so I guess I do owe you for that."

One of the movie watchers turned to shush them, but Sam just raised an eyebrow in a look that said *Try me*, and that was that.

"We know it's a big ask, bringing you back into all this, but you truly would be saving a life," Amber said. "And trust us, we'll make sure word never gets out that you helped us."

Liv looked at Amber so long it was almost uncomfortable.

"You know what's funny?" she finally said. "Even when they were at their most heinous—even when they told me, repeatedly, I was going to hell—I really believed that my parents loved me, somewhere deep down in there. That if I ran away, they would realize how wrong they were and come crawling back. But it never happened. They didn't even call. Emma keeps telling me I have to learn to trust other people regardless. That even after my parents, and what happened at the compound, I'm still supposed to try to see the best in each new person I meet, because not everyone's like *them*. But it's really fucking hard."

Sam knew what she meant. He didn't have it even a fraction as bad as she did, but he got where she was coming from. Eighteen years of living in Friedman had seen to that.

"Sorry, I guess it's not so much funny as sad," Liv said.

"It is sad," Sam said. "It totally sucks that all that happened to you. But Liv? You got out. And I can't promise that you'll always be safe. The faceless ones will be at the edges of your vision, always there in your head when you try to go to sleep. But you have help now. You have Emma. And you have us. And if you need us, we'll be there, just like we need to be there for our friend now. That's how this works."

"I really want to believe you," Liv said.

And then, with a deep breath, she told them the spell.

This time, when they reached the spot on the road where Sam remembered seeing the field open up onto the compound, he muttered the words Liv had told them, and then he let out a gasp. There it was, hidden in plain sight.

They'd driven straight here from Atlanta, and while it wasn't too late, it was already dark out. Knowing what he was looking at, he realized he could see a faint shimmer in the sky where the moonlight coming down should have been continuous but was broken instead, its glow split where it intersected with the cloaking spell.

"I think we should leave your car here," Denver said. "If we drive up to that parking lot, everyone inside is going to hear us coming."

"If they're as powerful as we think, they might know we're here anyway," Amber said.

"Let's hope that their numbers are down enough that they're

overwhelmed with other things, or at least distracted," Sam said.

"They weren't too overwhelmed to put up this insane cloaking spell," Amber said pessimistically.

"You can still turn back now if you want. I wouldn't judge you or hold it against you."

Neither of them budged from Sam's side.

"I don't suppose either of you knows even a low-level camouflage spell we could use on the walk? Delia taught us one ages ago, but I can never remember it."

Denver laughed darkly. "I think we'll just have to be as quiet as we can and cross our fingers."

Which was exactly what they did. Sam could hear the intense *kree-kree* of crickets and not much else as they crept along the short-grass field separating them from the compound. It was chilly enough that Sam felt his muscles constricting, though surely some of that was from nerves.

There was a large set of double-doors in the front of the compound, and Sam remembered from James's story there was a back door near the parking lot, but he figured both entrances would be watched and warded. Instead, he led them around to the side of the building, where there were no doors but there were windows on three distinct floors. They were boarded up, so all Sam could see was that lights were shining brightly on the first floor and less so on the upper floors. Sam remembered from James's description that the interior was shaped around a main room almost like a courtyard. Like a prison. What they were seeing would make sense if the light was coming from there.

"Maybe we should go in there with our white flag and beg," Amber said.

"No way," Denver said. "You didn't see them at the dance. These people don't care if you come in peace. They'll take you out without a second thought."

"There's a spell James did the night that we went to the fall festival—it lets you project your voice. If we can find a spell like that in one of the apps, maybe we can talk to Delia without alerting the others."

"I don't know about a spell *like* that," Amber said, "but I know that exact spell. James showed it to me before he got his cell phone back from his dad, just in case."

Denver watched Sam for his reaction, but Sam was past the point of being petty. Mostly, he was relieved.

He said, "Do you think you'd be able to do it now? To get Delia's attention?"

"I'm not sure," Amber said. "I never ended up doing it. In theory, if you know generally where a person is, you can target them pretty closely with what you want to say. But I've never seen the inside of that building. And if Delia is anywhere close to another person, they'll probably hear it, too."

"What if we do a finding spell first, to pinpoint Delia's location?" Sam suggested. "Would that help?"

"Maybe?" Amber said.

"Let's try it, then."

Sam reached out for their hands, and they formed a circle where they stood. Without the benefit of his singing bowl, he was hoping against hope that with their numbers and their power diminished, the True Light people wouldn't be ready and waiting for him.

"What object are we looking for?" Denver said. "I don't think the finding spell works on people. It works best if the object is unique."

"Her friendship bracelet," Sam said immediately. And then, considering it for a moment, he added, "I have to believe she's still wearing it."

Denver and Amber squinted, trying to remember and picture the bracelet Sam could see so clearly. When they were as ready as they were going to get, they all focused on the bracelet and let their minds wander. Perhaps because of the proximity, or perhaps because Sam had helped to create this bracelet in the first place, his mind went right away to a bedroom whose furnishings were a step below particleboard furniture out of a box, where Delia sat on the edge of a plywood bed with her head in her hands. Judging from the distant pine trees peeking through a window behind her, she was almost definitely in the compound, but it was so dark, it was hard to say exactly where.

"Good enough?" Denver said, snapping out of the vision before Sam and Amber had.

"I think so," Amber said, her eyes darting to the building beside them. She pointed to the far-right corner of the compound. "It seemed like she might be somewhere in there?"

"That's what I was getting, too," Denver said.

Sam shrugged, impressed.

"What exactly am I saying to her?" Amber asked.

"Tell her that she's not in trouble, but Sam is here, and James needs her help."

Amber covered her mouth as if she were one of those football coaches on TV, whispering a top-secret play into her microphone. It took her a full minute to say whatever she was saying, which meant the spell must have included all kinds of words beyond the message itself.

"Did it work?" Sam said when she finished.

"Hard to say," Amber said. "The only thing we can do now is wait."

"And maybe get your self-defense spells ready in case she doesn't come alone," Denver said, squaring his shoulders for a fight.

Sam couldn't bring himself to follow suit. He still hadn't fully processed what Delia had done at convention—what more she had been prepared to do—but if she came out here flinging spells, flanked by more of those people, well—Sam wasn't sure that was a world worth defending.

Fortunately, it didn't come to that.

They'd hardly waited five minutes before Delia stepped out of the darkness. Quite literally, at that. Sam had been watching the compound closely, but that wasn't the direction from which

Delia came; she appeared behind them suddenly, mists swirling about her feet.

She looked frightened to see them, and while at first Sam thought it was because she was afraid of what they might do, he quickly realized it was because she was afraid of what might happen to them.

"Are you insane? What the hell are you doing here?"

"Good to see you, too," Sam snapped back.

"James is unconscious," Amber said, trying to get them back on track. "We need whatever spell you did at convention so we can reverse it."

"Yeah, Arnold's Axiom," Sam said haughtily.

"Ar*nauld*'s," Delia corrected.

"Just give us the spell, please," Sam said. "Give us the spell, and we won't bother you anymore. We won't drag you down with our inferior high school magic. Because that's what this is about, right? The power? And in return, you won't have to lose sleep for the rest of your life, knowing that you killed James."

Delia winced. Which, good. Sam was going for the jugular. "No one was supposed to get hurt," she said quietly.

"And yet here we are. I don't understand it, Delia. I truly do not understand it. All you had to do was wait nine months, and you'd be long gone from here. Friedman. Me. James. You'd never have to see any of us again if you didn't want to, in your new life at Pinnacle. All that careful work. You just couldn't wait, huh?"

"I didn't get in, Sam."

"What?"

"To Pinnacle. I got my decision two weeks ago. I wasn't even wait-listed—just a short, sweet no."

"Aw, shit, Delia. You could have told me."

"Yeah? And what would you have said? No—what would you have *done*? I don't need sympathy. Not from anyone. I can take care of myself."

"Yes, I see you've done a bang-up job of that. Really set yourself up for life."

"What was it you said, Sam? 'You don't judge your friends by what they do one time'? I guess that only applies to boys you think are cute."

"How can you—"

"Guys?" Denver said. "Do we really have to do this now?"

"You're right," Delia said. "I don't have to explain myself to any of you. I'm leaving now, and I suggest you do the same."

"Not without that book," Sam said.

Delia frowned. "Even if I wanted to, there's no way in hell I could sneak that book out here. They are guarding it with everything they've got. I only made it out here by pretending to go to the bathroom."

Sam had suspected it would come to this eventually. There was no other option—they would have to make a run for the room. Hope they could get out with their lives.

But Amber put up a hand to stop him before he took his first step. She turned to Delia. "You don't have to sneak the book out here at all," she said, at first in surprise, then in bitterness. "You have a copy of the spell with you."

"What do you mean?" Sam said, looking back and forth between her and Delia, who had crossed her arms over her chest.

"Elements of Empathy. I may have bombed at convention from nerves, but I'm actually a pretty good empath when I put my mind to it. And you"—she said to Delia—"could give us the spell right now if you wanted. You just don't want to."

"Is that true?" Sam asked Delia.

In response, Delia sighed, then pulled out her phone and typed something quickly. Sam's phone dinged with a message, and when he opened it up, it was a series of photos. Zooming in, Sam saw that the photos were of the spell book. He remembered now that she'd taken one of the spells to post on the Pinnacle message boards—that was how she figured out the Enochian.

"Please be careful with those," Delia said. "You don't understand what they're like. How powerful they are. If they find out that I took those photos—let alone shared them with you—it would mean serious trouble for all of us."

"Dang, Delia," Sam said. "I hope the power is worth it."

"Not that I would ever expect you to understand," she said, "but it really, really is." Then she turned on her heel and vanished back into the night.

CHAPTER 23

THERE WERE TEN MINUTES LEFT OF VISITING HOURS when Sam, Amber, and Denver arrived at the Friedman Hospital, and they could tell from the annoyed look on the receptionist's face that he didn't trust the three of them to take only ten minutes.

"If it weren't crucially important, we'd come back tomorrow," Sam said.

The receptionist quirked a very world-weary eyebrow.

"We're his best friends," Amber cut in to explain, throwing Sam a look to remind him that they very purposefully were *not* mentioning their true intentions to anyone else, lest the doctors try to test their counter spell or get in their way. Sam felt sure that if even one more person caught wind of what they knew, True Light would come after their copy of the spell, and Delia really would be in more danger than she already was. In spite of everything, Sam wanted to avoid that at all costs.

"Room 103," the receptionist finally said. "You have nine minutes."

When they rounded the corner into the hallway where James's room was, they stopped short at the sight of James's dad, pacing outside his door. It might have been endearing, if he weren't an obstacle to their goal.

"No way he'll let me in there," Sam said.

"Maybe we should come back tomorrow?" Amber said. "Give ourselves more time to work on this counter spell?"

"As acting president, I honestly have no idea what to do," Sam said. "But if his parents are here now, they're probably going to be here tomorrow, too. We have no idea how long a person can live without their magic, and I'd rather not find out."

Denver said, "We can create a distraction for a few moments if you think that would give you enough time?"

Sam paused, considering. It was the kind of plan that would work only with superlatively good luck.

"Let's do it."

"All right." Denver nodded. "You stay here. When you hear me or Amber say, 'vegetarian lasagna,' that's your cue to make a dash for the room."

"It will definitely be Denver," Amber said. "I have no idea how I would work the words 'vegetarian lasagna' into a sentence."

"Duly noted," Denver said, and then the two of them were off.

Sam heard the moment they reached Mr. Dawson. It was hard to miss, because he had such a loud, deep voice. Even without hearing every word, Sam could tell that they were playing the concerned friend card, and he could also tell that Mr. Dawson didn't want to let them anywhere near his son.

"—and we would be happy to switch off with you this week, taking turns with him. Or if you even need us to bring food here one night, I make a mean vegetarian lasagna."

Denver was practically shouting that last bit, and Sam turned the corner at a near-sprint, afraid to miss his window. But the hardest part of staying hidden ended up being resisting the urge to laugh—the sight of Denver with his arm over Mr. Dawson's shoulder, forcibly turning him away from James's room so that he could tell him about vegetarian food, was pure comedy—the kind of gesture only someone as charming and lucky as Denver could get away with.

But Sam didn't laugh, and just like that, he slipped into James's room, where he had a powerful urge to sob.

James had severely diminished in the two days since Sam had seen him.

His skin was clammy and bruised. His hair was matted to his forehead. The tubes coming out of his mouth and nose made him look like some kind of android, more than anything. This couldn't wait another day. It couldn't even wait another minute.

The spell they'd prepared on the drive over here—Denver reading aloud the steps in the photo and then the three of them loudly debating the reverse of those steps, like this was one more convention category brief—was both tricky and demanding.

While the associations for the original spell were all about cutting and tearing, they'd agreed that the associations for the counter spell couldn't be as simple as mending or repairing. It was like a vein had been cut and James's magic had poured out; closing the vein now probably wouldn't do him much good. This was one of the points they'd debated—was magic a finite thing in the body, that needed to be replaced in the measure that was lost, or was it regenerative, self-restoring, so that if they *could* heal whatever part of James held it in, his own stores would resupply in time?

They weren't magic doctors, of course, but it was Amber who argued that since the magic doctors hadn't been able to fix James yet either, there probably *wasn't* a known healing spell that would do the trick. The piece of this True Light spell they needed to reverse was the piece that made True Light such an unprecedented horror—the taking of one person's magic for another. The counter spell needed to be a spell of giving.

Transcribing the words of the spell in reverse had been a touch easier, although it sounded like there were some instances of Arnauld's Axiom where it had been more effective to read the original words in reverse order, rather than to reverse every single letter. Who the hell had time to care about that? Sam had asked in the car and asked himself again now.

He needed to hurry, before Denver ran out of distractions.

Sam began to recite the words of the counter spell in a low whisper. He pictured his magic as a tangible thing, a thing he could give, and he pictured himself giving it. He remembered the time when he made James a playlist because the Schnauzer he'd had since he was a baby had died, and the time he gave James a sleeve of Rolos, for no other reason than that James had said he liked Rolos.

He conjured up all these moments of giving, and he kept reciting the words, and like anesthesia coursing its way fast and hot through his veins, he noticed that this spell was working, because he could feel its magic flowing through him.

And in the exact moments that he began to lose control of the spell—when the volume of his voice began to rise; and Mr. Dawson heard it and came in, shouting; and all the moments of giving started to become a blur—the spell took over, then took him out, then took him in.

Sam was back in the woods, that night after Bridget's party.

He and James were running, hand in hand, convinced that everyone was after them. They were being chased.

(No one was after them. They were not being chased.)

They reached the edge of the woods, and James stuck out his arm, ready to protect Sam from any Friedmanite who might want to hurt them.

(There was no one on the soccer field. No one in Friedman wanted to hurt them just then.)

James collapsed onto the grounds, and Sam lay down beside him. They looked up at the stars as if the stars existed only for the two of them.

(Countless people were looking up at those same stars at that same moment. All over the Western hemisphere.)

James leaned up on his elbow. He peered into Sam's eyes as if he was thinking about kissing him.

(He was thinking about kissing him. The boys felt so safe there.)

Sam didn't move, and James closed his eyes, and the moment passed.

(The moment passed. The moment passed. The moment passed.)

It was this summer at the bowling alley. The three of them had already bowled two rounds. This group of other Friedmanites had come over, because one of the guys, Jamal, had wanted to talk to Delia, and that meant everyone in one group was supposed to talk to everyone in the other.

One of the girls in Jamal's group, Bethany, had immediately started flirting with James. She wasn't even trying to hide it. She asked him what he thought of her fake tattoo, her new jeans. Sam kept getting cut out of the conversation, but James kept roping him back in, making it clear he didn't like the way this was going, and he was politely trying to correct it.

Finally, James had said, "Do you want to go?" And Sam and James had made up some excuse to say goodbye to Delia, who looked happy enough with Jamal. They'd tried to slip out without saying anything at all to Bethany. She had caught them outside. "Aren't we going to exchange numbers?"

James had made up some excuse there, too, which was the point when Bethany had said, "Oh, I get it. You two are fags together."

James's response, hardly missing a beat, was to lean over and kiss Sam, full on the mouth. It was a horrible moment that should have been wonderful. A kiss that felt more performative than genuine, that came as a shock when Sam was already shocked, that lasted both too long and not long enough, that only served its purpose if its purpose was to send Bethany away, and why would that ever be the purpose of a kiss?

Sam had been just caught up and confused enough that when it was done, he'd turned and continued leading the way to his car, laughing like *ha ha, didn't we do something great.* But the whole drive home, James's nervous monologue was about Bethany. The look on her face. How she had that coming.

There had never been a good moment for Sam to interject that he had some questions. That he was pretty sure he wanted to kiss James again, but alone this time. He'd dropped off James never asking those questions, and then he'd determined that he would stay home from Gulf Shores and ask James at Mike's party.

(He didn't stay home from Gulf Shores. He didn't go to Mike's party.)

The thing about dreams is, they are real and not real. Things happen without happening. Often, they don't make any sense.

Magic isn't like that. Sometimes people think it is, because one's associations are as personal as one's dreams. But magic is very real. It makes sense. It happens.

301

Magic isn't like a dream, but a memory is.

For a person who doesn't remember his dreams, a memory can be a hard thing to grasp. One wants it to be solid—a thing to build upon. One wants it to have really happened, and for the happening to matter. One wants it to make sense—to bear the weight of further examination.

But then one wakes up.

And when one does, at least one has the magic to fall back on. No one can take that away.

"Wake up, Sam. Sam, are you awake?"

That voice. Fractured and fragile, like a little boy scared of the dark.

Sam would know it anywhere.

"I'm awake."

Which made it so.

"You saved my life," James said. Pulling himself into himself, Sam realized that he was holding James's hand. He was lying in a hospital bed, and James was sitting in a chair beside him. The smell of plastic was strong, which made sense, because—*ah ha*—there was an oxygen tube in Sam's nose.

"We switched places," Sam said, his voice barely above a whisper, more like a high-pitched squeak.

"As usual, you overcorrected." James was smiling sadly.

"Best be glad I'm awake now, because if I had died trying to save you, my mom would have killed you."

"No lies detected. She actually just went to get a coffee. I think she was planning to put it into your IV."

"How long have I been out?"

James appeared to be doing some mental math.

"A day and a half? They're keeping me locked up in the room next door, so I'm losing track of time. But Denver and Amber are at school, so . . . yeah, I think it's been almost two days since I woke up."

"Damn."

"Yeah."

"I just remembered," Sam said. "When I was out, I think I had a dream. Or maybe it was memories. But they felt so real."

"Oh yeah?" James said, suddenly looking a little shy.

"It was in the woods by the soccer field. That night after Bridget's party. And then it was that night at the bowling alley. Do you remember?"

"I remember," James said.

Sam still felt a little woozy, as if he were waking up from anesthesia. It was making him bold.

"Amber told me about your dad losing his job."

"I heard. And . . . I'm glad you know. I wanted to tell you so many times, but I . . . I don't know what it's going to mean for me, you know? Next year and stuff."

"You want to be here for Benji. Make sure he's okay."

"Exactly," James said, sounding almost relieved.

"Always putting other people before yourself. Even when it

almost kills you. I guess that's what they teach you in that church of yours, huh?"

James searched Sam's face for a sign that he was joking, but Sam wasn't joking; his voice just defaulted in that direction.

"Magic can do an awful lot," James said. "But sometimes I think the more we try to understand it, the less we *get* it. And the more we try to control it, the more powerless we become. For me, that's where God comes in. Not to make you fear magic. But to make you appreciate it."

"I appreciate you, James," Sam said earnestly. There must truly have been some anesthesia in his system; he felt as if he were hovering outside his body, hearing someone else say these words with his mouth. His mind was already drifting back in the direction of sleep, a swift undertow that was difficult to resist. "That's why . . ." His words trailed off, giving way to the gentle hum of the machinery around him.

Finally, James leaned in.

"That's why what?"

"Honestly, James, I've already forgotten."

CHAPTER 24

THIRTY MILES NORTHWEST OF ATLANTA, IN THE PARKING lot of a Publix that looked like every other Publix in Georgia, Delia sat in the back seat of a silver Honda, picking at her nails.

Isaac sat in the front passenger seat, tapping his hands on the dashboard in a steady, maddening rhythm. Grace reclined in the driver's seat, her eyes closed, her legs pulled up and folded in—a deep state of concentration. Hank sat in the middle seat beside Delia in the back, staring at her hands as if, at any moment, he might reach out and try to make her stop. She almost wished he would. That would give her the excuse to fight back.

They'd been sitting like this for twenty-five minutes already, and Delia was starting to get cold. Grace swore she couldn't concentrate if the car was on and the heat was blasting in her face—or at least that's what Isaac *said* she said—and Delia's attempts to convince them that they could turn the heat on but point the vents in another direction had not gone over well.

Finally, chancing a look past Hank's creepy face and out his window, Delia saw the woman making her way to their car with her cart full of groceries. Isaac saw her, too, and he reached over and popped the trunk. When the woman reached them, she began loading the groceries one at a time. Gallons of milk, dozens of eggs, many pints of ice cream, sodas, beers. It took her at least five minutes to load all the groceries, in the state she was in. She looked a little bit like a zombie, so Delia decided to stop watching her.

The woman finished, closed the trunk, and then moved to stand next to their car. Grace opened her eyes and turned on the car, and they high-tailed it out of the parking lot before the spell fully wore off.

By the time the woman came to, the four of them would be long gone. At that point, she wouldn't remember a thing, according to Isaac, speaking on behalf of Grace. And Delia had every reason to believe them, seeing as how they hadn't been caught so far, after all these times.

Isaac turned on the radio. Lately, his paranoia was manifesting itself in attempts to get the news from every possible source. They didn't see any sign on social media or TV that the police were closer to tracing their whereabouts, but after the last rending, when it had seemed like the police must have been waiting for them—or else how could they have had so many officers at the mall?—Isaac had determined that the police were keeping what they knew from the press on purpose. That it was part of their strategy.

Isaac stopped on a channel that immediately sounded promising.

"—and all four victims were able to make a full recovery, with help from a spell devised by Dr. Greg Harris. If you witness an attack of this nature, please pick up the phone and call—"

Isaac switched the radio off. He eyed Delia in the rearview mirror, suspicion clouding his features.

He wasn't stupid. He knew as well as she did that all the full recoveries trailing in their wake wouldn't have been possible without help from someone on the inside, handing over the exact steps of their spell. Arnauld's Axiom. It was the only explanation that made sense.

But he also knew that the moving house of cards they'd all built together would come crumbling down at the first sign of infighting; they were at half capacity already. He also knew it was no skin off their backs for these victims to recover. Once a rending was successful, they had the magic they needed. If the victims wanted it back, they'd have to get it from somewhere—someone—else.

Most importantly, Isaac liked her.

Unfortunately for him, Delia didn't like him back. She never had, really. He was a bit of a brute. His magic was assertive and uncreative—his associations as dull as . . . well, dishwater. Grace had always been the real genius of their operation, Delia could see that now that Mr. Grender was in jail, but for whatever reason, Grace only shared her knowledge with Isaac. Once, late at night, in the bedroom Delia and Isaac were sharing at the motel where they'd stopped between compounds, Isaac had intimated that Grace really did get her magic from angels, and it was the angels who had told her she needed to speak through him.

That was the night Delia had confirmed her own long-standing suspicion—that these True Light members were all absolutely insane, and she couldn't respect herself if she stayed with them, no matter how powerful they were.

Which was why this was officially the last time that Delia would be sitting in the parking lot of a Publix for thirty minutes, while some rich, mind-controlled thrall did all their shopping.

She had enough power, surely. Enough to escape, to disappear—enough to erase every trace of her involvement with True Light, and to start over somewhere new where she could enjoy what she'd won in peace. Put it to good use as . . . something. She could figure out her next steps from wherever that was.

Somewhere far away from Georgia. Somewhere far away from Pinnacle.

And if the memories of what was and the dreams of what was supposed to be ever kept her awake, well—hopefully she would be powerful enough to erase those, too.

CHAPTER 25

IF IT WAS WEIRD TO TAKE A DATE OUT FOR BREAKFAST instead of dinner, the biscuits and gravy at Mary Ellen's were good enough that Sam was willing to accept any weirdness that came with them. Anyway, while it was true he was still getting used to the rules of dating, such as they were, from what he could tell you were sort of allowed to make up whatever rules you wanted, as long as you both agreed on them.

For example, not only were he and Denver out on a breakfast date at Mary Ellen's, once they were finished there, they were headed straight for Waffle House for an immediate comparison—not so that Denver could decide which was better, but so that Denver could see how truly excellent both restaurants were.

"Too bad they don't have Mary Ellen's on the UGA campus," Denver said, before taking another bite of his biscuits and gravy and letting out another obscene moan that—breakfast time or not—was making Sam want to jump across this table and start making out with him that second.

"That only means we'll have to take turns. One weekend you can drive to Athens and experience life as a cool college kid who has countless friends and plans every night. The next weekend I'll drive back to Friedman so I can remember how it feels to be bored out of my skull, dancing alone in my room."

"Please. I give it two weeks before you're dancing alone with your roommate. What did you say his name was? Henry Hipley? Yeah, you two are going to need all the help making plans you can get."

"I know this is just your way of showing your insecurity about long distance. But don't worry, I'm not like Arjun. I know you're worth a little effort."

Denver had nothing clever to say to that. He let his smile speak for him, and the two of them ate for a moment in the kind of comfortable silence that could only come with two truly compatible people. His dad said it was clear watching Sam and Denver that they'd been friends first and something more second. But Sam and his mom quickly corrected him—for Sam and Denver, the magic was that they'd been friends and something more from the very beginning.

"Amber and I were talking about recruitment for next year's Fascinators," Denver said.

"Already?"

"Well, that's the thing. With all due respect to your poster campaigns, we were thinking we should start the recruitment process early, especially since the briefs for next year's convention categories come out in March. Why not start practicing then? We thought we might even make a trip to the middle schools, like the Atlanta magnet schools do, so the freshmen aren't playing catch up."

"You really think you're going to find that many new members in Friedman?"

"We might. None as cute as you, though."

"You better not."

It was absolutely wild—flirting like this in Mary Ellen's. Mary Ellen herself kept looking over the counter and smiling at them, then pretending she hadn't been looking when Sam caught her eye. Friedman hadn't magically transformed into a liberal mecca overnight, but for the first time in a long time, Sam felt like he was hopeful about the future, instead of trying to freeze the present or lose himself in the past.

He remembered his dreams now.

He was living them.

ACKNOWLEDGMENTS

Books are high-level group spells indeed, and this one would not have been possible without the combined magic of . . .

Heather Alexander, my first reader and this book's first champion. Heather is the reason this book is not merely a series of conversations in coffee shops.

Sara Crowe, my brilliant literary agent. A world of thanks to Sara, Holly McGhee, and the whole team at Pippin. Their hard work and commitment to excellence is a continual source of inspiration, and Sara's love for these characters got me through many a dark night of the soul with this book.

Rosemary Brosnan, my peerless editor. Rosemary asks questions that point you in the direction of truth without ever making you feel judged for missing it in the first place, and if that's not real magic, I don't know what is. I am forever grateful to Rosemary, Courtney Stevenson, and the whole team at HarperCollins who helped make this book a reality.

Mary Auxier and Shona McCarthy, who made sure that Sam's (and my) hypotactic way of talking was never at the cost of clarity.

ACKNOWLEDGMENTS

Corey Brickley and David Curtis, whose cover art and design, respectively, are *unreal* good, like something out of a dream.

Will Walton, who generously confirmed that my memories of Georgia still held after fifteen years of my living in other places.

Nick, my husband, last but never least. Nick listened patiently while I reimagined plot points and read entire scenes of this book out loud, often at the same time; he is both string to my kite and kite to my string.